"Max," she m[...] opening her eyes and raising her head, "will you not remove your mask?"

Angel found she longed to see his face.

He shook his head slightly. "Better you remember me as I am now—your unknown cavalier, the man who is bewitched by your beauty. I would not have you think of me as I really am."

Angel did not have the first idea of what to make of his words. Her brain seemed to be fully occupied in dealing with her heightened senses and the odd reactions of her body. It had never betrayed her like this. Why on earth…?

His mouth descended on hers with the softness of a butterfly alighting on a flower. The last vestiges of rational thought deserted her. She wanted…she wanted so much more. She reached her arms up to him and pulled him closer, returning a man's kiss for the first time in her life.

* * *

My Lady Angel
Harlequin Historical #737—January 2005

Praise for Joanna Maitland's recent titles:

A Poor Relation
"Regency purists will note that Maitland has a fine command of the era's sensibilities."
—*Romantic Times*

JOANNA MAITLAND

My Lady Angel

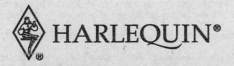

HARLEQUIN®

TORONTO • NEW YORK • LONDON
AMSTERDAM • PARIS • SYDNEY • HAMBURG
STOCKHOLM • ATHENS • TOKYO • MILAN • MADRID
PRAGUE • WARSAW • BUDAPEST • AUCKLAND

ISBN 0-373-29337-2

MY LADY ANGEL

First North American Publication 2005

www.eHarlequin.com

Printed in U.S.A.

Please address questions and book requests to:
Harlequin Reader Service
U.S.: 3010 Walden Ave., P.O. Box 1325, Buffalo, NY 14269
Canadian: P.O. Box 609, Fort Erie, Ont. L2A 5X3

Chapter One

'If I must take another husband, I suppose I could always marry Cousin Frederick.'

Lady Charlotte stared at her niece with narrowed eyes and pursed lips. She looked as if she had suddenly been confronted by a very bad smell. 'If I thought for one moment that you might do such a wicked thing, Angelina... Why, even you would deserve to be locked in the round tower till you came to your senses.'

Her niece rose swiftly from her spoon-back chair by the fireplace and came to sit on the sofa beside her aunt, taking the old lady's wrinkled hands in her own smooth white ones and stroking them reassuringly. 'Dearest Aunt, there is no need to threaten me with the tower. It is enough to hear you call me "Angelina" to know that I have offended you. I was only bamming you, I promise. You know I am in no hurry to marry again.' She managed to suppress the involuntary shudder that accompanied the word. 'I would certainly never marry another man called "Frederick",' she went on, assuming a teasing tone.

'Hmph,' snorted the old lady. 'You should not jest about Cousin Frederick and his family, Angel. They're a bad lot, every last one of 'em. And I'm sure they would all be delighted to see you dead and buried.'

'Aunt! You must not speak so. Truly, you must not. Especially of a man we have never met.'

'Don't need to meet him,' Lady Charlotte said roundly. 'Knowing your Great-uncle Augustus was quite enough for me, even if he *was* family. Never known a man so full of greed and envy. Couldn't ever accept the fact that his son remained plain Mr Rosevale while your father inherited all three titles.' Lady Charlotte had no qualms about speaking ill of the dead.

Angel tried another tack. 'Well, Cousin Frederick should be happy at last. After all, he is Lord Penrose now.' She smiled conspiratorially.

'Minx! If I didn't know you so well, I might have believed you meant that. What good is the earldom to Cousin Frederick when all the money and almost all the land goes with the barony? And to a mere slip of a girl at that?' She returned Angel's wicked smile with interest.

Angel dropped her gaze, trying to look like a demure young miss. She failed, as usual. 'He does have a seat in the House of Lords, Aunt Charlotte. Perhaps that will be some consolation to him.'

'I doubt it. The only law he would wish to enact would be to prohibit inheritance in the female line. Besides, he probably cannot afford to take his seat. It would not do for the Earl of Penrose to be threadbare.'

Angel tried not to smile at the picture her aunt's words had conjured up. Cousin Frederick, now the Earl of Penrose, had inherited a small impoverished estate in Cornwall, a seat in the Lords—and nothing else. As long as Angel and her aunt were alive, Frederick would have only an empty title.

But if Angel died without an heir, he stood to inherit everything.

'I think it is time we mended the feud, Aunt. After all, Frederick is head of the family now. We cannot refuse to receive him.'

'Nothing of the sort,' said the old lady. 'There are two families now. You hold the barony. As Lady Rosevale, *you* are head of the Rosevale family. Frederick may outrank you, being an Earl, but his is still the cadet branch. Let him head his own family. There is no need for us to receive him. No need at all. I, for one, shall never speak to him. It is impossible.'

Angel shook her head at her aunt's stubbornness. The Rosevale family was notorious for its short tempers and prolonged feuds, but neither her father nor her aunt had ever been prepared to explain the origins of this one. 'Aunt,' she said, 'I must ask you to tell me why Papa quarrelled with Great-uncle Augustus.'

'No, dear.' Aunt Charlotte looked decidedly mulish, but then, seeing Angel's set expression, she added, 'It was a very long time ago. It is best forgotten.'

Angel sat up even straighter. 'As *head* of the family,' she said, with emphasis, 'I need to be fully aware of such things. You must agree with that. You yourself said that—'

'No, I—' Aunt Charlotte was shaking her head.

'I insist, Aunt.' Angel looked meaningfully at her. The old lady was stubborn, but she also believed implicitly in the role of the head of the family. It was only a matter of waiting.

'Oh, very well. But it is not an edifying tale.' Aunt Charlotte took a lace-trimmed handkerchief from her pocket and touched it to her lips. 'Your papa... Er...your papa was not yet twenty when he inherited. I was already of age, of course, but your grandfather had appointed his younger brother, your Great-uncle Augustus, to be your papa's guardian and trustee. Uncle Augustus was very proud, very conscious of his rank. And grasping when it came to money.'

Angel's face must have shown some reaction to her aunt's outspoken description of the late Augustus Rosevale, for Lady Charlotte nodded bleakly and squeezed her niece's hand.

'You insisted on knowing, Angel, and so I must give you the truth with no bark on it. Augustus Rosevale was a miser...and a fortune-hunter to boot. Since he could not have the titles for himself, he did everything in his power to persuade your papa to marry his own daughter, Mary.

'Your papa would have none of it. And I encouraged him in his resistance, I freely admit. Uncle Augustus was a tyrant...and Mary was a plain little mouse, with neither spirit nor brains to recommend her. A marriage between them would have been a disaster from the first.'

'But I thought Papa's first marriage was a love match?'

Aunt Charlotte smiled fondly. 'Yes, indeed. Your papa had already met and fallen in love with Lady Jane Ellesmore. He paid no heed at all to Uncle Augustus's attempts to separate them or to advance the claims of his own daughter. The day your papa came of age, he proposed to Lady Jane. They were married within a month.'

'But she died.'

'Yes, she died. Although they did have twelve happy years together. In spite of Uncle Augustus.'

Angel looked at her aunt enquiringly.

'Your father's first marriage was not blessed with children, Angel. And Uncle Augustus took every possible opportunity of reminding your papa of the fact, never caring how much it might hurt him. It was even worse for poor Jane. It made her feel that she had failed as a wife.'

Angel turned her head away, biting her lip.

Aunt Charlotte was concentrating on her tale. 'She said to me once, not long before she died, that it might have been better if your father had married his cousin after all.'

Angel managed a nod. 'How terribly sad,' she said quietly.

Aunt Charlotte sighed. There was a faraway look in her eyes for a moment, but it was soon replaced by a martial glint. 'Poor Jane was barely cold in her grave when Augustus was back, trying yet again to persuade your father to wed Mary. Well! You will not be surprised to learn that your father sent him to the right about. Said Mary was too old to bear him an heir, even if he'd been able to stomach the sight of her, which he could not.'

Angel gasped.

'No, it was not well done of him, I agree. It was not Mary's fault, after all. But, you must understand, he had just buried his wife. And he had loved her dearly. Indeed, he was so distraught that, at one stage, I thought he...' She paused, swallowing hard. 'However, he did recover enough to decide that he must marry again, to ensure the succession, for it was clearly unwise to rely on Julian.'

'Julian? But...but surely he died when he was just a boy?'

'Is that what your papa told you?'

Angel nodded. Papa had spoken only once of his younger brother and it had seemed to give him pain. Angel had never felt able to press him for more information. And, apart from a single portrait of Julian as a child, there was no trace of him here at the Abbey.

'I can understand why he would have told you that but I...I fear it was not true, my love. Julian died, but... Oh, dear, this is very difficult.'

Angel waited.

Aunt Charlotte sighed. 'Julian was years younger than either of us, and so wild that we despaired of him. He did not see why he should pay any heed to your papa. They quarrelled all the time, I'm afraid. Your papa wanted Julian to marry in order to ensure the succession, but Julian refused to give up his wicked bachelor ways. Drinking and gambling, and—Julian said your papa was perfectly capable of getting an heir for himself. All he had to do was to find himself a better breeder than the one he had buried. You can imagine how your papa reacted to that! Yet another family rift, of course. Julian took himself off to France and never came back. I…I heard that he did marry there, but he and his wife, and all her family, were killed in the Terror. She was the daughter of the Comte d'Eury, you see, and—'

Lady Charlotte rose and walked to the window. Angel could tell, from the set of her shoulders, that she was trying to master a sudden surge of emotion.

'No matter how wild he was,' Aunt Charlotte said in a low, passionate voice, 'he did not deserve to die like that. No one did.'

Angel sat silent, wondering, waiting for her aunt to recover her composure. She had clearly loved Julian, in spite of his faults. Perhaps Papa had loved him too? Had he banished all the reminders of Julian from Rosevale Abbey because the memory was too painful? It certainly seemed to be so for Aunt Charlotte. Angel forced herself to resist the temptation to go to the old lady and put a comforting arm around her. Aunt Charlotte would have upbraided her severely for doing such a thing. A lady should never lose control of her emotions in public. Never. And if, by some mischance, she did, it was the height of bad manners for anyone present to notice.

'And Great-uncle Augustus?' prompted Angel, when Aunt Charlotte had turned back to face her once more.

'He and your father never spoke again. The breach was too deep to mend. Why, your father did not even go to the funeral when Augustus's son died. He didn't go to Augustus's funeral either.'

'Oh,' said Angel, considering. 'But I thought Cousin Frederick was Great-uncle Augustus's son.'

'No. Grandson.'

'Oh,' said Angel again. 'So...he is not an old man, then?'

'No, of course not. You knew that, surely? You said he might do as a husband for you. You were not planning—'

'Dear Aunt, I was only teasing you, I promise. I know nothing of Cousin Frederick. I supposed that he was... oh...fifty at least, and rather stout. With a large red nose,' she added, hoping her aunt would forget her momentary megrims.

'You, Angel, are most definitely in need of a spell in the tower,' said Aunt Charlotte bluntly, reverting to her normal self once more. 'I don't know why I— I'd do better to take myself off and leave you to your own devices.'

'But then you'd miss all the fun.'

Lady Charlotte raised both eyebrows.

'Since we are out of mourning at last, dear Aunt,' continued Angel, assuming a determined expression, 'it is time that we looked about us a little. I should so like to travel on the Continent, now that Boncy is safely disposed of. In a month or two, perhaps, once the weather is better. But I fancy we should open up the London house first, do not you?'

'I—'

'And if we should happen to encounter the new Earl of

Penrose, we will receive him with politeness, however stout his middle or florid his complexion.'

'Angel, we cannot—'

'As head of the family,' Angel said, with emphasis, 'I wish the breach to be healed. We must make the attempt. Both of us, Aunt.'

Lady Charlotte shook her head a little, but the look on Angel's face must have made an impact, for the old lady did not try to argue any further. 'Very well. If I must, I will receive him. Shouldn't think he'll be stout, though. His father and his grandfather were both as thin as rails. It suited their penny-pinching characters, I always thought.'

'Thin and florid, then.'

Lady Charlotte looked sideways at her niece. 'Well,' she said airily, 'you might be surprised on that front. Frederick is unlikely to be florid. Not yet. After all...' she paused, narrowing her eyes '...he's not that many years older than you are.'

'But, surely—?' Angel stopped in mid-sentence. The door had opened to admit old Willett, the family butler. His quiet entrance had been drowned by Angel's exclamation of surprise.

'There is a gentleman arrived, m'lady,' Willett said in his soft voice. He was making no attempt to conceal his disapproval of their visitor. 'He...he says he is related to your ladyship's family, but—'

Angel laughed. 'There, you see, Aunt. What did I tell you? It is Cousin Frederick, come to heal the breach himself.'

Willett coughed apologetically. 'The...er...gentleman gives his name as Rosevale. Julian Rosevale.'

Angel put her hand to her throat.

And in that same moment, Lady Charlotte, who never

allowed herself to show the slightest emotion in company, sank softly to the floor in a dead faint.

Hatless and head bowed, the Earl of Penrose remained on one knee by the graveside for several minutes more. He refused to acknowledge the rapidly waning winter light, or the steady rain that was soaking into his caped coat.

Ross Graham, standing awkwardly on the other side of the plain grey slab, seemed to be about to speak, but then thought better of it. He bowed his head once more, waiting.

At last, Penrose raised his head and stood up. His thick dark hair had been slicked down by the rain. He rubbed the back of his neck to wipe away the droplets that were now threatening to run down inside his shirt. Then, with a tiny shrug, he brushed the dirt from his pantaloons and resumed his beaver hat. 'Come, Ross,' he said, a little gruffly, 'let's get ourselves back to the inn. You look as if you are freezing.'

Ross smiled half-heartedly, but fell into step beside his friend. Their boots sank into the muddy grass. 'Every time I've come here, the weather has been foul.' His soft Scottish accent was unmistakable in almost every word he spoke. 'Do you think she's testing us?'

Penrose laughed in his throat. 'No, not she. Aunt Mary was kindness itself. You know that just as well as I do. She'd not ask us to put ourselves to the least inconvenience on her behalf.' He looked back at the tiny posy of snowdrops he had found to lay on Mary Rosevale's grave. She had always loved snowdrops. The rain was making them look bedraggled already, yet they seemed to glow against the drab stone. As much of a ray of sunshine as Aunt Mary had ever had in her grey existence.

'Penrose, I—'

'Do you have to call me that, Ross?' The Earl sounded more weary than angry.

'No. But it *is* your name.'

Penrose shook his head. 'Yes, I suppose... But I have plenty of others, too, as you know very well. If you must be so pompous, you could try Frederick, for example, or Maximilian, or even—heaven help me—Augustus!'

Ross laughed and clapped the Earl on his soggy shoulder. 'I think not. The last time I called you Augustus, as I remember, you threatened to knock me down.'

'Yes. You deserved it, too.' Ross was his oldest friend and one of the few who ever dared to tease him when he was in a fit of the sullens. They had grown up together. Aunt Mary had been like a mother to them, and the bonds remained strong, both to each other, and to her memory. 'You might be safer to stick with "Max".'

Ross merely nodded and continued to stride towards the carriage where the Earl's groom waited, hopping impatiently from one foot to the other.

'You're soaked to the skin, Cap'n,' he said bluntly.

'We've been through much worse, Sergeant,' replied Penrose, reverting to their army ways without a moment's thought. He and Sergeant Ramsey had shared many a flea-ridden billet in the Peninsula, in searing heat and in bitter cold. 'A little wet won't hurt me.'

'No, sir, but—'

'Might I suggest that you two continue your discussion once we are back under cover?' said Ross with a lift of his eyebrow. 'I, for one, am looking forward to a bowl of steaming hot punch. I am sure that his lordship feels the same.'

Ramsey looked nonplussed for a moment at the implied rebuke, but he was soon bustling his gentlemen into their seats. 'We'll have you back at the inn in a pig's whisper, m'lord,' he said, grinning as he pronounced the unfamiliar title. 'You, too, sir.'

Penrose leaned back in his seat and closed his eyes. It always affected him, the sight of Aunt Mary's grave. He should have come home earlier, helped her more... Her life had been so hard, at the beck and call first of her own father, and then of his. Neither of them had treated her as more than an unpaid servant. His own father, miser that he was, had insisted that Mary bring up his son so that he could be spared the inconvenience of finding another wife. For marriage, his father had said, was a plaguey expensive business. A new wife was always bent on finding ways of emptying a man's purse, whereas a spinster sister was easily controlled. Poor Mary. She had had so little of life's luxuries. And she had never had a home of her own, or children. Those joys had been denied her, by her own family, and by the heartless old man who had held the Penrose titles.

The new Earl of Penrose shifted uncomfortably in his seat at the thought of his hated predecessor. A pity there had been no chance to avenge Mary's wrongs. There was only a sister and a daughter left. He could not make war on women.

Old man Penrose had made war on Mary, had he not?

But Mary had had some consolation. She had been loved, and dearly so, by Penrose and by Ross Graham, the orphan she had taken in and defended against all the world, including her own family. Meek as a lamb where her own interests were concerned, she had become like a tigress when her boys were under attack. She had saved them, many and many a time. But, when it had come to saving her, Max and Ross had come too late.

'A penny for 'em.'

Max looked up. Rather against his will, he found him-

self returning Ross's smile. There was something about
those glinting blue eyes... Ross's sunny nature seemed to
admit neither defeat nor despair. And his optimism was
infectious on a dank February day by a graveyard.

'What you need, my friend,' said Ross, his smile broad-
ening into a grin, 'apart from the punch, of course, is a
battle to fight. Can't be brooding on your own troubles if
the enemy is marching over the ridge.'

Max laughed, but there was precious little humour in it.
'No chance of that, Ross. Boney's finished now.'

'I wasn't thinking of Boney, as it happens, though I, for
one, won't write him off till he's dead. Elba is too near
France for my liking.'

The Earl shrugged his shoulders, but said nothing.

'No, I was thinking about you, Max. You need to get
your teeth into something. Something worthwhile. Why
don't you do something in the House? You were talking
about the plight of the old soldiers begging in the streets.
Why not take up their cause?'

'Because I can't afford to take my seat, if you must
know. With no money, I'm a pretty sorry excuse for an
earl.' He realised he was sounding increasingly testy. It
was yet another lamentable Rosevale trait. He must make
more effort to curb it.

'Forgive me, but I don't understand. You were comfortable enough before.'

'I still am—for an anonymous captain in a marching
regiment. But an earl... That's entirely different, Ross. An
earl has houses, estates, retainers, obligations... I have the
title and the obligations, but nowhere near enough blunt to
meet them. That's just one more charge to lay at old man
Penrose's door. He and that daughter of his have tied me
hand and foot.'

'You speak almost as if he were still alive. What on earth is the matter with you? Old Penrose is dead more than a twelvemonth. You are the Earl of Penrose now.'

'Aye, but his daughter lives on to laugh in my face. The haughty—and wealthy—Baroness Rosevale carries on where her father left off. Both venting their spite on our family.'

'You—'

'Confound it, Ross. You know as well as I do how they treated Aunt Mary. Old Penrose was a black-hearted devil. I'd wager his daughter is the same.'

'Word is, she's barren.'

'What?'

'Married for years, but no children. Surely you knew that? So it's just a matter of time. One day the barony, and all that goes with it, will come to you. You'll be able to take your seat in the Lords then.'

Max shook his head. 'I doubt that very much, Ross. You've forgotten that her ladyship is several years younger than I am. Probably disgustingly healthy, to boot. No, I'm afraid that if I'm eventually to inherit, it will have to be through my children.'

'Er…doesn't that require you to have a wife, first?'

'You know perfectly well that it does,' his lordship said sharply, pressing his lips together into a tight, angry line.

'Mmm.' Ross paused. 'You know,' he said musingly, totally ignoring his friend's dark frown, 'you could always think about marrying the Baroness yourself. That way, you would get control of your inheritance all the sooner.'

Penrose merely shook his head wearily. He had his temper well in hand now. 'I had always thought you were out of your mind, Ross. Now, I'm sure of it. Must be the fiery red hair. Clearly all that heat addles the brain.'

* * *

'No more! No more!' Lady Charlotte pushed away the smelling salts that Angel had been waving under her nose. 'I am perfectly recovered, I assure you.'

Looking at her aunt's ashen features, Angel knew better. The old lady was still far from well, but argument would achieve nothing. Besides, there was still their astonishing visitor to consider.

'Shall I tell the gentleman that your ladyship is not at home? I—'

'No, Willett,' said Angel, glancing up from where she knelt by her aunt's chair, 'that will not do. Not if he is part of the family. Ask him to wait in the library. Tell him I shall join him there presently. Lady Charlotte will remain here until she is recovered.'

'As your ladyship wishes.'

The door had barely closed behind him when Lady Charlotte said urgently, 'He is an impostor. He must be. If Julian were still alive, he would have contacted us long ago. It's been more than twenty years. Why would he wait until now?'

Angel rose to her feet, still holding her aunt's slightly clammy hand. 'Because…because now he can claim the titles,' she said slowly.

Lady Charlotte started, and then nodded reluctantly. 'That would be true, of course. My brother was…is…was no fool. Though he would be nearly as poor as Frederick, since neither of them has any claim on the Barony. Oh, Julian…' She shook her head, frowning slightly, but suddenly her expression cleared. 'If it *is* Julian, just think how Frederick's nose will be put out of joint. He'll be mad as fire to be plain Mr Frederick Rosevale all over again. Why, it is famous!'

Angel released her aunt's hand and moved towards the door. 'Poor Frederick,' she said under her breath. She

closed it quietly behind her and started down the staircase
to the library.

Poor Frederick, indeed. His earldom might not be worth
much, but it did confer a certain standing in Society. To
have it whisked out of his fingers, barely months after he
had grasped it, would be humiliating in the extreme. Had
he done anything to deserve this kind of treatment? Aunt
Charlotte seemed to think so. But Aunt Charlotte's views
were not unbiased, judging by today's outburst of venom.
On occasion, she could be remarkably difficult. Why
did—?

Willett had already thrown open the library door. And,
as Angel reached it, the gentleman standing by the huge
stone fireplace turned round to greet her.

'Oh—' Angel stopped on the threshold, transfixed. The
man before her was certainly no newly discovered uncle.
This man was probably no older than Angel herself.

But he was, without doubt, the handsomest man she had
ever beheld.

Chapter Two

Angel's breath had caught in her throat. For a second, the two simply stared at each other. Neither seemed able to utter a word.

Then, with a tiny shrug, the apparition straightened and came towards her. An odd smile fluttered for a moment at the corner of his mouth as he made his bow, an old-fashioned courtly gesture, with an elaborate sweep of his arm. 'My lady, you do me too much honour.'

That bow belonged to a bygone age, Angel thought. How strange. This man might claim to be a Rosevale, but he could not be English. He—

Just then, he straightened and smiled at her. It was such a dazzling smile that, for a moment, she could neither think nor speak.

He took another step towards her.

Angel forced her tumbling thoughts into the beginnings of order. She must take charge of this encounter. She was the head of the Rosevale family, was she not?

She nodded politely towards her visitor and stepped further into the room. Behind her, the door closed with a tiny click. Willett was no doubt standing on the other side, ready to defend her against the foreign intruder. Willett had a profound distrust of all things foreign.

'Good afternoon, sir,' Angel said evenly. 'To what do we owe the honour of your visit?' She looked steadily at him, her head tilted slightly to one side as she assessed him more fully. Yes, there might be a slight family resemblance…but almost all the Rosevales were fair, like Angel herself, whereas this man had chestnut hair and dark eyes. And the features of a Greek god.

'My lady, I seek the Marquis Penrose.' He pronounced the title in the French fashion, but that barely registered with Angel.

She swallowed, trying to ignore the sudden thundering of her pulse at the visitor's question. He did not know! She took a deep breath. 'The Marquis of Penrose died more than a year ago, sir,' she said. 'Since my father left no male heirs, the title died with him. There is no longer a Marquis of Penrose.'

For a moment there was a shocked silence. Angel saw that her visitor's widening eyes were dark blue rather than brown, as she had first thought. Perhaps he was a Rosevale after all?

'Your pardon, my lady. I do not understand,' he said at last, shaking his head.

Angel motioned him to one of the wing chairs. He waited courteously until she had seated herself before following her lead. He moved with a degree of elegance that would draw every female eye.

'If you will have the goodness to explain your errand, sir, I am sure I shall be able to provide you with the information you seek. Tell me, why did you wish to see my father?' She tried to smile encouragingly at him.

'I am Julien Pierre Rosevale, my lady. I arrived from

France just a few days ago. The crossing was—' he closed his eyes for a second, and swallowed '—painful.'

Angel's mind was racing—a Frenchman called Rose-vale?—but she forced herself to nod in sympathy. Only the most urgent business would persuade any sane person to brave the Channel in the depths of winter.

'I came to seek help from the Marquis since he is…was my father's brother. It was not possible to travel before, because— Well, no matter. I think…you and I are cousins, I think?' It seemed that he was more than a little bewildered.

'You are Julian Rosevale's son? But—' Angel smoothed her silken skirts in an attempt to hide her consternation. 'Forgive me, *monsieur*, but I had understood that my uncle and all his family perished on the guillotine. How is it that you alone escaped?'

'Not I alone, my lady. I have a younger sister. Her name is Julie. Both of us escaped the terrible fate that took my father and mother, and all my mother's family. My father's servants saved us both and brought us up. They swore we were their own children.'

'Your father's servants?'

'Gaston, and his wife, Hannah,' he said, nodding. 'Gaston came from the d'Eury family estate at the time of my parents' marriage. But Hannah is English. She made us both speak English always when we were alone. Never outside the house, of course. We were always afraid that one of the spies might hear us. There were spies everywhere.'

That explained his remarkable command of English, Angel concluded. His use of the language was almost faultless. Only the occasional tiny slip betrayed his origins.

And the longer he talked, the less obvious it seemed to become.

* * *

Aunt Charlotte's tightly clasped fingers were almost as white as her face, but her back was ramrod-straight and her features were set.

'Aunt, you will allow me to present our visitor,' Angel said simply, drawing him into the room. 'He is lately arrived from France, in spite of the winter storms. He says his name is Julien Rosevale, son of your brother, Julian.' It was an odd way of performing an introduction, to be sure, but she was not about to accept this man's word as to his identity. Aunt Charlotte would be in a much better position to judge the truth of his claim. 'Sir,' Angel continued smoothly, 'this is my late father's sister, Lady Charlotte Clare.'

Aunt Charlotte had risen from her place, acknowledging the visitor's extravagant bow with only a slight nod. She did not extend her hand. Instead, she stared intently at him. 'You do not have the look of the Rosevales, *monsieur*,' she said at last.

'No, my lady. I take after my mother's family. The d'Eury family all have...had dark hair.'

Aunt Charlotte nodded thoughtfully and motioned the visitor to approach. 'You are much of a height with Julian, certainly. As to the rest...' She turned to Angel who had remained near the door, watching. 'My dear, would you be so good as to go to my chamber for me? In the drawer beside my bed you will find a carved ivory box.' She began to fumble inside the high neckline of her gown.

Angel hesitated. There were servants enough to run such errands, surely?

'Forgive me, my child, but I cannot entrust my box to a servant.' She finally succeeded in extracting a fine gold chain from under her gown and detached two keys from it. 'You will need the key,' she said, handing the larger one to Angel.

'Very well, Aunt.' Angel felt oddly reluctant to leave the old lady with the strange new arrival. There could be no danger, of course, with so many servants about, and yet…

'Thank you, Angelina,' said Lady Charlotte, with decided emphasis, nodding in the direction of the door. It seemed she had no qualms about being alone with the Frenchman.

Angel turned to leave. Her new-found cousin was before her, however, opening the door with a flourish. Where on earth had he learned such manners? They did not sit at all well with a child of the Revolution.

She ran lightly up the stairs to her aunt's bedchamber, wondering what could possibly be in this mysterious carved box. She was sure she had never set eyes on any such thing. It must have been kept well hidden.

The table alongside Aunt Charlotte's bed was nothing out of the ordinary. The brass key slid into the lock in the single drawer and turned easily. This drawer must have been opened many and many a time.

The drawer contained a bundle of letters tied with a black ribbon, a pressed posy encased in a protective sleeve of finest muslin, and a beautiful carved box.

The box was locked.

Lifting it out, Angel was struck by the warmth of the ivory in her hand. The box was very old. It was worn, particularly around the small brass lock, where it was only just possible to make out the tiny sprays of carved flowers. What could it contain? It seemed to weigh nothing at all.

She carefully closed and locked the drawer, casting a last glance at its contents. Such a pile of letters. And the posy looked fragile enough to shatter at a breath. Who had given it to Aunt Charlotte? Her late husband? Or was there perhaps a secret lover in the old lady's past? It was most intriguing.

She hurried back down to the drawing room, carrying the precious box. Willett was standing guard outside, just as before. He had been listening, of course, but he would never admit to it, not to her. If she wanted to know what had been discussed in her absence, she would have to ask her aunt.

The Frenchman jumped to his feet the moment the door opened. He had been sitting close by Lady Charlotte on the sofa. Angel fancied he had even been holding the old lady's hand. He was certainly quick to seize an opportunity. Angel had not been gone from the room above ten minutes.

'Thank you, my love,' said Lady Charlotte, reaching up to take the box. 'This is just what we need.' She busied herself with the tiny key, talking all the while. 'I am sure that Pierre is just what he says, but I shall produce the proof in a trice.'

'Pierre...?' Angel looked enquiringly towards the Frenchman.

'My family have always called me Pierre,' he said quickly. 'Since my father was Julian, and my sister is Julie, it seemed easier for everyone.' He smiled at her, as if he knew she would understand. And she found that she did.

'Here we are!' said Lady Charlotte.

The box was open. Its deeply cushioned interior contained two miniatures—of a man and a woman, both dressed in the elaborate style of the French court of decades before.

Lady Charlotte offered the man's portrait to Angel. 'This is Julian Rosevale, my dear. Your uncle...and Pierre's father.'

So that explained the locked drawer! Aunt Charlotte

must have found a way of keeping in touch with Julian, in spite of the family feud.

The portrait showed a Rosevale, no doubt of it, in spite of the powdered wig. He looked like a younger version of Angel's dead father. She felt a sudden sadness at the thought of her uncle's terrible end, and the fact that she had been told almost nothing about him until now. That cursed Rosevale temper!

'And this—' Lady Charlotte handed over the second portrait '—this is Amalie d'Eury, Julian's wife. And Pierre's mother. The likeness is very strong, I think.'

Angel studied the beautiful miniature. It was impossible to tell the colour of the lady's hair, since it was heavily powdered, but her brows were dark and her eyes were blue. She had the same fine features as Pierre, and the same determined chin. If the portrait was a true likeness, there could be no doubt that Pierre and Amalie d'Eury were related in some way.

And if Pierre was Julian's legitimate son, he was the rightful Marquis of Penrose, and the Earl of Penrose besides.

Poor Frederick, indeed!

Lady Charlotte was plying Pierre with questions. 'Tell me of your sister. Julie, you said? Heavens, I never learned that Julian had even one child, far less two. How old is she now?'

Pierre was gazing fondly at the miniature. For a second, he stared into the distance. Then he blinked, and said, 'Julie is twenty-four, *madame*, less than a year younger than I. She is—' he turned to look searchingly at Angel '—she has a great look of your niece. Julie's hair is perhaps not quite so silvery fair... But apart from that, they might almost be twins.'

'She would not come with you? We would have been

delighted to welcome her into the family, would we not, Angel?'

Pierre looked startled. 'Angel? Surely—?'

'My name, sir, is Angelina. It became something of a family joke to call me "Angel" when I was small, since I was definitely nothing of the kind. And later, it amused my father to use it still. You were speaking of your sister, however. Pray continue.' She refused to let herself be beguiled. As head of the family, it was her duty to judge his claim with a cool head. She must not let him change the subject. She needed a great deal more evidence before she would accept his story. He seemed to have charmed Aunt Charlotte in a trice—somehow—but he would soon learn that Angel was made of sterner stuff.

'The truth is, *madame*, that we have very little money. There was only enough for a single passage, and it was obviously out of the question for Julie to travel alone. I have promised to send for her, as soon as I am able.'

Angel thought he had begun to look a trifle uncomfortable. Poor man. It must be very difficult to admit to living in such poverty. 'You will understand, sir,' she said quickly, before her aunt had time to expose them further to a possible impostor, 'that I must ask you for proofs of your claims. Forgive me, but you must see that a physical likeness to my uncle's wife is not sufficient. Your relationship to the d'Eury family could be…er…other than the one you have described.' Out of the corner of her eye, she could see the beginnings of a flush on her aunt's neck. Lady Charlotte was outraged, of course, at even the subtlest suggestion that Pierre might have been born on the wrong side of the blanket.

'That is a trifle difficult at present,' he said brusquely, looking her directly in the eye. 'However, I am sure I shall be able to explain matters satisfactorily when I meet your father's heir. Where is he to be—?'

'*I* am my father's heir,' said Angel flatly. 'I am the Baroness Rosevale, and head of the family.'

'But you are a woman.' The words came out in a rush, and were followed by a look of acute embarrassment.

'Just so. No doubt things are managed differently in your country, *monsieur*, but in England a title as old as my father's may descend in the female line, in the absence of sons. You were about to explain…?'

He frowned and swallowed hard. 'Julie and I were born at the time of the Revolution, as you will know, my lady. Everything was in turmoil then. I do have the record of my parents' marriage, but, for the rest…' he shrugged eloquently '…I have nothing but my word, and the testimony of Gaston and Hannah. Just before he was taken, my father insisted we flee as far as possible from Paris to escape the guillotine. Julie and I…we were mere babes. We remember nothing of those times. It might be possible to find written proof if I went back to Paris to search, but I would not know where to begin. And I have no money to buy information.'

Angel chose to ignore that, for the moment. 'May I see the record of your parents' marriage?'

'It is at home. With Julie. We could not risk—'

'Yes, I quite see that you would not wish to bring it all the way to England. Tell me, where *is* your home?'

'We live in a small fishing village, between Marseilles and Toulon. It is called Cassis.'

'And Julie is there?'

'Yes, of course. With Gaston and Hannah. We could afford only one passage, as I told you, and even then by the slowest and cheapest route. We thought that, if I could reach the Marquis, he would help us…for his brother's sake.'

'Of course we will help you,' Lady Charlotte said, reaching out to touch Pierre's hand in an uncharacteristic gesture of affection. 'Angel—'

'We will be happy to help you to search for the proof you need, *monsieur*. But I must say I am a little surprised that you expected to receive help from my father. You must know, surely, that my father and his brother had had no contact since Uncle Julian left England? Forgiveness was not in my father's nature. Nor in Uncle Julian's either, according to my aunt.'

'I am aware of that. But I could not believe that any man would allow his dead brother's children to starve. Julie is an innocent. She is the niece of an English marquis and the granddaughter of a French count, yet she is almost destitute and living like a mere peasant. Do you tell me, my lady, that your family would have spurned her?'

'No, but—'

'Of course we would not!' Lady Charlotte seemed determined to take Pierre's side. 'We will help you both. *And* the servants who shielded you. You will understand, of course, that it is necessary to have the proof of your birth in order to establish your claim to the titles. Cousin Frederick will demand nothing less before he will relinquish his hold on the earldom. But have no fear, we shall send to Paris to search for the documents, and we shall—'

'I think I should discuss matters with my lawyer before we make any definite plans, Aunt Charlotte,' said Angel, interrupting quickly. 'If Mr Rosevale will tell us where he can be reached…?'

'Mr Rosevale, indeed! Why, Pierre is the Marquis of Penrose and should be addressed by that title. He—'

'I think it might be wise, Aunt, to make no such claim

at this stage. Forgive me, sir, but if you are the rightful Marquis, then you are also the Earl of Penrose. That title passed to my cousin Frederick after my father's death. I fancy it might be unwise to broadcast your claim until you have something more than a family likeness to substantiate it.' She watched him carefully, trying to judge the effect of her words. He now seemed totally open and unembarrassed. She could not detect the slightest sign of duplicity in his face.

Pierre smiled warmly at them both. Oh, he was a handsome man, no doubt of that. He had charming manners, too. When he smiled in just that way, with such warmth in his deep blue eyes, Angel found herself wanting to believe that he was exactly what he said. It would be so easy to take his part. And if she came to know him better, they might perhaps become friends, even— No! Angel pulled herself up short. She must not allow her judgement to be swayed by his looks and his charm. As head of the family, she must do her duty by this man, as calmly as—

'May we not invite Pierre to stay here at the Abbey, my dear? It must be very difficult for him, all alone in a strange country…'

Heavens, what would Aunt Charlotte say next? Such impropriety was quite unlike her. It seemed that even an old lady's head could be turned by a handsome face and old-fashioned courtesies. Pierre was certainly dangerous.

Pierre took Lady Charlotte's hand and bowed over it, almost touching it with his lips. 'You are most kind, my lady, but I could not accept. I am lodging in London. With Hannah's brother. I could not impose upon you both while my situation is…unresolved. It would be most improper.'

Lady Charlotte sighed deeply, but said nothing more. For a second, she looked a trifle chastened.

'I thank you for your understanding, sir,' Angel said

with sincerity. 'If you will furnish me with your direction, I shall ensure that you are kept informed of any developments. I cannot promise you that you will have news quickly, however, no matter how many envoys I send to Paris.'

'But you will send them, Angel?' Aunt Charlotte was beaming now. 'That is splendid. Just think what a blow it will be for Frederick. He will be reduced to plain Mr Rosevale all over again. I declare, we shall soon have Great-uncle Augustus turning in his grave.'

'Max?'

He groaned a little, not opening his eyes.

'Max, it is morning. You said you had to leave early.' Louisa laid a gentle hand on his dark stubbled cheek. 'And you are much in need of a shave,' she whispered, trying to hide the smile in her voice.

His eyes remained stubbornly closed. He did not move an inch.

She lay back on her soft pillows, luxuriating in the warmth of the bed and the closeness of the man at her side. She knew better than to continue when he so clearly did not wish to be roused. He would—

In less than the space of a heartbeat, he had pulled her into his arms! 'What I am in need of, my dear one, is much more urgent than a shave.'

'Indeed, sir? And what, pray, is that? You—'

She was not permitted to say another word. His mouth came down on hers for a long and increasingly passionate kiss that made her forget the advancing hour and the winter chills outside. He was on fire already, and he knew exactly how to light an answering flame in her.

Louisa groaned in her turn.

He stilled immediately. 'What is it? Did I hurt you?'

She groaned again, deliberately. 'You are an idiot, Max.' She ran her free hand down his back and began to trail her fingers over the soft skin of his buttocks. 'After all these years, you really should have learned a little more about me, you know.'

'Impossible,' he said. Her hand moved again, raking the nails across his flesh. He gasped and rolled on to his back, taking her with him and trapping that roving hand. 'It is impossible to understand any woman, my sweet. No man should even begin to try. But then again—' he put his hands around her waist and settled her astride him '—there are certain things that can usually provoke a reaction.' He reached up to cup her breast, weighing it in his hand and then delicately skimming the rough skin of his thumb over her nipple.

Louisa closed her eyes, trying not to moan at the pleasure of it. In some things, he understood her only too well.

'Mmm, yes. That is most certainly a reaction.'

With her eyes closed, Louisa could no longer tell precisely what he was doing to her. All her skin seemed to be burning, as if he was stroking every inch of her body at the same time. That was impossible, and yet…

'And now, my sweet,' he said softly, in a voice so thick with desire that it reached into her very heart, 'you may do with me what you will.'

'For a man who cannot understand women, you manage remarkably well, I think.'

Max paused in the act of arranging his cravat and turned to gaze down at her. In the aftermath of their lovemaking, she looked particularly beautiful, her skin still slightly flushed, her dark hair pooled on the rumpled pillows. He was tempted to rip off his clothes and return to her.

'No, Max.' She shook her head and sat up, pulling the

covers up to her chin. She could read him much too well. 'You know you must go. But I may expect you to come back tonight?'

'No,' he snapped.

'Max—?'

'Forgive me, Louisa, that was uncalled for. I am not angry at you. I have…other things on my mind. I have to go out of town today. On…family business. I do not expect it to be pleasant.'

She did not ask for any further explanation. She never pried. She was truly a woman in a thousand and he was lucky to have found her. He smiled affectionately at her and returned to the matter of his cravat.

He heard her give a long, deep sigh. What on earth—?

'Max, there is something I must say to you, my dear. I ask you to hear me out.'

He turned back to her. He had never heard her use quite that tone of voice before. And she was suddenly very pale, almost as white as the sheet she held against her neck.

'I know you will not say this, so I must. Max, my dear… When you marry—and I know it must be soon—you must give me up. You are a man of honour. You should not betray your wife with a woman like me.' She was twisting the sheet in her fingers as she spoke.

He felt an enormous surge of fury as the full import of her words dawned on him. His Louisa was worth a dozen simpering Society wives! She gave him friendship, and laughter, and the shared delight of their joining. Now, for perhaps the first time in their long relationship, she was giving him advice—to leave her.

'My wife, whoever she may be, will know better than to interfere in what I choose to do. If she marries me to gain a title—and what other reason could there be?—she would be well advised to learn to content herself with that, and to concentrate on giving me the heir I need. She will do as I bid her, Louisa, and that includes turning a blind eye to my relationship with you.' He managed to stop the rush of angry words. She was staring down at the coverlet now. 'Unless you wish to be rid of me?'

'Oh, Max, you know very well that I do not. But I understand you better than you think. Perhaps better than you understand yourself. The marriage you have described is a stony-hearted business alliance. If you go that route, you will end up hating your wife, and hating yourself, too. You need to marry where there is love…or affection, at least.'

He shook his head wonderingly. In the course of their long liaison, she had never presumed. On his rare visits to England, on leave from the Peninsula, she had always been warm and welcoming. She had treated him as if he were her only lover, though he had known full well that he was not. Without a protector, she would have starved.

And when he had returned for good and was able to afford—just—to set her up for himself alone, she had not changed. She took his money, but she was generous of herself. She was a diamond. He would never give her up.

'Marriage is a matter of business, Louisa. You know that as well as I do. You are right that I shall have to take a wife. And since my earldom is threadbare, she must be richly dowered. I do not doubt I shall find a rich father who is willing to sell me his daughter in exchange for a title. Believe me, I plan to drive a hard bargain in return for assuming the shackles. I must have control of her fortune; and she must be biddable. I do not insist on any great degree of beauty, though it would not go amiss if—'

He stopped short. Louisa was gazing up at him with an expression of profound distaste on her lovely face.

'Confound it, I sound like a coxcomb, do I not? Whoever she is, I shall treat her well, I promise you. There have been quite enough downtrodden women in my family—' a vivid picture of poor Mary Rosevalc came immediately to mind '—and I have no intention of forcing another into that sorry state. She will have money, and influence, and, God willing, children at her skirts.'

'But she will not have your love.'

He laughed harshly. 'Come, Louisa, do you really think me capable of that? Is any man of my station? I never saw a love match, neither in my own family nor in all my time in the army. The poets have much to answer for. Love, if it exists at all, comes between a man and his mistress.' He lifted her hand from the ruined sheet and raised it to his lips. Her eyes widened in surprise at such an unusual display of affection.

A sharp knock interrupted them. The door did not open, however. Louisa's servants were too well trained to intrude.

'What is it?' called Louisa.

'His lordship's carriage is at the door, ma'am.'

Max settled Louisa's hand gently on the coverlet and looked towards the door. 'Tell Ramsey to walk the horses. I will be down presently.'

'Aye, m'lord.'

'I must go, my dear. I will…think on what you have said.'

'You will consider it for the space of a second or two, you mean, and then discard it.'

He shook his head, smiling wryly.

'What is more, you have had no breakfast.'

Trust Louisa to know exactly when to change an unwelcome subject. She was a companion that any man would envy. 'I shall take something when we stop to bait the horses.' He bent to put a hand on her cheek and drop a tiny kiss on her lips. 'And, in any case,' he went on, straightening and turning for the door, 'what need have I of food? I am already very well satisfied this morning.'

She was blushing deliciously. It was a good memory to take with him on this unwelcome journey.

'Goodbye, my dear. I shall return as soon as I may.'

He ran lightly down the stairs to the tiny hallway where the servant was waiting with his heavy driving coat and his hat and gloves. At this time of year, he could not complete the journey in the day. There was too little daylight and the roads were always bad. Curse the woman! With her background, she could not help but be a thorn in his flesh, but why did she have to choose the middle of winter to inflict her scheming ways on him? He shook his head impatiently. He had no alternative. It would be a long, cold journey but he must confront her now, while he had the advantage of surprise.

The servant opened the door. Outside, the streets were white with frost. The horses' breath rose in great clouds in the half-hearted winter light.

By the time he reached Rosevale Abbey—if he ever did reach it in such weather—he would have devised some very choice words for his unknown cousin. Very choice indeed.

Chapter Three

'Have you seen my thimble, Angel? I seem to have mislaid it and I cannot possibly go to London without my canvas work.'

Angel sighed. Aunt Charlotte had been getting worse and worse since Pierre's visit. For days, she had talked almost non-stop about how she planned to help Pierre to oust Cousin Frederick. Only Angel's announcement that they were leaving for London, no matter what the weather, had served to divert the old lady's mind. Now the subject of her endless lectures was London Society and the need for her niece to make her mark there. Angel had become heartily tired of hearing about modistes, and fripperies, and Almack's.

'It is probably at the bottom of your workbag, Aunt. I am sure your woman will be able to find it for you.' She rose from her desk and crossed to the library door to give her aunt an affectionate peck on the cheek. 'Forgive me, dear Aunt, but I must finish these letters or we shall never be able to leave. I will join you for a nuncheon in an hour or so.' She patted Lady Charlotte's hand and turned back to her desk, forcing herself to give all her attention to the paper before her.

Angel waited, trying to read, until at last she heard the click of the door. Aunt Charlotte had gone. She began to write swiftly then. Her instructions must be quite clear or—

A sudden cramp bent her almost double. Oh, no! Not again. It was not even three weeks since the last time. She threw down her pen and put both hands to her belly, kneading her flesh in an attempt to allay the pain. The spasm receded. But she knew it would soon come again. She would have to go upstairs to her abigail. Benton was as bad—worse—than Aunt Charlotte. She meant well, but she would go on and on about Angel's erratic courses even though they both knew that there was no remedy to be had.

Angel shuddered at the sudden memory invading her mind. She tried to push it away but it was too vivid—the midwife's filthy hands forcing her legs apart, probing into the most secret recesses of her body, ignoring her screams of pain. And the doctor's sneering voice in the background, bidding her to be silent. She shuddered again. She could almost feel those freezing fingers tearing at her body.

Another spasm racked her. Dear God, why was she so cursed? It made no sense to have to suffer so. For years they had said she was barren. Everyone had told her so, the doctors, the cackling midwife, her husband, the Honourable John Frederick Worthington, and even her father—

No. Her father had never used that word. He was infinitely sad that she did not conceive, but he had never used that word. Not to her face, at least. Perhaps Papa had simply thought she was a slow breeder, like most of the Rosevales. He himself had had only one child in two long marriages. And Aunt Charlotte had none.

But the doctors had been so sure. And her husband had been so very angry, so insistent that she try every possible cure. John Frederick had forced her to give up her riding and almost all other kinds of exercise, and shut her up at home under the watchful eye of that tipsy midwife. He had given her disgusting food to eat and stood over her to make sure she swallowed every last bite. And he had come to her bed at every opportunity, insisting that she do her duty as his wife. 'You are mine,' he would always say. 'Mine!' There had been times when she had even been glad of the untimely arrival of her courses, in spite of the unbearable pain.

Except for that last time.

Her courses had been more than seven weeks late. Her body had felt…different. She had dared to hope…and made the fatal mistake of telling John Fredcrick of those hopes.

Too soon. Within a fortnight, she had lost the babe.

Ignoring Angel's terrible distress, the hovering midwife had immediately declared that she would never be able to carry a child to term. Worse, the woman had told her husband, too.

John Frederick was coldly furious. He said not a single word. He simply ordered the servants out of the room and then laid into Angel's pain-filled body with his riding crop. She thought he was going to kill her.

But some vestige of humanity must have remained, for he threw down the crop and stalked off to the stables in the pouring rain, to vent his rage by galloping full tilt to the furthest reaches of the estate.

The resulting chill was probably inevitable. It went to his lungs. And in the end, it had killed him.

Angel had buried the grief for her child deep within her heart. She had said nothing to anyone about her loss or about what her husband had done, though she knew that her abigail suspected. There was no point in distressing

Papa, who knew Angel too well to think that she was happy with the man he had chosen for her. If he noticed that her mourning was less than sincere, he never said so. And, crucially, he told her that there was no need for her to rush to take another husband.

I shall continue to follow his advice, Angel resolved, waiting for the pain to subside so that she could rise from her chair. I shall not allow Aunt Charlotte, or anyone else, to push me into marriage, for what would it bring me but pain and even more grief? The chances of my bearing an heir must be very slim indeed. I should be trading my new-found independence for—for what? At best, companionship. At worst…at worst, yet another enslavement of body and soul.

No. It is out of the question. I shall never marry again. Never.

'My lady…'

Angel struggled to open her eyes. How long had she been asleep?

'My lady, the Earl is here. He insists on seeing you. Says he will not leave unless you come down.'

Angel shook her head, trying to clear her thoughts. What on earth was the abigail talking about? 'Earl, Benton? I do not understand.'

'The Earl of Penrose. Your ladyship's cousin.'

Angel sat bolt upright, moving so fast that for a moment she was quite dizzy. She put a hand on the back of the *chaise-longue* for support. 'I… The Earl of Penrose? Here? What can he possibly want with me?'

'Willett told him your ladyship was indisposed, but he still refused to leave. Said as how he'd come up here to see you in your bedchamber if you would not go down to him.'

Angel swung her legs round and put her feet on to the floor. Yes, that was better; she was steadier now. Thank goodness she had not taken the laudanum that Benton had been pressing on her. She took a deep breath, waiting for the return of the pain. It seemed to have gone. Aunt Charlotte's tisane had worked, for once.

'Does my aunt know that the Earl is here?'

'I am not sure, m'lady. Willett offered to fetch her, seeing as you was asleep, but the Earl said—' Benton blushed rosily. 'The Earl said that his business was with your ladyship, and that no one else would do.'

Angel frowned. It was clear that the Earl's choice of words had been somewhat less circumspect than the abigail's version. Whatever Cousin Frederick's errand, he was in no friendly mood. She stood up and straightened her shoulders. She would go and meet this unknown cousin. And she would make it clear that, as head of the Rosevale family, she was not to be browbeaten by anyone, even a belted earl.

'You had best fetch me a fresh gown and tidy my hair, Benton. I would not have his lordship think that I have been dragged through a hedge.'

Benton smiled uncertainly, but did as she was bid. 'Shall I ask her ladyship to join you?' she said as she patted the last silver curl into place.

'No. Yes...' Angel thought back to Aunt Charlotte's uncharitable opinion of Cousin Frederick and her rash enthusiasm for Pierre's claim. The old lady was quite capable of saying more than she ought, especially when she found herself face to face with a man she believed to be an enemy. 'No,' she said with determination. 'If his lordship wishes to discuss a matter of business with me, I shall meet him alone. I am the head of the family. I am perfectly capable of handling my own affairs.'

She headed for the door, throwing a sideways glance at the glass to ensure her gown was presentable. She was no longer in mourning but, for this encounter, the dove-grey gown felt exactly right—demure and quietly elegant, as befitted a widow and a lady of rank.

Max had been pacing up and down in the drawing room for fully half an hour. The delay was doing nothing for his temper. Trust a woman to pretend to be indisposed in order to avoid an unwelcome visitor. She would learn that he was not so easily gulled. He would force her to receive him, even if he had to pace this room for a week.

He only hoped that she would come alone, when she did finally arrive, for he was not sure that he would be able to curb his temper if she brought her aunt. The old hag had encouraged the Marquis's unforgivable insults to Aunt Mary. And now she had produced a French pretender, like a rabbit from a hat. Did she really think she could succeed with such an obvious deception? She had probably helped her niece to start all these confounded rumours, too. No doubt these two harpies thought that it would improve their protégé's chances if all London was buzzing with gossip about the long-lost heir.

Long-lost impostor, more like! If the Frenchman—

The double doors opened. For a second, a tall stately lady dressed in half-mourning stood framed within the opening. Then she nodded slightly and took a pace forward, allowing the butler to close the doors at her back.

She did not speak, nor did she offer her hand. She was assessing him, just as he was assessing her. He would not have called her beautiful—her expression was much too severe for beauty—but her colouring was striking. She had hair like spun silver. He recognised it as the famous Rose-vale hair, inherited from the first Baroness, centuries before, but not found in anyone on his side of the family. Would she think him a changeling, with his dark locks?

No. She would not give a thought to such a detail. A warrior entering the lists did not concern himself with his opponent's colouring, but with his ability to fight. The woman who was coolly appraising him had the look of a doughty adversary. He would do well to be on his guard.

He bowed from the neck, not lowering his eyes. It was important to watch every move she made.

She dropped him a quick curtsy, the very minimum demanded by good manners. 'I understand you wished to see me, Cousin Frederick?'

Her voice was low, with a hard edge that was not pleasing to the ear. Had she deliberately chosen the mode of address that he most hated? Only his father and his grandfather had ever called him Frederick. He had despised them both; and he detested the name they had bestowed on him.

'I am obliged, ma'am, that you have felt able to rise from your sickbed to receive me. I trust you are quite recovered?' He saw a flash of anger in her eyes. A hit! Excellent. It was important to keep her on the defensive.

'You are too kind, sir. I understand you have important business you wished to discuss with me? Business that could not be delayed?'

'Indeed, ma'am.' Max waited for her to invite him to sit, but she did not. She simply stood there, glaring at him. It seemed he had caught her on the raw. So, that was to be the way of it. If she wanted a bout with the buttons off, he would happily oblige her. 'I must ask you for an explanation of this disreputable imposture you are promoting. You—'

'I am promoting nothing of the sort,' she snapped. 'How dare you suggest such a thing?'

'Do not think to play me for a fool, Cousin,' Max replied. 'I am perfectly well aware that you and your aunt are behind the rumours that are circulating in London. I am only surprised that you have not arrived in town already, with your French puppet in tow. I warn you now, I will not tolerate any attempt to undermine my position. Even from a woman.' The last few words came out in a hard, rasping voice that he barely recognised. He stopped abruptly, conscious that he was allowing his temper to get the better of him after all. What was it about this woman? He prided himself on his self-control with the female sex, but with her…

She lifted her chin and stared at him, with astonishingly dark blue eyes that were alight with fury. Her skin seemed to have grown paler; or perhaps it was the contrast with the spots of anger now burning on her cheeks. She took a step forward as though she might like to strike him, but her arms were held rigidly at her sides. She was controlling herself with difficulty. 'I take it you have proof of your outrageous allegations?' she said.

'Do I need proof? The fact that you do not need to ask for details of them is proof enough for me, Cousin.' Confound the woman, she was as bad as he had expected. Worse, perhaps. Why had he bothered to make this journey? He should have known better. He was struck by the irony of it all. 'Like father, like daughter,' he said acidly. 'It is perhaps as well that one title, at least, is no longer the preserve of the more dubious side of the Rosevale family.'

She gasped and turned completely white.

He had never felt such searing anger. He had gone much too far, and he knew it. By attacking her dishonourable behaviour in such terms, he had sunk to her level. He should apologise. But his throat was so constricted that, for a moment, he could not utter a word.

She had reached out a hand to clutch the back of a chair. A spasm crossed her face. It looked almost like pain. Then she straightened again and said, with an obvious effort, 'This discussion is now at an end, sir. I will thank you to leave. My aunt and I plan to travel to London next week. If you have anything more to say to me, you may say it there. And you may be sure that I shall take the greatest of pleasure in introducing you to my cousin, the rightful Earl of Penrose.' She spun on her heel and started to move to the door without giving him any chance to reply.

'Not so fast, Cousin.' Max strode forward and grasped her wrist, forcing her to stop in her tracks. 'We have not finished this interview yet.'

'Release me this instant.' Her voice was a furious hiss. She kept her head turned towards the door as if she could not bear to look at him.

Max took a long slow breath and then deliberately reached round to grasp her other wrist. Her bones felt tiny and fragile. He had no intention of injuring her, but he was determined that she would hear him out. For several seconds, they both stood motionless. Then Max exerted just enough pressure to turn her back to face him.

She did not try to pull herself free. She simply stood there, refusing to look at him. Her extraordinary silver hair was on a level with his chin.

'So, madam, you have decided to pit your French impostor against me, have you? Are you sure that is wise?'

'I am sure that the rightful Earl of Penrose is a gentleman, sir,' she replied evenly, gazing fixedly at her trapped wrists, 'which you are not.'

Max had recovered just enough control over his temper to recognise that she was deliberately trying to provoke him. He resisted the immediate temptation to let her go. 'Clever,' he said softly. 'But also rash. If you are so sure I am no gentleman, ma'am, why did you consent to this private interview?'

He paused. She did not reply.

'Quite. However, I am gentleman enough to remember that you are a lady, in spite of this fraud you are intent upon. I ask you, as a lady, to abandon it, for your own sake. It will do you, and the Rosevale family, nothing but harm.'

She looked up then. For a moment, Max thought he saw real pain in her eyes, but it was quickly replaced by black anger. '*My* position is unassailable, sir,' she retorted. 'Yours, on the other hand, is somewhat precarious. I will thank you to release me and leave my house. We have nothing more to say to each other.'

The woman was impossible! Why had he ever thought to reason with her? It was a waste of words!

'You are foolish, madam,' he said, dropping her wrists abruptly. 'Your family already has enemies enough. You cannot afford more. But, I promise you, you have added another today.'

He stalked to the door and wrenched it open. Then he turned and bowed mockingly. 'Good day to you, Cousin. Be sure that we shall continue this discussion at a later date.'

Then he walked smartly down the stairs to the entrance hall to retrieve his coat and hat. The butler was waiting for him, with a look of alarm on his face. It was almost as if he expected Max to strike him!

Max caught the reflection of a black-browed man with a face like thunder in the glass near the bottom of the stairs. Good God! It was himself! No wonder the old butler was quaking in his boots.

Taking a long deep breath, Max willed his heart to slow. It had been pounding fit to burst, as if he were about to charge the enemy. That silver-haired woman must be a witch to have affected him so.

The butler silently helped Max into his coat. Then he held out Max's hat and gloves, without raising his eyes from them, as if he could not trust himself to look Max in the face.

Max was not about to enter into an altercation with a mere servant. He took his things with a brief nod of thanks and hurried out into the gathering gloom where Ramsey was waiting with his carriage.

'Drive back to Speenhamland, Ramsey. There is nothing more for us here.' He flung himself inside and threw his hat and gloves into the furthest corner, the moment the carriage began to move down the driveway.

What on earth had come over him?

He stared unseeingly ahead. He must have run stark mad to allow his temper to rule him in such a way. With a lady, too. What had happened to his manners? Dear God, if Aunt Mary could have heard him...

Aunt Mary. Yes. There was something about the Baroness that reminded him of Aunt Mary. The two were totally unlike in looks, to be sure, but still there was something in their manner... Perhaps that had been the spark? The contrast between Aunt Mary's honesty and the Baroness's flagrant disregard for it had been too much. His temper had gone off like a rocket. In all those years as a soldier, Max had never lost his temper with anyone weaker than himself but, faced with a single silver-haired Jezebel, he had forgotten every vestige of how a gentleman should behave.

He should be ashamed. It did not matter what she had

done. Or what she might still do. He owed it to himself—
to his own honour—to behave like a gentleman.

He would have to apologise.

He let his shoulders droop and let out a long sigh. Yes,
he would apologise. Eventually. But certainly not today.
He could not face her again today.

Besides, she was ill…

He sat up sharply, his senses all on the alert. No. He
had not imagined it. There *had* been pain in her face.

She really was ill.

And he had forced her to meet him, forced her to listen
to his insults, forced her to remain when she wished only
to flee from him.

His behaviour had been totally unforgivable.

Angel stood rigid until the door closed behind him, and
then she collapsed into the nearest chair, moaning softly.
She was in too much pain to move.

But she was just lucid enough to curse her cousin. He
was even worse than Aunt Charlotte had suggested. He
was the devil!

'My lady—'

Angel looked up to see the butler standing in the doorway, aghast.

'I'll fetch Benton at once, m'lady,' he said, almost slam-
ming the door behind him in his haste.

Angel closed her eyes and leaned her cheek against the
cool damask of the chair. That was a little better. Her head
ached so.

'My lady, let me help you to your chamber.'

Angel breathed a sigh of relief at the welcome sound of
Benton's voice. She could not have faced Aunt Charlotte's
incessant questions. Not now. Benton would keep Aunt
Charlotte at bay. In a very short space of time, Angel was

upstairs and in her own bed, and Benton was gently cooling her brow with a cloth soaked in lavender water.

Angel opened her eyes a fraction. The curtains were closed and the room was dim, lit only by the fire. It was blissfully peaceful.

'Have the pains returned, m'lady?'

'Yes. And I have the headache now, too.'

'Shall I fetch you a little laudanum?'

'No, Benton. You know how I hate it. Sleep is all I need.' Angel smiled weakly at her faithful abigail. 'You may ask my aunt to prepare one of her tisanes. It will make her feel useful.'

Benton rose obediently.

'You need not tell her whether or not I drink it,' Angel added softly, snuggling down into the welcoming softness. She really ought to stop to consider what Cousin Frederick had said, but her head ached so much that she could not begin to order her thoughts. She would just close her eyes for a space. In a moment or two, her mind would be clearer, and then she could...

Angel woke with a start. She lay for a moment, listening.

There was no sound at all. The house was totally silent. Everyone must be abed. The faint glow from the dying fire showed that she must have been asleep for hours. And the pain was gone.

She lay back on her pillows and gazed up at the silken canopy. In the gloom, it seemed to be floating.

So that was Cousin Frederick.

She closed her eyes, trying to picture him in her mind. She could not. She ought to be able to do so, surely? It was very strange. But Cousin Frederick's character was so overpowering that she had only the vaguest memory of his face. She could remember little more than his fierce anger. That, and his voice—taut as a tempered steel sword blade, whipping at her skin. No, she would not soon forget that hard, merciless voice.

For the rest, he was tall and strong—strong enough to master a mere woman, at least—and he had dark hair. In fact, from what little she could remember, he had not looked like a Rosevale at all. Why, Pierre was more a Rosevale than Frederick!

Was he? The question hit Angel like a blow.

She turned on her side and fixed her gaze on the fireplace as she strove to remember Cousin Frederick's exact words. He had said… He had accused her— Good God, he already knew about Pierre! But how…?

Aunt Charlotte. Of course. Who else?

It did not matter that Angel had counselled caution. Pierre had promised to do, and say, nothing, but Aunt Charlotte had given no such undertaking. She would probably have broken it, even if she had. No doubt she had written to only her dearest friends, and in strictest confidence. No wonder the rumours were flying all over London.

And what of Pierre? Had he heard? Angel did not know which circles he now moved in. Perhaps he had been spared the covert looks and sly whispers. She must see him as soon as possible, warn him of the dangers of speaking out of turn.

She must warn Aunt Charlotte, too. And take her to task for her lack of discretion. That would not be easy. Since her father's death, Angel had gradually learned to take on the responsibilities of her new status, but it was incredibly difficult to play the part of the stern head of the family with an old lady who had been like a mother to her for years.

None the less, it must be done. Tomorrow.

And the moment Angel was well enough to travel, they must set out for London, in hopes of saving Pierre from Cousin Frederick's wrath.

Chapter Four

'So it was a waste of time?'

'Completely. I learned nothing more than we already knew. Perhaps if I hadn't lost my temper with her...'

Ross shook his head. 'It never was your most attractive feature, I will admit. And just lately...' He held up a hand. 'No, do not turn that wicked tongue of yours on me, if you please. I promise you that I should not respond, so it would be a waste of energy. You would do better to spend some time in the ring. Do you good to hit someone.'

Max strode over to the window and stared down into Dover Street. Why was he so bad-tempered these days? He'd learned to control it when he was in the army, dammit, so why couldn't he do it since his visit to the Abbey? 'She's coming to town,' he said at last, willing his tense muscles to relax. He turned back to Ross. 'She's out of mourning now, of course. I fancy she plans to set herself up in Rosevale House and start introducing that cursed Frenchman to the *ton* as the rightful Earl of Penrose. It makes my blood boil, Ross. I could cheerfully strangle her.'

'Why? You said yourself that the title is worthless.'

'Aye, but I'll not have it stripped from me to provide

amusement for a…for a…' Words failed him when he thought of her. He felt that all-consuming anger again. What was it about that woman…?

'It's understandable that you are angry,' Ross said calmly. 'But have you thought that she might be an innocent victim in this? She may have been taken in by a plausible rogue.'

Max made no attempt to hide his disbelief.

'It wouldn't be surprising,' Ross said, 'considering the kind of life she's led. She's by no means fly to the time of day. She's been in mourning for years, remember, first for her husband and then for her father. And she was kept pretty close before that—married out of the schoolroom, by all accounts. Her husband never permitted her to come to town, you know.'

'How on earth did you learn that?'

'I have made it my business to find out,' Ross replied with a rather satisfied smile. 'While you were posting off to confront the wicked Baroness, I decided there might be subtler ways of handling the situation.'

Max nodded somewhat reluctantly.

'There is plenty of speculation about your Baroness, Max. She may not have spent time in Society, but her aunt appears to be a gossip of the first order. Since the Baroness is a very wealthy woman, every gazetted fortune-hunter in London will be after her, I imagine. The Frenchman may well be one of them. Had you thought of that?'

Max ran an unsteady hand through his hair. 'No, I hadn't.' He paused, thinking. 'It's more than possible, as you say, that the Frenchman is a fraud who means to trap her into marriage. She's a wealthy prize—rich enough to set any man up. I should have thought of that. I'm afraid I have not been thinking straight at all since I met her.'

Ross looked at him in surprise. 'So Captain Rosevale,

the consummate tactician, is no more? Pity. I'm sure cold logic would be a better weapon than blind anger.'

'You're right, of course. As usual. And, for once, I shall take your advice to heart. We need to plan our assault like a military campaign. And the first thing we need is intelligence. What have your subtle enquiries discovered about the Frenchman?'

'Unfortunately for us, he is playing his cards very close to his chest. I've found out where he comes from—somewhere near Toulon—but nothing more. If we are to smoke him out, we'll need to do a deal more digging.'

Max nodded. 'That means a trip to France. But I'm loath to leave London while that—while my dear cousin is in residence. Even if she has been duped—though she struck me as too strong-minded for that—she could create a great deal of mischief. I don't think I can risk leaving the field to her.'

'I don't suggest that you should.' Ross put a hand on Max's shoulder. 'Look, Max, there is no call for both of us to go. Provided you trust me to—'

'Devil take it, Ross! You know very well—'

'If you trust me with such a delicate mission, old friend, I will gladly go to France and do your spying for you.' He laughed infectiously. 'Could be quite like old times, eh? Creeping around among the Frenchies, trying to discover the lie of the land.'

Max smiled back. He felt as if a weight had been lifted from him. 'I do believe you intended to go all along, you rogue.'

'Yes, well, perhaps…'

'Believe me, Ross, I am very much in your debt. There is no one else in the world I would permit to do this for me. You—'

'I am nowhere near repaying everything that I owe you,

Max, so I suggest you stop praising me to the skies. Besides, I've a notion that a trip through France would just suit me. What we saw of it last time was not exactly... ideal, was it?'

They exchanged a look of shared understanding. The memory was very real to them both. The whole of Wellington's army had been glad to leave the Pyrenees behind and start across the French plain. Conditions had been harsh, for everyone, but the army had known that victory was almost within reach, after so many years of struggle.

'I think I begin to envy you, my friend,' said Max after a moment.

'I am sure I have the easier task. I have only to make my way to the south of France and bribe my way to the information we need. Whereas you must brave the drawing rooms of the *ton* and this impostor's nefarious schemes...and the matchmaking mamas, too, of course.' Ross grinned. 'You are become an eligible bachelor at last.'

'You think you are jesting, Ross, but it is no joke, believe me. The acquisition of a title seems to change even a man's appearance. When I was a mere Captain Rosevale, I had neither face nor fortune to commend me. I have little more by way of fortune now, heaven knows, but it appears that an unmarried earl will always be described as handsome by the ladies of the *ton*—especially those with unmarried daughters. I heard it with my own ears.' He shuddered. 'Downright nauseating.'

'Don't worry, Max. I promise to keep reminding you to look in the glass. Besides, if your impostor has his way, you will be plain Mr Rosevale again...in more senses than one.'

'It does have its attractions, Ross. I'd be lying if I said otherwise.'

'You are too modest, Max.' Ross gave his friend a long appraising look. 'And you are not ugly... Well, not really...'

Max grinned, refusing to rise to Ross's bait.

'More seriously, though,' Ross continued, 'I ought to warn you that your impostor really will turn the ladies' heads. He is quite disgustingly handsome. And he has the manners to match, too, I'm afraid. I suppose we're lucky he isn't wearing regimentals. If he were, the ladies would be falling at his feet.'

Max grunted. It seemed the odds were stacked against him. He could rely on Ross to ferret out what information there was to the Frenchman's discredit, but it would take time. Meanwhile, Max himself would have to find ways of undermining the man here in London. Or, if not the man, then the woman... That blasted woman! She—

He refused to let his temper rule him, this time. He must plan his next moves with the utmost care. If necessary, he must be all smiles and soft words. Logic and cold calculation were what he needed now. In hot blood, a man made mistakes.

And after all, Ross could well be right. She might be innocent of any wrongdoing. She might be the prey, not the predator.

'If the Frenchman *is* after her money, will you protect her?' said Ross, echoing Max's unspoken thoughts.

'I should, of course...' Max had a mental picture of the silver-haired harridan with a temper as fiery as his own. 'But, having met her, I doubt if she'd accept protection from me. I can't force her to spurn him, can I?'

'No. You'd have to marry her yourself to do that.'

'That's the second time you have suggested I marry Angelina Rosevale. What's got into you, Ross?'

Ross shrugged eloquently.

Max thought back to that tempestuous encounter at the Abbey. He had not behaved well—and he knew it. She was only a woman, after all, and an unworldly one, into the bargain. She had neither husband nor brother to defend her. So it was his duty to do so.

His duty did not extend to marrying her!

'After our recent encounter at the Abbey, I think I am the last man on earth that Lady Rosevale would marry. In fact,' Max added, remembering her exact words, 'I'm sure of it. She told me I was no gentleman. I'd have to drag her to the altar by the hair.'

Ross's eyebrows rose. 'I hadn't thought of abduction. But now you come to mention it…' He grinned wickedly.

Max raised his eyes to heaven. He knew better than to respond when Ross was in one of his rollicking moods.

'As a matter of fact,' said Ross after a moment, looking rather more solemn, 'you would not need to resort to abduction. Much better to make the lady fall in love with you. She—'

'Confound it, Ross, I—'

'She wouldn't be the first, would she?'

Max clamped his lips tight together.

'Seriously, Max, you know very well how to turn her up sweet. After all your practice in Spain, an unworldly widow should be like wax in your hands. Charm her into favouring you over the Frenchman.'

Max began to shake his head, but stopped. It was true that he could make himself attractive to women. It was just that he had never tried it when the stakes were so high. In Spain, a little dalliance had been a light-hearted thing, a fleeting pleasure for both parties. But this? This was too important. His cousin was pursuing a dangerous path.

If she was being cozened by a plausible impostor, it was

Max's duty, as a gentleman and her closest male relative, to do everything in his power to save her.

And he would. Somehow. Whether she willed it or no.

Aunt Charlotte had fallen asleep. At last! Angel offered up a silent prayer of thanks, even though it had taken a long time. They would be in London in little over an hour from now. Not much of an opportunity for Angel to order her thoughts and decide what she was to do.

She had had time enough to reflect on Cousin Frederick. Days of time. It had not helped. She still could not make up her mind about him. She could not even remember him properly. His temper had been so overwhelming that she had thought of little else…apart from his strength when he had held her fast.

He had threatened her, had he not? And he had accused her of conspiring with Pierre to steal his title. Not in quite such stark terms, of course, but that had surely been the import of his words.

He had been furious. He had said things that were unforgivable. So she had every right to hate him, just as Aunt Charlotte did. And yet…

Angel glanced across to where Lady Charlotte slept in the corner of the carriage. Her mouth hung slightly open. Every now and then, a little noise emerged. How mortified the old lady would be to be told that she snored!

Angel smiled to herself. Poor Aunt Charlotte. She hated the idea of growing old and losing control. She prided herself on her self-control—except where Cousin Frederick was concerned. There she had no control at all. She had nothing but cold, implacable hatred for him, and for all his family. That, Angel supposed, must be the reason for her aunt's unaccountably sudden acceptance of Pierre, too. Nothing else made any sense. It all seemed totally out of character for such a refined lady.

Angel shook her head. There was no point in brooding about Aunt Charlotte. She was impossible to fathom. Besides, Angel still had to decide what she was going to do in London. About Pierre. And about Cousin Frederick.

She did not fully trust Pierre, though she was not sure why. Perhaps it was because of Aunt Charlotte's lightning conversion to his cause. On the other hand, he might be exactly what he said. Angel owed it to her honour, and to her family, to give Pierre every opportunity to establish his credentials. If he proved to be her Uncle Julian's son, it would be Angel's duty to take his part against Cousin Frederick.

A little tremor ran through her at the thought of taking on a man who could outface her in her own drawing room. She quelled it very deliberately, putting the odd sensation out of her mind, and reminding herself that she was wealthy enough—as Cousin Frederick was not—to call on all the resources of the law to back her. She could do it. But it was daunting, none the less. She—

The carriage hit a bump. Aunt Charlotte woke up with a start.

'Oh, dear, have I been asleep?' she asked, putting her hands up to straighten her lace cap. 'I do apologise, my love. How boring for you to have no one to talk to. I promise I shall try to keep awake for the rest of the journey.' Another bump jolted them both. 'And if the road continues like this, I shall have no difficulty,' she added waspishly. 'Considering how high the tolls are, it is too bad that the road is in such an appalling state. Do you not think so, Angel?'

Angel nodded absently.

'I wonder how soon Pierre will call on us. You did write to tell him we were coming to town, did you not, Angel?'

'Yes, Aunt. I asked him to call on us the day after to-morrow.'

'But why so long? We—'

'I have asked my man of business to call on me tomorrow. I must discuss matters with him before we see Mr Rosevale again. I would not have Mr Rosevale cherish false hopes.'

'Nonsense. There can be no question of that. You yourself saw the likeness to the portrait.'

Angel took a deep breath. Patience!

'And he is such a delightful young man. So handsome! So charming! And so eligible, too. I predict he will have half the ladies in London dropping the handkerchief.'

'Quite possibly, Aunt, though his looks will not avail him much without a title or an estate. He told us they were living like peasants, remember?'

'Yes, and it is quite shocking. You must help him, my dear!'

'Must I?' said Angel warningly.

The old lady began to look a little flustered. 'I very much hope you will help him. You cannot take Cousin Frederick's part, surely? From what little you told me, he behaved to you like an absolute blackguard. Exactly what I should have expected from Augustus Rosevale's grandson, of course. Not an ounce of good in any of 'em.'

Angel kept silent. She was not about to encourage her aunt's intemperate outbursts even though, in this case, she was right. Her cousin had behaved in an appalling fashion. He was foul-tempered...and a little frightening, too. She felt that odd tremor again, running down her spine. She forced herself to ignore it and to focus on Pierre. Pierre was gentle, and charming, and understood exactly how to make a lady feel…valued.

'They are certainly not at all alike, Aunt. But I wonder whether Mr Rosevale will be able to stand against Cousin Frederick. He will be a formidable opponent, I think.'

'But Pierre will have you to stand with him. Will he not? He is exactly what a young man should be, you know, and you—'

'If he were as perfect as you say, Aunt Charlotte, I should marry him myself!' cried Angel, in exasperation. 'He—'

Aunt Charlotte clapped her hands in delight. 'Of course! That is exactly the solution! If you marry him, there can be no question about his place in Society. Your position would be unassailable, too, and—'

Angel closed her eyes in despair, trying to shut out Aunt Charlotte's excited chatter.

What on earth had she said? She was mad, totally mad, to have even hinted at such a thing to Aunt Charlotte. The old lady was annoying, certainly, but there had been no justification for Angel's loss of control. It was the curse of the Rosevales! In hot blood, the Rosevales said and did things that no sane person would ever dream of doing.

Now Aunt Charlotte would treat it as settled. And the last thing Angel wanted to think about was marriage. To anyone.

'Dear Aunt,' she said gently, 'pray do not throw yourself into transports. I was teasing you—and I apologise for it. It was not well done of me. You know well enough that I have no desire to take another husband. Even one who is absolutely perfect.' She smiled hopefully at the old lady, who was looking very disappointed.

Lady Charlotte frowned for a second, but then her brow cleared. 'Let us not make any hasty decisions, my dear,' she said brightly. 'It is too soon to decide—of course it is—but nothing is impossible, especially with such an exceptional young man. We must wait and see. But I have a feeling that something special will come of your relationship with him. You mark my words! Just wait and see what happens!'

Angel groaned. 'Thank you, Aunt,' she said in clipped tones. 'I think we have said quite enough on this subject.' She stared meaningfully at the old lady until, finally, Lady Charlotte nodded and looked away.

Angel breathed a gentle sigh of relief. 'I think I shall go to Célestine's tomorrow,' she said lightly. 'If I am to go into Society, I need something to wear apart from half-mourning. I must say, it will be quite a treat to wear bright colours again.'

Lady Charlotte beamed and nodded, as if nothing had happened. 'Indeed so, my dear. And, for a lady of rank, Célestine is the only possible modiste. She is particularly talented when it comes to gowns for great occasions, like Court presentations. Or weddings…'

'Aunt…' Angel warned.

'But it is true, my love. Why, only last year, three of the grandest brides of the Season were dressed by Célestine and—'

'It does not apply to me. I am a widow, not a new bride. And I am *not* planning to remarry. I must ask you to speak of something else, Aunt.'

There was an awkward silence for several minutes. But, as the carriage was now travelling through the villages on the outskirts of London, there was much to distract the ladies, especially Angel, who had not visited London for years.

'My goodness,' she said, when the carriage slowed to negotiate the increasingly heavy traffic, 'I had not remembered that the city was as busy as this. At this rate, we shall not reach Rosevale House before dark.'

'Don't worry, my dear. John Coachman will find our way. Besides, some of the streets are now lit by gas lamps. I am told that it is as bright as day.'

Angel did not attempt to contradict her.

'It makes the streets much safer, too, I hear. Not that you would be out in the streets after dark, of course. No lady of quality would ever do that. Which reminds me, Angel. I know you are a widow, but you are new to Society and you do have a reputation to lose. It is important that you know exactly how to go on. I shall help you, naturally, but I…er…I ought to remind you, my dear, that you must never go out alone. In fact, it would be best if you always took the carriage—'

'I must take *some* exercise, Aunt.'

'But not by striding around the countryside like a peasant searching for…for…'

'Lost sheep?' said Angel mischievously.

Lady Charlotte tut-tutted. She was in her element now. 'You may take exercise on horseback. In the park. It is a splendid place to see and be seen.'

'No doubt. But a quiet amble in the park, stopping to chat at every other moment, provides little by way of exercise, Aunt. I shall continue to walk.'

'But—'

'But, to please you, dear Aunt, I shall take a maid with me. Let us hope she can keep up!'

'Angel, no! You must not make such a spectacle of yourself. Truly you must not! If you stride about like a…like a man, you will do your reputation no good at all. Imagine what Society would say of you! You must behave like a lady at all times. You really must. You know how important it is.'

Angel swallowed the hot words that rose to her lips. She would not let her irritation show, not this time. She must try to be fair to Aunt Charlotte, who certainly had Angel's best interests at heart. Unfortunately, there would never be a meeting of minds on what those best interests were. Aunt Charlotte was convinced that Angel should behave, in almost all respects, as if she were a demure débutante. And she would continue to urge restraint on Angel at every opportunity. It was intolerable! But it was also understandable. Aunt Charlotte loved her and wanted her to find happiness. Sadly, they disagreed on the role of a husband in that blissful state.

Angel forced herself to smile at Lady Charlotte. Let the old lady believe she had won the argument and that Angel would behave exactly as her aunt wished. After all, Angel was mistress of her own household. She should certainly be able to find ways of escaping from the oppressive rules her aunt wished to impose.

There must be a way. She would not be caged!

Angel stood in the imposing entrance hall of Rosevale House in Berkeley Square, watching her aunt mount the stairs and disappear in the direction of her bedchamber. Angel was still inwardly fuming, but she was determined to control her ire in front of the servants.

She turned a friendly smile on the waiting butler. 'Good evening to you, Willett. I am glad to see that you made much better time than we did. I am afraid we were delayed by the traffic. I hope that Cook's efforts will not be spoiled if dinner is delayed for an hour.'

'Your ladyship's wishes will be conveyed to the kitchen at once,' Willett said.

Angel looked hard at the man. He sounded rather more pompous than usual. And he seemed to be lacking his normal composure. Strange. She would quiz Benton about what was going on. But first, she needed a bath. She felt hot and dirty from the journey.

As Angel turned towards the staircase, Willett coughed delicately. 'Your ladyship has a visitor.'

Angel spun round. Who would be so rude as to intrude on a lady at such a moment? After more than a day on the road, she was in no fit state to greet a guest. Unless it was Pierre? Was he in trouble?

'The Earl of Penrose, m'lady. He is waiting in the bookroom.'

With a sharp intake of breath, Angel picked up her dusty skirts and marched smartly towards the bookroom. Willett only just reached the door in time to open it for her.

Cousin Frederick turned as she entered. He was immaculate in a blue coat and pale pantaloons. There was not a speck of dust on his shining hessians. And there was a superior smile on his face that made her want to slap him!

'To what do I owe this singularly ill-timed visit, Cousin? An emergency of some kind, I collect?'

Penrose's smile vanished and was instantly replaced by a black scowl. Then his gaze travelled over her dust-stained clothing. She thought she detected a sneer at the corner of his mouth as he bowed to her. It was intolerable!

Angel did not offer even a nod in reply. She was much too angry. 'I will thank you to state your business, Cousin, and allow me to go about mine. As you have clearly observed, I am in no fit state to entertain casual callers.'

Cousin Frederick's eyes narrowed as he straightened once more. He looked coldly furious. 'Your pardon, my lady,' he said in clipped, formal tones. 'I will relieve you of my unwelcome presence on the instant. I should not wish to inconvenience you in any way.'

With another perfunctory bow, he strode towards the

door where Angel was standing, effectively forcing her to make way for him. How dare he?

'Sir! You—!'

It was too late. Her impossible cousin had thrown open the door and marched out into the hallway. She heard the click of his heels on the marble floor, and then the sound of the front door.

Angel sank into the nearest chair and let out a long slow breath. Stupid! Stupid! Why had she not stopped to think before she spoke? She, after all, was the one who had said that they must make peace with Cousin Frederick's branch of the family. Instead, she had taken one look at his haughty face and lost her temper. Again! What was it about that man? He made her behave like a foolish child rather than a grown woman.

Whatever the cause, there was no hope of reconciliation after an encounter like that. Her own hasty tongue had made an enemy of the man who was both her cousin and her heir.

Max strode off round the square at a cracking pace. Ross had had the right of it. Max needed to hit something—or someone—soon, or he would explode. So much for his good intentions! What was the point in trying to make peace with such a termagant? The benighted woman was utterly without manners or common decency. Just wait until the tabbies started in on her! Then she would reap the rewards of her unladylike behaviour.

And he would happily watch from the sidelines while the lady's nemesis approached. If she continued in this vein, she would find herself ostracised from Society.

Did she not deserve it?

Max did not attempt to pursue that question. He knew that reflection was impossible when he was in a black temper. He would do better to follow Ross's advice. Unfortunately, at this time of day, he could not go to Jackson's Boxing Saloon.

With an exasperated grunt, he turned his steps towards St James's and his club. If he could not punch his way out of his temper, he would drown it instead.

Chapter Five

Lady Charlotte gazed across to where Angel sat at the pianoforte, playing exquisitely, as usual. Angel looked calm, poised and quite beautiful in a sapphire and silver gown, one of Célestine's fabulous creations. Lady Charlotte sighed with pleasure.

'Your niece plays quite delightfully, my dear Lady Charlotte.'

Lady Charlotte turned to the elderly dowager at her elbow. 'Yes, indeed, Lady Perrimer,' she said, nodding.

'She is come up to town in search of a husband, I collect?'

Lady Charlotte swallowed a gasp. The old tabby was nothing if not direct. 'The Baroness Rosevale has a position in Society to fulfil,' she responded in a crushing tone. 'It was not possible for my niece to do so while we were in mourning for her father, as I'm sure you, ma'am, would be the first to agree.'

Lady Perrimer bowed her grey head a fraction. The two enormous plumes in her purple turban wafted down and then up again, rather as an afterthought. She raised her lorgnette to scrutinise Angel yet more closely. 'Whatever your niece's intentions may be,' she said, lifting her glass to indicate the young gallant who was bending over Angel's shoulder to turn her music, 'it is a pound to a penny that every fortune-hunter in London will be trying to win her. Young Rotherwell there is but the first.' At that moment, Angel smiled gratefully up at her escort, and Lady Perrimer snorted in disgust. 'Should have thought you would have taught her not to bestow her favours on just anyone. Rotherwell hasn't a feather to fly with…and is a rakehell, besides.'

'My niece was taught manners from the cradle, ma'am,' Lady Charlotte said acidly, 'and that included the importance of being polite to any gentleman who renders a service to her.' She tried to ignore the fact that Angel now seemed to be openly flirting with her cavalier. Confound the girl! She should know better than to expose herself, and her relations, to the criticism of tabbies like Lady Perrimer. Just wait till they were alone!

'Outrageous!' Lady Perrimer was clearly paying more attention to the evidence of her eyes than to Lady Charlotte's quelling words.

'Are your own family arrived in town, ma'am?' said Lady Charlotte, with a tight smile. She refused to be drawn further on the subject of Angel's behaviour. 'Your two younger sons are as yet unmarried, are they not?' She was gratified to see a tiny flush on the dowager's neck. Let her have a taste of her own nasty medicine.

Lady Perrimer raised her eyebrows haughtily. 'My three eldest sons are already well married, ma'am. As for the two youngest…I dare say they will be settled eventually. It is of little importance, since the succession is in no danger. When one has a fine family of sons…' She smiled in a particularly condescending way. 'Such a pity that your brother did not succeed in siring even one son. In spite of having two wives.'

Lady Charlotte knew when she was outgunned. Fortunately, Angel had just risen from the instrument and seemed to be moving in the general direction of the supper room on the arm of young Rotherwell. 'Excuse me, ma'am, but I fear I must leave you. I promised to join my niece for supper.' With a slight nod, she moved rapidly away, trying to ignore the fact that she had certainly lost that encounter. She must warn Angel about her behaviour before her niece's reputation suffered irreparably. Angel might be a widow, and a Baroness into the bargain, but even she should not encourage the attentions of reprobates such as Rotherwell…or Lady Perrimer's younger sons.

Max watched with distaste. His cousin was continuing to flirt openly with Rotherwell. Rotherwell, of all people! Was the woman so naïve, or so lacking in self-esteem, that she must stoop to consorting with Rotherwell?

She was laughing up at her companion now, reaching out to touch his sleeve in a revoltingly familiar way. Women! Did she have any idea of the risks she was taking with a man like Rotherwell? Probably not. She had led a sheltered life until now. Perhaps no one had warned her about the dregs of Society and the harm they might seek to do her.

He was relieved when Lady Charlotte drew her niece aside and began whispering urgently to her. High time the chit learned what was what.

But the Baroness was clearly in no mood to heed her aunt's advice, for she was shaking her head and cutting short the old lady's words. Lady Charlotte was beginning to look quite indignant. Was the chit so determined on her folly that she would dismiss her companion's warnings without a hearing?

Max watched, astonished to see that his cousin would

abruptly desert her aunt and return to resume her flirtatious tête-à-tête with Rotherwell. After only a few minutes, they were joined by two more of London's most notorious fortune-hunters. Max was not in the least surprised. Such men would never willingly leave the field to only one of their number.

Max's disgust grew. The haughty Baroness was clearly basking in the false compliments being showered upon her by her three money-grubbing suitors. Somewhat unwillingly, he admitted to himself that it was not only her money that was drawing them to her like wasps to a pool of honey. Her person, too, was more attractive than he had remembered. She seemed to have blossomed since he had last seen her. It was not simply that she was beautifully gowned. There was something more. Some men might even have called her beautiful—but only if they knew nothing of the character beneath.

Suddenly he was no longer in any doubt. She *must* be perfectly aware of what she was doing. She was sparkling with animation, smiling and laughing with the gentlemen and occasionally gazing coyly up at one of them through her lashes. So much for Ross's warning that she might be an innocent in need of protection. She was nothing of the sort! And he would take pleasure in saying as much to Ross, as soon as his friend returned from France.

The longer Max watched, the angrier he became. The woman was drawing the censure of all the tabbies for her outrageous behaviour. Every eye was upon her! If she was not stopped, the Rosevale family would have no reputation left!

Max was striding across the floor to her before he was fully aware of what he was doing—or what he planned.

Rotherwell and his companions reluctantly made way for Max's approach. He offered them only the briefest military bow. 'Gentlemen,' he said frostily, 'you will allow me to deprive you of my cousin's delightful company.' He held out his arm imperiously, frowning down at the Baroness until she placed her gloved fingers on his sleeve. Then, with a curt nod to the three rakes, Max moved her away, leading her to the far side of the main saloon where empty sofas stood against the wall.

'Will it please you to sit for a while, ma'am?'

She glowered up at him. 'It pleases me not at all, sir. Why did you insist on bringing me apart, pray? We can have nothing to say to each other.'

'Smile, Cousin,' Max said coolly. 'There is already enough conjecture in this room about your behaviour without adding the speculation that you and I are at outs.'

'How dare—?'

'Smile, Cousin.' He waited, but she did not respond. 'Watch. It is not so very difficult to do.' He affected to smile down at her.

'That is not a smile, sir. That is a grimace,' she said sharply. 'However, since you clearly wish to have speech with me, I can grant you…a few moments. I take it that will suffice?'

Max said nothing. He simply waited while she took her seat. She arranged her skirts demurely, taking much more time than was necessary, and then she looked up at him with a spark of challenge in her eye and a tiny smile on her lips. 'You are squandering your allotted time, sir. I am waiting to hear what it is you wish to say to me…but my patience is not infinite.'

'Neither is mine, madam,' he said flatly, taking his seat beside her and stretching out his legs with an appearance of nonchalance. He refused to let her suspect how much she exasperated him.

He raised a hand to beckon a waiter with a tray of champagne. Without saying a word to the Baroness, he took two glasses and offered one to her. 'I am sure you are in need of something to drink now.'

She raised her brows but did not make any move to take the champagne. 'How so?'

He offered the glass once again. 'After so much animated discussion with that trio of ne'er-do-wells...'

She threw a long, bleak look at him but said nothing. However, she did at last take the crystal flute from his hand. In truth, she had no choice, for those eyes were still watching them from across the room.

'Whatever you may think of me, Cousin,' Max said smoothly, 'you would do well to make it appear that we are simply having an amicable discussion about matters of mutual interest. The tabbies will be quick to fix on the slightest sign of acrimony between us.' He leant back carelessly and took a mouthful of champagne. 'Mmm. Not bad. I suggest you try it, Cousin.'

He watched her face as she sipped. It was a fine vintage, but she did not look as if she were enjoying it. What on earth had she been doing since her come-out? 'Not to your liking, Cousin?'

'It is palatable enough, sir,' she replied, her gaze fixed on her wine.

There was a long awkward silence, and then she raised her eyes to his. Max recognised the same dark blue Rosevale eyes that stared back at him every morning from the glass. He might not have the famous silver hair, but they both had the Rosevale eyes.

Except that hers were sparkling with anger.

Angel looked quickly away. She had no desire to allow the Earl to see how furious he had made her, or how oddly uncertain. Everything he did and said appeared to have an ulterior motive. That question about the champagne, for example... From anyone else, she would have laughed it off, perhaps even pretending that she had drunk it often, but Penrose seemed to have guessed at her inexperience of Society ways. Had he seen through her attempts at playing the flirt, too?

She wished she could simply rise and walk away, but that was impossible. They were being watched; they both knew that. If she deserted him, he would no doubt give some indication of his displeasure, enough to start the tongues wagging even faster. No, she must not let her temper rule her. She must best him...and cool logic was the answer.

She took another tiny sip of champagne and smiled a company smile, as if she were enjoying the sour taste and the prickle in her nose. The bubbles were racing each other up the side of her glass like tiny sparkling rivers, rushing to the freedom of the sea. It looked much prettier than it tasted, she decided.

Keeping her eyes fixed on the rim of her crystal flute, she said, as calmly as she could, 'You wished to say something to me, Cousin?'

He waited a long time before replying, but she refused to raise her head. Those penetrating eyes of his could see altogether too much.

'It is not for me to govern your conduct, ma'am, but—'

'Indeed it is not!' Her fingers tightened involuntarily round the stem of her wineglass.

'It is not my place to govern your conduct, ma'am,' he said again, in exactly the same tone of voice, 'but I should be failing in my duty to the Rosevale family if I did not warn you against those...gentlemen. A lady such as yourself, who has been out of Society for some time, may be unaware of the risks of openly consorting with such reprobates. I must tell you they are not gentlemen that I would expect a member of my family to acknowledge. You will forgive my plain speaking, I am sure.'

Angel's stomach was twisting itself into knots even before the last of his words was out. She could feel a pulse drumming in her temple. How dare he presume to tell her whom she might acknowledge? As if he were head of the family and she a mere nothing...a poor pensioner, dependent on his bounty. Oh, he was hateful, and arrogant. If only she were a man...

But she was not a man, and she had few weapons to use against him.

With difficulty, she succeeded in mastering her temper. Had he spoken those words deliberately, in order to provoke her in public? She would not give him that satisfaction.

Taking a deep breath, she rose as elegantly as she could, trying to hide the tension that pervaded her body. With exaggerated care, she placed the almost untouched champagne on the side table. Then she turned to her cousin and extended her hand politely, smiling for the benefit of the spying eyes, but keeping her own gaze fixed on her fingers. 'If I am to forgive *your* plain speaking, sir, you must forgive *me* for ending our conversation at this point. Your intentions have been made abundantly clear, but I must tell you, frankly, that I have no desire to hear one word more of your concern for the reputation of *my* family. I am prepared to end this discussion in an appearance of amity—as much to protect your reputation as my own, I may add—but I will not be constrained to continue it, not by you, nor by any man. Goodnight, Cousin.'

She glanced up then and saw a flash of burning anger cross his face, but it was immediately replaced by a bland, expressionless mask. Without a word, he returned her empty smile and bowed briefly over her hand, barely touching her gloved fingers.

Angel dipped a polite curtsy in return. She must retreat with dignity while she still could. This time, at least, she had not been bested...even though she knew she had not actually won.

Max clenched his jaw and cursed inwardly. Damn the woman! Why on earth must she insist on refusing to see sense? She was not a complete fool, surely? She had taken charge of her own estates, after all. But she would not acknowledge the risks she was running, risks to her reputation and, quite possibly, to her person.

He was still standing by the sofa, not having moved so much as a single step since her abrupt departure. Did he look thunderstruck? That would not do. He retrieved his own glass from the table and sipped meditatively, smiling a little to himself, as if he were mulling over a pleasurable exchange.

At the far end of the huge saloon, his cousin made her farewells to their hostess, Lady Bridge, and then calmly took Lady Charlotte's elbow to steer her towards the door. The Baroness had obviously decided to leave, to avoid any threat of a further encounter with her obnoxious cousin.

Had he been obnoxious?

Probably. His intentions had been of the best, but the execution... She certainly did not respond well to being lectured about her behaviour, especially by him.

One of Aunt Mary's sayings came into his head, unprompted. He had not thought of it for years. What was it? Something about catching more flies with sugar than vinegar. Was that what she needed? Sugar? She had certainly seemed to be enjoying the syrup that those confounded rakes were pouring around her.

Flattery. Sweet words. Make her warm to him first. And then persuade her to listen to his advice. He could not afford to alienate her completely, for there was still the matter of the French impostor. There, he was prepared to admit, he had probably done her an injustice. She had not introduced the French Adonis to the *ton* as the rightful Earl of Penrose. At least, not yet. In fact, she had not even been seen with the man, as far as Max was aware.

Strange. What on earth was she up to?

Max resolved to send for the ex-Runner he had employed to watch the Frenchman. A report on the man's activities was now overdue. It was such a pity that Ross was no longer around to take charge of such matters. He had always been a much better spy than Max—more patient, and much more painstaking. By now, Ross must be at least halfway across France. With luck, it would not be long before he returned with the truth about the Baroness's French pretender, and then—

Lord Bridge chose that moment to enter the main saloon. He had been ensconced in the card room for almost the whole evening. Now he looked remarkably agitated. What could possibly be up with the man?

'Ladies and gentlemen,' Lord Bridge said in a voice calculated to be heard over the hubbub of noise in the huge room, 'I am afraid I must crave your indulgence for a few moments. I should be most grateful if all the gentlemen would join me in the library. Immediately.'

The hush that had greeted his words was immediately replaced by a babble of excited voices, questioning, wondering. One or two of the ladies looked as if they were about to swoon. Max heard the words 'the King' mentioned more than once. Had the poor old King finally succumbed to the madness that had afflicted him for so long?

With all the other gentlemen, Max filed out into the

corridor and then into the library. Behind them, in the saloon, the ladies' voices were rising even more. They
wanted to know what was going on. And they were, no
doubt, annoyed to be excluded from Lord Bridge's announcement.

Lord Bridge had stationed himself in front of one of the
huge fireplaces in the library. His hands were clasped behind his back. His lips were clamped tightly together as if
he were afraid that some word might escape him before
its due time. He waited until the last man had arrived and
the great oak door had been firmly closed.

'Gentlemen,' he said solemnly, 'I have grave news. I do
not know how we shall be able to impart it to the ladies.
They will be stricken. Stricken. We must do our best to
protect them from the shock.'

Several gentlemen shuffled their feet impatiently. Would
he never get to the point?

'Gentlemen.' Lord Bridge paused dramatically. Then he
took a deep breath and said, 'Gentlemen, Bonaparte has
escaped from Elba. He has raised his standard again in
France.'

Chapter Six

Angel sank gratefully on to the *chaise-longue* in her bed-chamber. Thank goodness she had escaped from that encounter...and from Aunt Charlotte's constant questioning!

She sipped her tisane and gazed into the flickering flames, wriggling her toes against the warmth. Mmm. Better, much better. The tension had begun to leave her almost as soon as she stepped into her carriage. The thundering pulse had slowed again, instead of turning into a headache, as she had feared. Why should an encounter with her arrogant cousin produce such an odd—almost painful—effect? She was fully in control with every other man she met. Why not with Frederick?

She must try to avoid him. She could not afford to be provoked into impropriety by his acid tongue, not when she was in the process of establishing herself in Society. Besides, she had made such plans for the next few weeks...

One of the coals sent up a burst of bluish-purple flame. It flickered for a second or two, and then died.

Angel was reminded of that quick flash of fury in Cousin Frederick's dark eyes. They were expressive eyes, most of the time, but he also knew how to hide his emotions. Perhaps she was able to read him because she was a Rosevale, too? They were very much alike—quick to anger and slow to forgive.

Or were they?

Staring into the flames, Angel forced herself to think more clearly. What did she really know of him? Apart from Aunt Charlotte's blackening of his character, Angel really knew very little. He had served as a soldier in the Peninsula. So he was probably brave…and resourceful. He certainly had the habit of command—as he had now shown on more than one occasion—though he assumed it at quite inappropriate moments, and with quite the wrong people! What on earth made him think he could order Angel's behaviour in that arrogant way? It was outrageous! And not the conduct of a gentleman.

On the other hand, she herself had not been behaving quite as a lady should. She had known that perfectly well, long before Aunt Charlotte's warning.

Angel sipped guiltily at her tisane. She should not have been so sharp with the old lady, whose intentions had been of the best. It was just that… Oh, why was it wrong to want to live, just a little? Angel was a widow now. Surely Society's rules were just a little less rigid for a widow? For what law had she broken? She had practised a little flirtation, nothing more. In all her life, she had never before had the opportunity to do so. First her father had watched her, and then her husband. Was it so very dreadful, now that she was her own mistress, if she wished to discover whether she could learn the wiles that would attract a man? After all, it was only a game. She had no desire to go beyond a light flirtation.

She shuddered. Nothing beyond a light flirtation. Absolutely not.

But flirtation was delightful. To be surrounded by cavaliers, hanging on her every word, telling her how beautiful she looked, trying to kiss her hand... Oh, yes, quite delightful.

And if her burgeoning plans came to fruition, there would be plenty more opportunities to perfect her technique...without the slightest risk of being upbraided by Aunt Charlotte.

Or by her hateful, arrogant cousin!

'Do stop pacing, Max. You will wear out the carpet.'

With a grunt of suppressed laughter, Max subsided into one of Louisa's comfortable armchairs. 'Forgive me, Louisa. I am behaving like a bear.'

Louisa's silence was eloquent.

'Dammit, Louisa, I feel so powerless!'

'I do understand, Max. But worrying about Ross will achieve nothing, you know.'

Max nodded, reaching for his glass of madeira. Louisa was perfectly right. Ross was an experienced soldier, well used to surviving in enemy country. In spite of that red hair, he could always melt into the background when it was necessary.

But there was still Bonaparte! The Allies should have known better than to exile him to Elba. It was much too close to mainland France. No doubt his spies and supporters had found it easy to keep their Emperor informed of the plots to free him. But to have succeeded so soon...!

'Besides,' Louisa continued, 'this panic is bound to be over very quickly. Has not Marshal Ney sworn to King Louis that he will bring Bonaparte to Paris in an iron cage?'

'So I have heard,' Max muttered. He would not voice his doubts to Louisa, but he had little faith in Ney's word to the King. Ney was Bonaparte's man, bred in the bone.

'There you are then. Bonaparte will be taken. Peace will be restored. And Ross will soon return with the information that you need.' She smiled fondly across at him.

'I pray you may be right, my dear. But, none the less, I feel…anxious. It would be unwise for any of us to underestimate Bonaparte. Upstart Corsican to Emperor of France and ruler of most of Europe—that takes a very special kind of man. I would not be surprised to learn that they have sent for Wellington already.'

'But that cannot be necessary. The latest despatches from Paris are clear that Bonaparte is receiving no assistance.'

'Indeed? Your sources are better than mine, my dear.' Max was not surprised that Louisa knew more about the government's intelligence than he did. She always ensured she was well informed about politics, and her judgements were very sound. It was one of the reasons he enjoyed her company so much. She offered everything a man could wish for…except the breeding he needed in a wife.

'The Duke's place must surely be in Vienna,' she said firmly. 'Who else can be relied upon to defend England's interests against the Hapsburgs and the Tsar?'

Max nodded. 'I am sure the Duke will not be summoned unless it is absolutely necessary—which I pray it will not be.'

'Would you return to the colours, Max? And Ross, too?'

'I cannot speak for Ross, Louisa. For myself…it is very difficult. Truly, I do not know.' He paused, pondering. 'If I were to return to the colours, my cousin and her protégé would have the field to themselves here in England. And if I were to fall, there would be no one to prevent them from setting up that man-milliner as the new Earl. I am not sure that it would be wise for me to go.'

'You distrust Lady Rosevale so very much?'

'Yes, I think. To be frank, Louisa, I know precious little of her. Our every encounter seems to resemble a cock-fight. My cousin is a termagant, I fear.'

Louisa laughed gently. 'You mean, my dear, that she has the Rosevale temper, just as you have.' When Max said nothing, she went on, 'You are well matched, I think.'

Max grunted. 'I might have been a little hasty, I suppose…'

'Mmm. Your cousin does not have the look of a termagant.'

'You have seen her?' The words were out before he stopped to think. Of course. Louisa would have made it her business to get the measure of the enemy. If the Baroness was likely to be a threat to Max, Louisa would do everything in her power to help his defence. She was as true as steel.

'She is very beautiful. And resolute, I think. You will not easily get the better of her, Max. Indeed, she may get the better of you.'

'Nonsense!'

'My dear, she does not have to advance on you with sword drawn and pennants flying. A woman has other weapons. And even you have a heart that can be touched, especially by a beautiful woman who longs to be loved.'

'What on earth gave you that idea? It is not like you to allow sentiment to overcome your judgement. I may tell you that my cousin is out for what she can get. She plans to install that damned Frenchman in my room and then to marry him. I am sure of it. Her only concern is to maintain her line and the Rosevale fortune. And to do me down.'

Louisa shook her head, smiling affectionately at him. 'Since you are so very sure that I am wrong, I challenge you to prove it. You yourself said that you barely know her. Well…find out more. Get close to her. Test her. Then

you will learn which of us is in the right of it.' She rose
from her chair and came to perch on the arm of his, laying
her hand on his shoulder. 'I saw a lonely, rather frightened
woman who needs to be loved, not a grasping harpy. Besides, what would be the point of her marrying the Frenchman, even if he did seize your title? Such a union would
bring her nothing she needs.'

'She needs an heir.'

'She needs a husband, and then an heir. The identity of
the husband is largely immaterial. Any gentleman would
do...even you.'

'Good God, why is it that all my friends are bent on
marrying me off to that confounded woman? First Ross,
and now you, Louisa. I should have thought better of you.'

Louisa allowed herself to slide gracefully from the arm
of the chair on to his lap. She put her hands to his face
and gazed up into his troubled eyes. 'Oh, Max. Dearest
Max, you know that is unfair. I would never betray you.
Never. What I want for you is...' She swallowed. 'What
I want for you is what you want for yourself...even though
you may not yet recognise it.'

He frowned and shook his head at her. What on earth
was Louisa talking about? It made no sense at all. The
Baroness was the last woman he would ever want. Apart
from her odious wealth, she could offer him nothing, not
even children—and certainly not the warm and loving
friendship he shared with Louisa. Life with the Baroness
would never be comfortable. No man in his right mind
would marry her.

Louisa said nothing more for several moments. Then she
simply placed a gentle kiss on his lips, waiting for the
response she knew must come. He trusted her, and he had
never yet been able to resist her.

Just as she had never been able to resist him.

The kiss was long and soon deepened into passion. 'Blast you, Louisa,' he said hoarsely, raising his head at last, 'why must you talk in riddles? Lord preserve me from scheming women!'

She laughed up at him.

With a rueful grin, he said, 'Some things are much more important than scheming, my dear. Do you not think?'

He waited for her nod of agreement and then, in a single powerful movement, rose from the chair with her in his arms and made for the stairs that led to her bedchamber.

'My dear boy, there is nothing you can do. Try not to worry. I am sure your sister will be perfectly safe. Why should that Corsican upstart pose any danger to her? His only interest is in reaching Paris and proclaiming himself Emperor all over again.'

Pierre nodded glumly. He did not look convinced, Angel decided, in spite of all Aunt Charlotte's fine words. 'That may well be true, Aunt,' she said, 'but what then? At this rate, he will be in Paris, and victorious, in no time at all. Once all France is in his grasp again, who knows what he may do?'

Pierre nodded again. 'They are cowards and turncoats. All of them. And as for Ney—' The look on Pierre's face was an eloquent combination of anger and disgust. 'Ney swore to bring Bonaparte to Paris in an iron cage. But his iron melted soon enough, did it not?'

'King Louis should never have trusted Ney's word,' said Lady Charlotte vehemently. 'Ney may call himself a Marshal, but he is only a peasant, after all. No amount of gold braid could ever turn such a mushroom into a gentleman. A gentleman's word can *always* be trusted. Do you not agree, Pierre?'

Pierre muttered something that might have been agreement and turned away, staring out of the window at the dark and ominous skies. It would surely rain soon.

Angel put a restraining hand on her aunt's arm. 'It is natural that he should worry, Aunt,' she said softly. 'Especially as he is now stranded in England, and unable to go to his sister's aid. We can only pray that Bonaparte is soon stopped. Surely there are *some* Frenchmen who will stand against him?'

'Spineless, the lot of them!' hissed Lady Charlotte.

'Hush, Aunt!' Angel cast a quick glance over her shoulder to where Pierre stood, apparently lost in thought. Perhaps he had not heard. 'Remember that Pierre is a Frenchman, too.'

'Yes, but Pierre is a gentleman,' said Aunt Charlotte stubbornly. 'Even a French gentleman understands about honour.'

Angel nodded, grateful that her aunt had not raised her voice this time. The old lady was becoming increasingly outspoken and no longer seemed to care much whom she offended. And yet she constantly upbraided Angel for speaking out of turn! It would have been quite amusing...if it had not been so very provoking.

'Angel.' Aunt Charlotte was whispering now. 'Since Pierre is missing his sister so much, he would probably respond to some young, female companionship. Take a walk with him. I am sure you will be able to relieve him of his blue-devils.'

Angel's eyes narrowed. Aunt Charlotte was plotting yet again. She seemed to be for ever trying to throw Angel and Pierre together, even though Angel had made it perfectly clear that he must not be recognised as more than a distant member of the family until his claim had been proved.

And now that the route to and from Paris was closed, the proof might be very long in coming.

Aunt Charlotte was not to be denied. She had already crossed the room to where Pierre stood. 'Angel is looking a little pale, do you not think? I am sure she needs some fresh air and exercise. I am not up to walking myself, I am afraid,' she said, telling the untruth without even a trace of a blush. 'Perhaps you would give her your arm around the square, dear boy?'

Pierre looked more than a little flustered, but he bowed his agreement. What else could he do?

'Go and fetch your hat, my dear,' said Aunt Charlotte. Then, seeing that Angel was still unwilling, she added, 'You have not been out of the house these last two days, child. And that is not at all like you. Go along, do. Before it comes on to rain.' She glanced out of the window. The sky was getting darker by the minute.

There was no point in arguing, Angel decided. It was true that she had been feeling a little out of sorts these last few days, but it must be simple fatigue. She had been doing too much since she came to London, that was all. She would soon recover her normal appetite and zest for life. And it certainly would not do to remonstrate with Aunt Charlotte in front of Pierre, no matter how much the old busybody deserved it. She was quite determined to make a match between Angel and Pierre. Well, Angel would make it crystal clear to Pierre, as soon as she had an opportunity, that her aunt's schemes would never come to fruition. Never.

On the other hand…

Minutes later, Angel paused in the act of tying her bonnet. Of course! Pierre might provide just the answer she needed. She should have thought of this before. After all, he was dependent on Angel's goodwill in order to pursue his claim. He was in no position to refuse her request.

Aunt Charlotte would be outraged, if she ever found out. But Pierre could be sworn to secrecy. Angel could insist on that.

Aunt Charlotte would never know.

With a satisfied smile, Angel tied the ribbons in a co-quettish bow under her ear and stopped to survey the effect in the glass. Aunt Charlotte wanted her to flirt with Pierre? Well, now she certainly looked the part. And she was de-termined to make the most of it. She descended to the entrance hall with something of a bounce in her step.

Pierre was waiting for her at the foot of the stairs. Ob-viously, he had been dragooned into obedience by Aunt Charlotte. It was difficult to stand against the old lady when she was really determined, especially if one was not prepared to be rude to her. Poor Pierre. He could not afford to alienate any of his potential supporters.

Angel smiled warmly at him and tucked her gloved hand under his arm. 'We must make haste, sir, if we are not to be caught in the rain.'

He nodded, but he did not return her smile. He seemed to be fully absorbed in putting on his new beaver hat and ensuring that it sat at just the correct angle. However, he was more than considerate of her as they descended to the flagway and crossed to the gardens in the centre of the square.

'Such a pity that the trees are not yet in leaf,' she began. 'It still seems like winter.'

'Indeed.'

'I suppose that, in the south of France, the landscape is very different?'

'Indeed, yes.'

Angel waited for him to continue, but he did not. The

man seemed determined to allow his black mood to rule him. Well, she would not allow it to rule her! 'I can understand that you are concerned about your sister...about Julie. And also that the proofs of your claim will be delayed even more. It is vexatious in the extreme, of course, but my agents cannot be expected to put themselves in harm's way at such an uncertain time. You do accept that?'

'I have no choice in the matter.'

That was true, but it was less than polite of him to remind her of it. 'Pray, do not be concerned. Even if your compatriots do not stand against the usurper, the Duke will soon return and then all will be well. I am sure of it. In no time at all, we will have the proofs you need. I promise you that I shall send for Julie at the very earliest opportunity.'

Now, for the first time that day, he looked more like his normal self. His relieved smile lit up his countenance, reminding Angel of just how handsome he was. 'My lady, I cannot tell you how grateful I am to you. That Julie should be brought to England, accorded the status she has been so long denied... We have waited a very long time for this. It is like...a miracle. I only wish there was some way of repaying your kindness.'

Angel managed—just—to conceal her smile of triumph. 'As it happens, there is one small service you might render me,' she said quietly. 'Shall we take another turn while we discuss it?'

Angel was feeling rather hot. It must be the thrill of her plan. She lay back on her pillows and gazed up at the canopy, visualising how it would be. It was so very exciting. And rather shocking, too. She had wanted to experience a little freedom, but she would never have thought of this! She had not even dreamt that such things existed.

Pierre, of course, had been learning a great deal about parts of London that no Society lady would ever frequent. And so he had been able to suggest the perfect solution, for she would be guarded by her own cousin. It was a pity that she had so little time to prepare, but the opportunity was much too good to miss.

Tomorrow, Angel would have her moment of freedom at last!

Chapter Seven

'I don't believe it. Is that really you, Max?'

His answering laugh was unmistakable. He was clearly enjoying himself after all.

'But you look completely different. I swear I should never have known you. Your face…that wig…and those clothes! You even seem to have grown taller.'

Max lifted one foot to display the red high heels on his buckled shoes. 'Gentlemen used to wear high heels, too, you know. *And* the face paint. Why should you ladies have all the fun? I decided that it would be better to make myself totally unrecognisable for this little…masquerade. It is not, after all, the sort of occasion that should be graced by the presence of a belted earl.'

Louisa grimaced. 'Would you prefer not to attend? We could still cry off, if you really feel it is not quite the thing and—'

'My dear, I beg you not to tempt me to play the coxcomb. I could so easily tell you that I agreed to attend simply to please you. Then I should have you in my debt—'

'Even more in your debt, you mean.'

'But it would not be true. And I will not lie to you, even

over such a matter as this. It is not quite the thing for the Earl of Penrose, to be sure, but when I was plain Captain Max Rosevale, it was exactly the sort of occasion I delighted in...especially in the company of a beautiful lady.' He made an extravagant leg, with such a wicked grin on his face that Louisa was forced to laugh. 'So the Earl shall remain at home and, if you permit, dear madam, you will be escorted by poor old Captain Max, a penniless lover in a macaroni's garb and a plain carriage.'

He held out both his hands to her and then danced her round the tiny sitting room.

'Stop! Stop! Max, you are gone stark mad!'

'No. Not mad. Enjoying a little lost freedom, perhaps. For this one night, I intend to forget all about the responsibilities of my new status and pretend that I really am still a simple soldier, bent on enjoying himself. If you are ready, my dear? I must say that you look absolutely entrancing in that gown. Good enough to eat, almost.' He bent his head and dropped a playful kiss on her bare shoulder.

'Later,' she said softly, drawing her evening cloak around her neck to thwart his next move. 'I really *do* wish to attend this ridotto, Max, so you must restrain yourself. If I were to allow you liberties now...we both know what would happen. And then your wig and your high heels would not have a chance to astonish the assembled company. Others may not know that there is an earl under the powder and paint, but I shall. And I intend to relish the joke.'

He grinned and bowed again. 'Your wish is my command, *madame*. If you are ready, shall we go?'

Louisa picked up her fan and her velvet mask from the side table. 'You can tie this on for me when we are in the carriage. Did you bring one for yourself?'

He nodded. 'I did think I might simply rely on all this paint, but…' He pulled a slim black mask from the capacious pocket of his sky-blue satin coat. 'It seemed wisest to take no risks.' He offered his arm. 'Come then, Madame Louisa.'

She smiled up at him. 'It will be my pleasure, Captain Max.'

Angel stood at the edge of the dance floor and marvelled. She had never seen such a colourful throng of people. Almost all were dressed in the extravagant fashions of the previous century. And almost all were masked. They were whirling round to the strains of the waltz.

She clasped Pierre's arm in delight. 'Oh, is it not wonderful?' she exclaimed. 'I do wish I had been able to procure a costume like some of these.' With her fan, she pointed to a passing couple. The lady was dressed very much in the style of the French aristocracy of forty years before. Then Angel looked regretfully at her own gown. It was beautiful, of course—it had been designed by Célestine—but it was remarkably plain by comparison with those of the other ladies present. Angel had had no opportunity to buy fancy dress. Nor had she dared to take the risk that Aunt Charlotte would discover her plans, for the old lady would have done her best to thwart them. 'The next time, I shall ensure I have just such an ensemble,' she said firmly.

'That would be a pity,' Pierre said in a low voice. 'You would have to powder your beautiful hair, which would be a crime.'

Angel flushed behind her mask. 'You are too kind, sir,' she said. He was looking down at her in a most disconcerting way. Even through the slits of his black mask, she could see that his eyes were glittering strangely.

'You look quite beautiful, *madame*,' he said slowly, 'and…so very much like Julie.'

'Oh. But—'

'Shall we join the dance?' He held out his hand to lead her on to the floor.

Angel gulped, and took it. A waltz! Heavens! She had never yet danced it. She knew the steps, of course—Aunt Charlotte had made sure of that—but she had never, in her life, been twirled around a dance floor in the arms of a man.

Within a minute or two, she was quite light-headed with the speed and excitement of it all. Why, it was wonderful! Pierre was an excellent dancer, so very light on his feet. He held her firmly, but not so near to his body that she was in any way embarrassed. In fact, to be held in such a way was quite thrilling to her senses. To be so close, to feel the heat of his hand in the middle of her back, even through his glove and her gown…

She had wanted to find out how it felt to be truly alive. And as he spun her round and round, she knew that her longings were beginning to be fulfilled. She had taken control of her own life…and it was exhilarating.

At length, the music stopped and they found themselves standing near the edge of the dance floor. Pierre seemed quite his normal self—handsome and composed, looking every inch the French aristocrat in his eighteenth-century dress. But Angel was out of breath and really rather hot. Strange. It was not at all like her to react in such a way. Most unbecoming. Surreptitiously, she wiped her face with her handkerchief.

'You are not used to so much dancing?'

'Well, no. But I am perfectly used to exercise. I do not quite understand why I should feel so hot.'

'It is very warm in here. Should you like to take some air?'

'No, no. There is no need. I am sure it will soon pass. Perhaps something to drink?'

'Of course.' Pierre beckoned a passing waiter and took two tall glasses from his tray. 'Drink this, my lady. Then you will feel cooler.'

The chilled flute felt wonderfully soothing against her lips. In next to no time, the glass was empty. She sighed her pleasure. Then she sneezed. 'Oh, my goodness! I am afraid I am not used to so many bubbles.'

Pierre beckoned again and soon there was a second glass in Angel's gloved hand.

'I shall take this one more slowly,' she said, glancing up at him through her mask. 'If I continue to sneeze, I shall scare away all my potential partners, for fear that I may be ill.' She took a long sip. Somehow, it tasted even better than the first glass.

'Come, *madame*,' said Pierre, offering his arm. 'Let us walk a little, so that you may take the cooler air and enjoy your wine.'

The orchestra was just striking up for another waltz. Angel looked longingly over her shoulder towards the dancers, but decided that Pierre's advice was probably wise. A little air would surely cool her…and calm her disordered senses, too. There could be no harm in walking apart with one's own cousin for a space, especially since no one would recognise either of them.

The waltz would wait. There was still plenty of time for dancing. The ridotto was to continue for hours yet.

'She's here!'

'I beg your pardon?'

'Forgive me, Louisa, but Baroness Rosevale is here. In

the flesh.' From their place in the middle of the dance floor, Max nodded towards a couple who was moving down the side of the room in the direction of one of the exits.

'Surely not. I cannot believe that a lady of her standing would dare to attend a function here. Our host may be almost as rich as Golden Ball, but in Society it matters only that his father was a butcher and his money is made from trade. I believe you must be mistaken, my dear.'

'I am not.'

'But how can you tell? Your cousin is masked, is she not?'

'I am not wrong, Louisa. She is wearing a mask, I grant you, but that silver hair is unmistakable. That, and the way she holds herself... No, I am not wrong.' He shook his head angrily. 'And that French blackguard has had the temerity to bring her *here*!'

Louisa turned in his arms to catch another glimpse of the pair. 'So that is your Frenchman. He looks... interesting.'

'He looks like a buffoon in that outrageous costume.'

Louisa allowed her gaze to travel slowly down from Max's wig and painted face to his satin coat. She said only, 'Almost every man here is dressed in just such a fashion. It is, after all, the theme of the ridotto. So you are perhaps a little harsh to single out one Frenchman as the only buffoon in the company.'

'Oh, very well,' he said, with a rueful smile. 'You are in the right of it, as usual. Come.' He pulled her a little closer. 'Let us enjoy the dance. Whatever Lady Rosevale may be doing with her French cavalier, it is nothing to us.'

He pulled her closer and deliberately spun her into the crush.

Louisa gasped aloud, but then gave herself up to enjoyment of the waltz, for Max was an expert dancer and she had no reason to fear any mishap while she was in his arms. They rarely had an opportunity to dance. That was why she had been determined to attend this ridotto, for here she need share him with no one.

Pierre led Angel through the double doors and down a long corridor to a small deserted room. It seemed to have been fitted up as some kind of retiring room, for a fire was burning and there were comfortable sofas around the walls. He crossed to a window and threw it wide.

Angel watched him from the open door. She noted vaguely that he seemed to know his way about this huge, over-decorated house. Had he visited it before? It was possible, of course, for he had now been many weeks in London, and a single gentleman was bound to seek out the pleasures of the capital.

He guided her to a sofa near the fire, watching rather anxiously while she set her glass down and took her seat. She sighed with relief and put her hands to the strings of her mask. They seemed to be tied in knots.

'No!'

When Angel looked up, startled, he sat down beside her and removed her hand from the mask. 'No. You look like... It is best if you continue to wear it.'

'But—'

'Someone might walk in upon us. It is too dangerous.'

She nodded. He was right. She could not afford to be recognised in such a house as this. She reached for her half-empty glass instead, but he forestalled her, taking her hand and raising it to his lips. No other man had ever treated her with such gentleness...such reverence. She smiled a little hazily at him.

'You trusted me to escort you to this masquerade, my

lady, and I am honoured that you do…but, in spite of the ties between us, you persist in treating me like a stranger. You have never yet called me by name.' His voice sounded very deep suddenly. 'Will you not do so? We are quite alone, after all.'

Angel could not completely fix on the import of his words. She was sure there was something…but her brain did not seem to be able to function normally this evening. 'I…I am grateful to you…Pierre…for acting as my escort.' She stopped. She knew she must sound like a tongue-tied schoolgirl. An awkward silence ensued. He seemed to be waiting, expectant, gazing at her profile.

He must be waiting for her to give him permission to address her as 'Angel' in return, but, in spite of the warmth she felt for him tonight, she could not quite bring herself to say the words. It was such an intimate thing… He was handsome and charming, of course, but he guarded his feelings very well. In truth, she knew very little of him. She did not know if he was even a Rosevale at all.

The words dried on her tongue. She sat immobile, waiting. If he was truly a Rosevale, he would be furious.

Pierre gave a long sigh. Very gently, he turned her to face him and placed a tiny kiss on her lips. She did not have time to be shocked. It was over so quickly that she almost thought she must have imagined it. But her lips remembered. She closed her eyes on the unfamiliar tingle. Ah, that was good. Something told her that, provided she did not open her eyes again, this new and pleasurable feeling would linger on. Just a little longer.

He feathered a kiss on the corner of her mouth and then more, along the line of her jaw. His touch was so unthreatening, so gentle that it might not be happening at all. The sensation was wholly new to her. She allowed it to flow through her limbs, marvelling at the way her skin prickled under the touch of his lips and his fingers. Pierre was kissing her, touching her, as if he wanted to give her pleasure, as if he valued her for herself alone. No man had ever touched her with tenderness. Her husband had never shown her gentleness in any form. His touch had been a demand for possession, a prelude to his painful invasion of her body. This…this was a different world.

Pierre muttered something unintelligible. Was it French? It did not seem to matter. She wanted to revel in this delightful new experience, to explore this strange intimacy between man and woman.

His kisses had reached the side of her neck. He pushed aside the long curl by her ear and touched his lips to the spot below her earlobe. She shivered with the pleasure of it.

He drew her closer. She did not resist. It seemed to be what was expected. She allowed herself to continue to float on this strange new sea of pleasurable sensation.

Then he began to kiss her in earnest. And it was no longer gentle or pleasurable. His mouth fastened on hers. He forced her lips open so that he could explore the tender recesses of her mouth.

A knot of fear formed in Angel's belly and her eyes flew open. She wanted to pull away, but he was holding her firmly. At the first indication of resistance, he deepened the kiss even more. She could not escape.

After what seemed a long time, he broke away and lifted his head a fraction. His dark eyes were unfocused. He muttered, heatedly, 'Ah, Julie! Julie!'

The shock of his words gave her a strength she had not known she possessed. She tore herself away from him and thrust him back against the furthest arm of the sofa.

'It is not your *sister* you are kissing, sir!' In her disgust, she spat the words at him. She jumped to her feet and glowered down at him. 'What kind of man *are* you?' She could see that he was bright red under his maquillage. 'I will thank you to leave this place, sir. And at once.' She waved his objections aside. 'You need have no concern for me. I will make my own way home. I should rather be escorted by the meanest Englishman alive than by a man such as you.'

She turned smartly on her heel and marched out of the room, closing the door behind her and leaning her head against its smooth panels. Good God! What did it all mean? He was attracted to her because she resembled his sister? Was that why he had refused to allow her to remove her mask? Was that why—?

She shook her head in bewilderment. If only she were not so very hot. Now her head was beginning to throb fit to burst. And she felt quite dizzy. She should go home. Her hired carriage was outside. She was at no risk if she simply took her place in it and ordered the coachman to drive to Berkeley Square. She would be safe.

But her moment of escape would be over.

The sound of the dancing and the excited chatter filtered down the corridor to her. She stood undecided. She had so enjoyed that waltz. That was why she had come, was it not? To find out what it was like to be free to follow her own desires—to dance, to flirt a little, to enjoy life as she had never before been able to do. Must it all be over so soon?

Her headache seemed to be receding with the music. In spite of her concerns, her body had begun to sway to the seductive rhythm of the waltz. She hesitated, trying to focus her fuddled mind.

Well, why not? She could return to the ballroom for a space, to watch and listen for a little longer. It had been cooler in the retiring room with Pierre, but she dare not return there. She must resort to the welcome effects of a glass of chilled wine. Yes. She would return to the dancing, take another glass of wine, and enjoy the spectacle from the sidelines. Pierre would not dare to return to her side, so she had nothing to fear. She might even be invited to dance. At a ridotto, introductions were never made. Everyone hid their identity. A little quiver of excitement ran down her spine. She would steal just a few more moments of freedom. There was no need to leave quite yet.

She put her hands to her hair in an attempt to tidy it. With no mirror, it was difficult, but it felt as if most of her curls were still in place. She took a deep breath, smiled for the benefit of anyone who might be watching and walked quickly down the corridor, back to the ballroom.

'Max!'

He did not seem to have heard above the hubbub.

Louisa stretched up to speak directly into his ear. 'Max, look there! Your cousin is in some difficulty, I fear.' She nodded in the direction of the exit where they had last seen the Baroness and her companion. Now, there was only the Baroness herself, looking both perturbed and somewhat dishevelled. She had caught up a fresh champagne flute and was taking a long draught.

'By God, that villain has attacked her!' Max exclaimed, much too loudly.

'Hush!' said Louisa, looking around quickly to see whether anyone had heard.

Max was relieved to see that no one was paying any attention to them. His thoughtless words had been lost in the incredible noise of the room. But that was now the least of his worries. 'Louisa, I—'

'You must go to her, Max. Of course you must.' When he hesitated, she seemed to sense his dilemma in an instant and said firmly, 'Do not concern yourself about me, my dear. I am well able to look after myself. You must look to your cousin now. It is best that I leave, immediately. If you permit, I shall take the carriage.'

Max found he had a lump in his throat. 'Louisa, you are a woman in a thousand,' he said hoarsely, bending to kiss her hand. Then, shielding her with his powerful body, he began to force a path through the press of people to reach the main entrance.

Louisa was smiling proudly when they at last reached the doorway. 'Be sure I shall send the carriage back for you,' she said. 'I would not have you rely on any conveyance provided by that impostor.' Then, with an impudent little curtsy, she turned to leave. 'Treat her kindly,' she whispered over her shoulder.

Max was feeling anything but kind. His cousin had come to the sort of masquerade that no respectable woman should ever attend. She had ruined Louisa's enjoyment of the evening. And now he was in honour bound to rescue her from whatever predicament she was in. No, he did not feel at all kindly disposed towards her.

The Baroness was still standing near the double doors. Of her companion there was no sign. She looked somewhat heated, her hair was no longer perfect, and her mask was a little awry; but her dress did not appear to have been disarranged. Perhaps it had not gone as far as attempted rape, then.

He strode over to her side. 'Good evening, *madame,*' he said, keeping his voice even and controlled. This time, he was determined not to allow his anger to show. He was almost certain that he sounded perfectly normal. That was something.

She looked up at him, but there was no sign of recognition in her face. For the moment, he had forgotten how much trouble he had taken to disguise his features. It was not surprising, in truth, if she did not know who he was.

He opened his mouth to tell her, but she forestalled him. 'Good evening, sir,' she said, curtsying. 'This is a splendid assembly, is it not?'

Max realised that she was gazing up at him provocatively over the rim of her wineglass. What on earth was the woman about? Had she no idea of the risks she ran in a place like this?

With difficulty, he resisted the temptation to rage at her as she deserved. Had she not just escaped from one man's unwelcome attentions?

She smiled up at him then. It was a remarkably flirtatious smile.

Max did his best to return it and reached for her hand, carrying it to his lips in a grand gesture that was in keeping with his costume. The lady seemed to be positively seeking his attentions. Perhaps he had misread her looks earlier? Perhaps she had not fled from her French lover after all? He had one sure way of finding out. He could offer her another.

'Would *madame* care to dance?'

She gave a tiny giggle. 'Why, yes, sir. I should be delighted.' She put down the now empty glass and allowed him to lead her on to the floor.

Max took her into his arms, deliberately holding her much too close. It was time his foolish cousin learned her lesson. Better that she learn it from him than from any other man.

Angel found that the constant turning was making her feel truly light-headed. It must be the dance, must it not? She vaguely recalled warnings against the waltz, as a dangerous dance that would make fragile young ladies swoon. Yes, that must be it.

But her latest cavalier gave no indication that he might let her fall. Indeed, he seemed to dance as if he had been born to it. The sensation was unlike anything she had ever experienced before. She felt protected, but daring, both at the same time. If only she did not feel so hot...

'Are you enjoying the dance, *madame?*'

Angel fancied she detected just the trace of a foreign accent. He had an attractive voice. It was rich and mellow, like the fine oak panelling at the Abbey. As a child, she had often stroked it, loving its smooth carved surface.

'*Madame?*'

Oh, dear. He was expecting an answer. 'Thank you, sir. It is...delightful. Though I have never before danced among such a press of couples.'

He laughed, deep in his throat. It made her look up at his face and reminded her of just how tall he was. She was sure she had never met such a tall man in all her life. She wondered how he would look with neither wig nor maquillage. Who might he be? He had such an air...

'I collect that you have not attended a ridotto here before?'

Angel shook her head.

'May I ask why you chose to attend on this occasion?'

'You may ask, sir, but I do not choose to answer,' she replied quickly, swallowing her annoyance at the impertinence of his question. How dare he question her like a...like a...husband?

His eyes opened wide behind his mask. They were very dark eyes. 'As you wish, *madame,*' he said simply. 'I can see that you do not intend to be questioned. But you will tell me your name, perhaps?'

'If you will first tell me yours,' she replied, without

hesitation. She gazed up at him through her lashes, practising the look she had determined to copy from the best Society flirts.

'Very well. But I shall hold you to that. My name is… Max.'

'Max,' she repeated. It was a strong name. It suited him. She had never before met anyone with that name.

'And your name, *madame?*'

'Oh. Yes. My name is—' She stopped, aghast. She could not possibly tell him her name was 'Angel'. That would certainly betray her identity. She must think of something…

'Your name is…?'

'Rose. My name is Rose.' She beamed with satisfaction. It was not quite a lie, even if it was not the whole truth. 'But some of my family call me Rosa,' she added, unable to resist the embellishment.

'Rose. Rosa. But yes, a very pretty conceit.'

Angel frowned. She had a vague feeling that there must be a hidden meaning to his words but, just at the moment, her head was spinning so much that she could not apply herself to the puzzle. She would be glad when the dance came to an end. It was so very hot and, yet again, she was desperately thirsty.

After only a few minutes, the waltz ended. Angel gave a sigh of relief.

'I take it that you have no desire to continue dancing with me, *madame?*'

Oh, dear. He was beginning to sound annoyed. She had been very rude. And without cause. 'Forgive me, sir… Max… It was not my intention to… It is just that…it is very hot. Perhaps we might find somewhere a little cooler?'

A strange expression crossed his face, but it was gone

again in a split second. Tucking her hand in his arm, he ushered her politely from the floor and escorted her towards an open window. Angel shook her head slightly, trying to clear it. Something very odd was happening.

Her companion put a tall glass into her hand. 'I am sure that a cool drink will help,' he said simply, touching her glass with his own. 'To your beauty, *madame*.'

If Angel had not been so hot, she would certainly have blushed at his words. No, not at his words. It was the way he was looking at her...

Chapter Eight

Max forced himself to smile down at her as he watched her drink. How many glasses had she had? And this, from a woman who had claimed to dislike the taste? She was clearly well on the way to being foxed. Was that why she had made that highly improper suggestion to go apart with him? If not, she was either out of her mind, or a woman quite without morals. She was alone in the company of complete strangers. And she seemed to be prepared to make advances to a man she had never before set eyes on.

Now thoroughly exasperated, he decided there was no point in trying to pursue the riddle of her outrageous behaviour. His cousin had already made it perfectly clear that she would not answer his questions unless it suited her to do so. No, this was no time for talk. His only option was to show her the error of her ways. Since her mind was already befuddled, the lesson would have to be stark enough to remain with her, even when the effects of the alcohol had worn off.

He took a slow sip of his own champagne. He was planning to enjoy this encounter. She thought he was a stranger…and a foreigner into the bargain. He would enjoy it even more—later—when he revealed his identity to his haughty cousin. The satisfying thought of that confrontation brought a thread of laughter into his throat.

'You have found something amusing, sir?'

She was trying to look provocative, though she was hampered by her mask. Her fluttering eyelashes kept catching on it. Against the black velvet, her eyes seemed intensely blue, like the dark of a starry sky. There seemed to be more colour than usual in her complexion, too. It must be a trick of the light.

'Not amusing, no. I was thinking only that this champagne is of a very indifferent vintage. Hardly worth drinking, do you not agree?'

'I…I do not hold myself out as a judge of champagne, sir.' With the utmost care, she set her glass down. It was almost empty. 'But I do find it extremely hot in here. Chilled champagne can be very…refreshing, I think.'

Max said nothing, but he looked at her with a degree of scepticism. If she was not totally foxed, she ought to notice.

It appeared that she did not, for she said, 'Do you not find it uncomfortably hot here, Max?'

'I admit that I am not used to wearing a wig. It is not only hot, it is also d…decidedly uncomfortable.' He only just succeeded in biting back the oath that had risen to his lips.

She giggled. 'You could always remove it, I suppose.'

'I think not, my Lady Rose.' He had an almost uncontrollable urge to scratch his head under the wig, but he refused to give in to it. Instead, he waited for her to make the next move. If she had a jot of sense left, she would either leave the house at once or return to the dance floor, but he was prepared to wager she would do neither. She seemed determined, this evening, to throw caution to the winds. It made him want to rail at her…or to strangle her with his bare hands.

'I think perhaps I should have n…no more champagne,' she said, a little unsteadily. 'If I have too much, who knows what might happen?' She giggled again. Then she put a hand to her brow.

'Are you quite well, *madame?*' Max asked quietly. To be honest, she did look a little flushed.

She turned towards the window, but there was precious little fresh air to be had. 'If only there were somewhere cooler…' she said wistfully.

Max glared at her. He was hardly able to contain his increasing fury. What on earth did she think she was doing? She sounded like a child barely out of the schoolroom, asking a favour of some besotted old uncle, rather than a grown woman—and a widow, besides—inviting a complete stranger to take her into the shadows.

She smiled up at him then. In spite of the mask, she looked…alluring. This was no schoolroom miss. This was a grown woman who wished, it seemed, to become a siren. Her silver hair, her dark glowing eyes, her heightened complexion—everything combined to entice a man into her domain. Max could not say a word or move an inch. He just stared down at her.

She bit her lip and lowered her gaze from his face. Max, his anger forgotten for the moment, could not tear his eyes away from her mouth. It had been rosy before, but now her lower lip was bright red. She was almost pouting. It would be a crime not to kiss that mouth.

'Come, Rose,' he said hoarsely, taking her arm. 'Let us find somewhere cooler so that you may recover a little.' He ushered her through the double doors and along the dimly lit corridor. Somewhere in this part of the mansion, there was a conservatory, he was sure. It would probably be empty. At least, he fervently hoped that it would. For he now felt an urgent need to be alone, quite alone, with his silver-haired companion. He would not harm her—even she could not make him descend to the level of that French blackguard—but it would do her good to be frightened a little. A few kisses, certainly. Perhaps on more than just her lips… He smiled into the darkness when he came to the door he had been seeking and saw that there was a key in the lock.

Angel was relieved to be out of that oppressive heat. Her tall companion seemed to be most anxious to accommodate her wishes. He had perfect manners, too. Yet again, she wondered who he might be and where he came from. She was sure she had never met him before. She would have remembered. Would she not? Even without the wig, he would be much larger than any man of her acquaintance.

She looked round the room they had entered, grateful that it was not the retiring room where Pierre had taken her. She could not bear the thought of being in that place ever again.

'Are you fond of plants, Rose?'

His voice seemed lower than before. Or perhaps it was just that here, in this deserted conservatory, he no longer had to compete against an orchestra and scores of chattering voices.

'Rose?'

'I beg your pardon, Max. I am afraid I was not paying attention. You asked…?'

'I asked if you were fond of plants, *madame*. Roses, perhaps, to match your name? They would be hard pressed to match your beauty.'

'Oh…' Her stomach turned over at his words, spoken

in that deep, musical voice. She felt as if she had been caressed. Without further thought, she put her hand to the strings of her mask. Before, they had seemed determined to resist her questing fingers. Now they came undone at a touch. The mask fell to the floor.

'Thank you,' he said simply. There was a long pause. He was staring at her as if he wanted to imprint her features on his memory.

Angel found she could not hold his gaze. Suddenly, she felt hotter than ever. 'I…I…'

He touched a finger to her lips and allowed it to rest there. 'Hush.' Then he raised her hand to his lips and placed a tiny kiss on each finger in turn.

Angel shivered. She could not speak. Her throat was too tight. And his silencing finger still lay across her lips. Boldly, she touched her tongue to his skin.

He became totally still for a long moment. And then he used that same finger to trace the line of her lower lip. She longed to taste him again, but she did not dare. He was too silent, too dark, too overwhelmingly powerful. Her hand—which he still held—felt tiny within the strength of his. An odd tremor ran down her spine. She ought to know what it meant… She ought to know…

Angel closed her eyes, wishing she had not removed her mask. Behind it, she had felt safe, hidden, anonymous. Without it, she felt naked to him.

She knew when he bent his head to hers. She could feel his nearness. Her skin seemed to tingle with awareness of him. And there was a subtle male scent, too—a mixture of soap and cologne, with a hint of tobacco and leather.

He is going to kiss me, she thought, and I shall not resist him. He finds me beautiful…and I…

She tried to swallow to ease the tightness of her throat.

Her lips parted a fraction. She ran her tongue over them, waiting...

His lips touched her closed eyelids, first one, then the other, with the lightness of a sigh. She shivered again. Her whole body seemed to have been awakened by that touch and was trying to reach out for more, like a parched man lost in the desert and offered only a single drop of life-giving water. One drop, one touch, was not enough.

She waited. A tiny moan escaped her.

'Mmm.' He kissed her lids again, more slowly and deliberately this time, before moving to her temple. 'Mmm,' he murmured again. 'You have beautiful skin. So delicate. And it tastes of...violets.'

Angel felt her knees buckling under the combined onslaught of his touch and his extraordinary voice. It made her think of new honey from the comb—sweet and rich and oh! so very tempting.

He must have sensed her weakness, for he put his arm around her to take her weight and steered her to a padded bench overhung with greenery. She sank down gratefully. She turned to find that he was sitting beside her, his arm still around her and his body so close that she could feel the warmth of his muscular thigh through the thin silk of her gown. Out of the blue, it occurred to her that if she had been in fancy dress, her panniers and petticoats would have impeded him. She found she was not sorry for her choice of garb. Not now.

Gently, he pulled her to him until her head rested against his shoulder. Her eyes closed once more. With his free hand, he began to stroke her hair, lightly at first, but then plunging his fingers into its heavy mass so that most of the pins popped out and fell to the stone floor, ringing tiny metallic notes.

'Max,' she managed at last, opening her eyes and raising

her head, 'will you not remove your mask?' She found she longed to see his face.

He shook his head slightly. 'No, Rose, for there is nothing to see. Better you remember me as I am now—your unknown cavalier, the man who is bewitched by your beauty. I would not have you think of me as I really am, lest it repulse you.'

Angel did not have the first idea of what to make of his words. Was he disfigured under his mask? Her brain was unwilling to begin to tackle anything that required coherent thought. It seemed to be fully occupied in dealing with her heightened senses and the odd reactions of her body. It had never before betrayed her like this. Her legs still felt incapable of supporting her. And the churning in her belly was extraordinary, as if all her insides had turned to thick cream, turning over and over as it was whipped into peaks. She felt extremely strange…quite light-headed. Why on earth…?

His mouth descended on hers with the softness of a butterfly alighting on a flower. The last vestiges of rational thought deserted her. She wanted…she wanted so much more. She reached her arms up to him and pulled him closer, returning a man's kiss for the first time in her life.

It was a revelation. This man did not demand possession. He toyed and teased with his lips and his tongue for what seemed like hours until she was almost screaming in frustration. She wanted… She did not know what she wanted. But when, at last, he deepened the kiss, she groaned low in her throat and pressed herself more closely into his hard body. She wanted…she needed to touch him.

Her fingers were on his cheek. She could feel the beginnings of stubble there. She slid her fingers round to the smoother skin beneath his ear and to the back of his neck, under his wig. Here was his own hair—thick and silky.

She wanted to run her fingers through it, but it was too tightly tied. She moaned in disappointment.

Max lifted her wandering hand and brought it to his lips. 'Fear not, my beauty,' he murmured, kissing her fingers again, 'you shall not be disappointed. I promise.' He laid her hand on the buttons of his shirt.

She trembled. She had never, in her life, disrobed a man. Her fingers would not obey her.

A rumble of laughter in his chest made her raise her eyes to his. They were dark and their expression was unreadable. There was a tiny smile on his lips as he gazed at her.

And then he kissed her again. She was lost. Her body yearned for him. She felt him begin to undo the tiny buttons on the front of her gown. She felt the cool air on her naked breasts when he pushed aside the silken layers. But she felt no shame, only an overwhelming desire for the touch of his fingers on her skin.

It seemed he would not give her what she wanted. He continued to kiss her, deeply and passionately, but made no move to touch her aching breasts. At last, she could stand it no longer. 'Max…' she pleaded. 'Please…'

That tantalising smile still hovered around his mouth. 'Show me what it is you want, my beautiful Rose.' He put his hand, gentle and yielding, into hers. He was leaving the choice to her.

Angel had no choice at all. She carried his hand to her naked breast and held it there. She could feel the rapid beating of her own heart against her splayed fingers. He must be able to feel it, too.

He grazed a thumb across her nipple. It was almost painful. Angel sobbed aloud. Then her voice was swallowed in the return of his kiss. This…this was what she wanted. His mouth on hers, his hands on her naked body, touching, exploring, heating her skin until she was ready to burst into flames.

He lifted his lips from hers. His fingers were still exploring her naked skin, now touching her breasts, now stroking the sensitive skin of her belly under her chemise. Her gown lay in a pool around her hips. She saw that she was almost naked in his arms. It was as if she were looking down at her own body from a great height. It seemed unreal. Only his touch was real.

'What do you want now, my sweet lady?'

She leaned into him to recapture his mouth with her own, but he swayed back from her, just out of reach.

'Ah, no, Rosa. Not like that. You must tell me in words. Tell me what you want.'

'You, Max,' she cried, suddenly desperate that he might not kiss her again. She need not have feared that. Her words were barely uttered when he pulled her back into a fierce embrace, kissing her with even greater passion than before. Now, he was demanding, but Angel wanted nothing less of him. She needed this man.

He lifted her a fraction. She felt the silk of her gown and petticoats slither over her thighs to the floor. She reached for the buttons of his waistcoat. He should be as naked as she!

'Not yet, my sweet,' he said throatily, transferring her arms to his neck so that he could reach round to undo her stay laces. 'First, I must see you. All of you. Your beauty should not be veiled.'

That was too much. 'No,' she groaned. 'No. I need you now, Max.' She began to kiss him with an urgency she would not have believed possible. Now she was no longer prepared to be passive, accepting. She danced her tongue over his lips and into his mouth, advancing and retreating, daring him to respond to her challenge.

'As you wish.' It was almost a groan. Carefully, he laid her down on the bench, pillowing her head on the jacket that he had, at last, removed.

She closed her eyes, waiting, longing. She needed him. She needed him now.

But he did not respond as she expected. Instead, he trailed an idle finger up the inside of her bare leg, from the top of her silk stocking to the junction of her thighs. She could not stifle the gasp of pleasure that escaped her. She did not want to try. She wanted him to know what he was doing to her.

When she felt the first touch of his lips where his hand had been, she caught her breath in shock. But then he laughed softly against her flesh and the sound vibrated into the core of her, like the plucking of the strings of a harp. The chords he struck were perfect. She was floating in the air, surrounded by music that only she could hear. And she wanted it to continue for ever.

It did not. He stopped. He moved his body so that his mouth was on hers once more and his clothed body was covering her nakedness. With a deep rumble of satisfaction, he spread her thighs a little wider. He took a sharp breath. 'Mine,' he said in a strange, harsh voice.

The word hit her like a blow. John Frederick! It was John Frederick under the mask! Her husband was alive! And he was going to punish her again!

No! The word echoed in her head. Had she screamed aloud? He was still kissing her, urgently now. She tried to free her mouth, tried to push him away, tried to fight. But she was securely imprisoned under his weight. There was no way of avoiding the pain to come. She understood that with the blinding clarity of a lightning flash.

And then she descended into darkness.

* * *

Max hastily readjusted his clothing, frowning down at the dishevelled beauty on the bench. She had led him on—she was the worst kind of tease—but he would never stoop to take an unwilling woman. Not even this one.

He lifted her gown from the floor and shook it out, waiting for her to regain her senses. She would demand her clothing before anything else. Women always did. They were incapable of functioning when unclad.

'Rose. Wake up, Rose.' He waited…but she did not recover. She was in a very deep swoon. Strange. Perhaps she…?

He pushed all questions out of his mind. First, he must revive her and then he must help to return her to some measure of decency. She must have some smelling salts. Women always carried them, did they not? He searched in the pockets of her gown, but found nothing. Her reticule, long since abandoned by the bench, was of no help either. Lady Rosevale, it appeared, was the one woman in London who did not carry a vinaigrette.

Max prided himself on being a man of decision. A soldier needed that to survive. Without a second's pause, he set about restoring her clothes. First, he retrieved the velvet mask and replaced it, for that, above all, would ensure her anonymity if they were interrupted. Resting her head against his chest to tie the strings behind, he forced himself to ignore the sight and feel of her glorious breasts, pressed against him. He focused, instead, on the intricacies of her clothing, a problem that was yet to come. Thank God he had not succeeded in removing her stays. Putting those back on an inert body would have been impossible.

It took him too many precious minutes to restore her petticoats and her gown. He noted wryly that it had taken him far less time to remove them, even though she had not actively helped him to do so. Then, he had been grate-

ful that she had chosen to wear a gown with front fastenings, since it had made the disrobing so much more pleasurable, face to face and breast to breast. Now, he was
grateful in a much more practical way, since he could lie
her down gently on the bench on top of her gown, while
he forced her arms through the short sleeves and tussled
with the myriad of tiny buttons. He swore softly but vehemently as he struggled. Gowns like these were not made
for men's fingers. The loops were too small and too tight.
He wondered how he had ever undone them in the first
place, but he had no time to devote to such idle questions.
Now that she was relatively decent once more, he must
revive her.

His cousin lay as one dead. Max could not believe that
a mere swoon would continue so long. She must truly be
ill.

And then he remembered just how much champagne she
had consumed. No wonder she had passed out. The woman
was probably dead drunk!

'Rose!' He shook her gently. No response. 'Rose! You
must wake up!' Still no response.

Max ground his teeth in frustration. He could not leave
her here; but neither could he carry her out and drive her
home. It would betray the fact that he knew who she was.
And in any case, her hair was tumbled down her back—
almost of its own accord, his hand reached out to stroke
the silken strands—and her dress was only just decent. It
would be clear to any observer what she and Max had been
doing…and eventually, that fabulous silver hair would
lead to her unmasking.

'Rose!' he said again, more loudly. Nothing. No wonder. It was not her name. He put his mouth close to her
ear, resisting the temptation to touch his tongue to her

creamy skin. 'Lady Rosevale!' he said. 'Angelina! If you stay here, you will be ruined. You must wake up!'

Even that had no effect on her. He shook his head, desperately trying to think of something else. He dare not leave her to seek help. Unless…

Louisa! Louisa would help. And Louisa was very discreet. Ramsey would have returned by now from taking Louisa home. Max would send him to fetch Louisa…and her smelling salts. He would have to leave his cousin where she lay, but only for a very few moments. There was a risk, but it was a small one, especially if he locked the door once more. No one would disturb the Baroness in his absence.

He made her as comfortable as he could on the bench. Unfortunately, he had to retrieve his coat from under her head, since he did not dare to venture out among the guests without it. But her mass of hair was pillow enough, especially now that her pins were gone. It was a pillow any man would be happy to share.

With a last glance at her sleeping body, he went quietly out into the corridor and locked the door behind him, pocketing the key. Then, straightening his coat, he hurried off in search of the faithful Ramsey and his plain carriage.

'Where am I?' Angel put a hand to her aching head. She was wearing a mask. What was she doing here in a…?

John Frederick! He was here! He had—!

From somewhere deep in her hot and fuddled mind, a sharp voice scolded her roundly. She had imagined it. John Frederick was dead. Long dead. She had been dreaming that he was…that he had—

Oh, God! Now she remembered…not everything, but enough. She had gone apart with a man she had never met, and she had… It was he who had…

She struggled to her feet, holding on to the bench for support. She must get away from this place! Looking down, she saw that some of the tiny buttons of her gown were in the wrong loops. Someone else—the masked man—had dressed her. She shut her eyes against the horror of it. Then, with trembling fingers, she fixed the buttons and straightened the petticoat beneath. As long as she was fully masked—she put up her hands to check—she could make her way to her carriage and escape from this terrible ordeal.

There were hairpins all over the floor. Her hair! She could not go out with her hair down her back. She grabbed some of the pins and tried to make her hair presentable, but it was useless. There was too much weight in it and she did not have the knack. She could tie it back with a ribbon—if only she had one—but that was the extent of her skill.

She scanned the conservatory. There must be something... A piece of twine, perhaps? Nothing.

She would not, she could not go out into the ballroom. Even with a mask, it would mean ruin. Leaving the pins where they lay, she grabbed her reticule and pushed her way through the exotic greenery. There must be a window, at least. She would climb out. She had no choice if she was to escape.

She found, not a window, but a concealed door leading to the garden. Almost, she could not believe it. She pushed her hair back over her shoulders, turned the key and opened the door very slowly. She listened. Nothing. No voices. It was only to be expected. No one would be in the garden at night so early in the year. It was much too cold.

After the heavy warmth of the conservatory, the spring night was very chill indeed on her bare neck and arms.

Without her cloak, she might well take cold. She did not give it another thought. Her cloak had been given up at the entrance, and there it must stay.

She relocked the door, removed the key and dropped it on to the path. Then, picking up her skirts, she felt her way round the wall of the house. Twice her feet strayed into flower beds and she sank into soft, wet soil. Her evening slippers and stockings were soon soaked. They would be filthy, too, though she could not see that in the dark. At last, she came to the corner of the house. There seemed to be a passageway. At the end of it, she could see the roadway. Carriages stood, their lamps glowing dully. She could hear voices, too.

She put up her hands to check her mask one last time and walked carefully down the side of the house, casting about for her own carriage. It was there, just a little way away. She had only to make her way to it, ignoring the stares of the gossiping grooms and coachmen, and climb in. Then she would be safe, where her masked lover could not find her.

Chapter Nine

Angel cowered back into the darkest corner of the carriage, trying to make herself as small as possible and covering her face with her hands. She recoiled instantly. She could smell the scent of him on her fingers.

Oh, what a fool she had been! With Pierre, she had been in control. And so she had imagined that she could control an encounter with any man. She remembered every move Pierre had made. It had been delightful—at first—but her feelings had not been engaged in any way. It had been as if he were coldly practising on her, like an eager student repeating a piece of music over and over, until it reached the point of perfection that touched the heart. She had known it was false, every single second of it.

But, with Max, she could not even remember what he had done or fathom how he had done it. She remembered the feelings: the heat, the desire… She had encouraged him…shamelessly, like a wanton. Her body had seemed to have a will of its own, totally divorced from conscious thought or morality…

Until that fearful moment when everything had changed. When her masked lover had seemed to turn into John Frederick…

It was not the first time she had fainted away. Twice, when John Frederick had been particularly violent, she had swooned under him. He had roundly abused her for it, but it had not stopped him from taking his pleasure of her. He had said it made no difference to him whether her eyes were open or closed.

With Max…with Max she had thought everything was different. He had been so caring and gentle… He had made her feel so—

But now her whole body ached, as it always had after her husband had come to her bed. So much for Max's gentleness! His gentleness must have turned into invasion, even while she was senseless.

A sob of anger escaped her lips. She had been wicked. Now, she was paying the price. She wanted to scream her fury to the whole of London. How could something so tender, so beautiful, turn in an instant into dross?

Max wrestled with the lock. It made a great deal of noise, but the confounded thing refused to budge. If she had regained her senses, his cousin might assume that some stranger was trying to force an entry. He tried the key again, more slowly this time. The lock turned at last.

He flung open the door and strode into the conservatory. He had left her lying on the bench. It was empty. The Baroness had disappeared. Even her reticule was gone. All that remained was a scatter of hairpins on the floor.

He cursed aloud. It was not possible! The door had been securely locked when he returned. She must be hiding somewhere among the greenery.

Max was not about to be cozened by a mere female, especially not by this one. He would search methodically but, before he started, he would relock the only door. She would have no opportunity to slip out into the corridor while he was searching for her. He nodded to himself, sure that he had guessed her plan. It was a good plan, too—for a woman—but not good enough to be used against a seasoned campaigner.

He began his search in the corner nearest the entrance, the most likely hiding place for someone about to try for the door. Then he quartered the conservatory with precision. He looked in every possible hiding place. The Baroness was nowhere to be found.

In the final corner, he discovered a hidden door to the garden. He cursed his luck to have found it only at the very last. He had wasted precious minutes. The door was locked. There was no key, but he felt sure that it had provided his cousin's escape route. She had probably had the presence of mind to lock it behind her and take the key. Had he not done the same to her?

He had no need to follow her out into the garden, for he knew exactly what she would do. She would make her way to the front of the house where the carriages waited. She would try to escape. Alone. How much of a head start did she have? He could perhaps cut her off via the front door.

He hurried back to the main entrance and out on to the flagway, casting around for the Baroness's carriage. It was bound to be a plain, hired vehicle, like his own. She would not have wished to advertise her presence at this house.

There was no sign that any of the line of vehicles was about to leave. Blast the woman! He had missed her. She was gone. She must have escaped while he was still searching the conservatory. Unless she was hiding…

He summoned one of the gossiping grooms with a sharp gesture. The lad confirmed that a plain carriage had indeed driven off some ten minutes earlier, but he had not noticed its passenger.

Max swallowed an oath and tipped the groom, before walking slowly back to the brightly lit entrance to the mansion. Louisa would arrive soon. No doubt she would have been intrigued by his summons. He would have to explain something of what had happened, and then escort Louisa home again.

What was he going to tell her about his encounter with the Baroness in the conservatory? Not the truth. It could not be the whole truth. He had been faithful to Louisa since his return from the Peninsula, as she had been faithful to him. He could never bring himself to tell her that, confronted by a frivolous, scheming and vindictive beauty, he had forgotten all about his understanding with his mistress. He had tried to seduce his cousin out of ungovernable anger and—he had to admit—lust. She was beautiful. She was tempting. And when she had responded so passionately to his advances, she had become irresistible. It was only when she fainted away that he had succeeded in regaining a vestige of control over his heated body. She had swooned at the prospect of coupling with him. That alone was an unforgivable insult. Enough to dampen any right-thinking man's ardour.

Max lounged against a mock Greek column in the hallway, waiting for Louisa's return. At least *she* was faithful and open about her desires. The Baroness, by contrast, was coy one moment and behaving like a cheap doxy the next. No doubt she had been practising on the impostor, earlier. Max found himself wondering whether the Frenchman had had more success than he. If the woman flirted like that with every man who paid court to her, she must be spending most of her life on her back. And she should have been big-bellied long before now.

But she was barren. That fact had probably turned her

into a total wanton. Even more reason not to allow her to triumph in the battle between himself and the Frenchman.

At the sound of carriage wheels outside, Max straightened. It was almost certainly Louisa. He started towards the entrance, still undecided about what he should say to her.

'Your stockings are ruined, my lady. And your slippers.' Benton pursed her lips in disapproval. 'And you have come home without your fine evening cloak…and with your hair hanging down your back, never a pin in sight. I declare, it is—'

'Benton,' said Angel rather hoarsely, 'that will do. I am perfectly well aware of the state I am in.' She wiped the back of her hand across her damp forehead. 'And I know exactly the mistakes I have made. I pray you—no more.'

'You have a fever, m'lady, I don't doubt. I've seen it coming these last two days, but you wouldn't listen, would you? Gadding off to heaven knows where, and you without a morsel of food inside you since the day before yesterday. Even then t'were barely a mouthful.'

'Benton. Please. Let it rest. I have the headache.'

Benton put down the hairbrush she had been using to remove the tangles from Angel's hair. 'Best if I leave that till you're feeling better, then. You won't want your hair touched if you have the headache.'

'Thank you.' Benton loved to fuss and scold, but she had a kind and understanding heart. During Angel's marriage, Benton had often held her mistress while she wept. The abigail was the only person who knew even a fraction of what Angel had been made to suffer.

Benton fetched a basin of warm violet-scented water and gently washed Angel's face and neck. Then she put the basin on the floor and bathed her mistress's dirty, bruised

fcct. Angel sighed in satisfaction at Benton's gentle
strokes, massaging her skin. 'That feels very soothing.'

'Bed now, my lady. I shall make sure no one disturbs
you in the morning. Not even her ladyship. I shall tell her
you are unwell and must be left to sleep.'

Angel lay down on the crisp, cool sheets and let her
aching head sink into the pillows. She closed her eyes
gratefully.

'I will bring you a tisane, m'lady. It will help the headache. And the fever.' Benton laid a hand on Angel's brow.
'Lavender water to bathe your forehead, too.'

'Mmm. That would be wonderful.'

Benton tucked the covers around her. 'I shall not be
gone but a few minutes, m'lady. Try if you can get a little
sleep.'

When she heard the click of the closing door, Angel
turned her face to the wall. She could never sleep, not with
all these terrible thoughts going round and round in her
mind. Why had she responded like a harlot…to a complete
stranger? What was it about him? Their encounter had become so hazy that she could not put her finger on any
single detail, but she knew she had not resisted his advances. She knew, too, that he was a practised seducer. He
had known exactly how to make her respond to him. It
was almost laughable. Her husband had accused her of
lying like a block of wood in his bed. With Max, she had
swayed and bent like a tender sapling. Until that terrible
moment when…

Angel felt the hot tears running down her cheeks and
on to the pillow. They were tears of anger, and of shame.
Yes, she was unwell. Yes, she had been in no fit state to
attend any public gathering, but *she* was the one who had
drunk all those glasses of champagne. And she was the
one who had invited a tall, masked stranger to seduce her.

Oh, she deserved every single pain that she was now to endure, whether mental or physical.

Her headache was getting worse. Someone seemed to be pounding on her skull with a hammer, just above her eyes. She put the heel of her hand to the place and pressed hard, trying to push away the pain. It would not go. It was her penance.

She was still awake when Benton returned with the promised tisane, creeping in quietly in case her mistress was already asleep. Angel opened her eyes as Benton carefully placed the tisane on the bedside table. 'Thank you.' She struggled to sit up.

Benton put a gentle arm around her shoulders and eased her into a sitting position, adding an extra pillow behind her back. 'Drink it, m'lady. It will help you to sleep.'

It tasted slightly different from Benton's usual tisane, Angel thought. What had she added to it this time? There was no point in asking, for Benton would deny everything. Besides, whatever it was, it would be worth it if it helped her to sleep and to forget what she had done. Angel drank gratefully and then sank down among her pillows once more, closing her heavy eyes.

The room was dark. There was barely any light from the dying fire; the candles had all been snuffed. The darkness surrounded her like velvet. She could feel herself drifting, beginning to dream. She could feel the touch of a man's fingers on her skin, of a mouth at her breast. She could feel the pain of penetration, of harsh selfish thrusts. She could hear the satisfied grunts of her husband reaching his climax and spilling his seed into her helpless, useless body.

Angel's insides twisted painfully at the recurring memory. The child… If only she had borne the child… If only she *could* have borne the child… That was impossible. It could never come to pass. Yet with Max, she felt…

Angel sat up with a start. The nightmare dissolved into the familiar darkness of her bedchamber. It was not real, after all. She was in her own room. And she was alone in her own bed. Her husband was dead and there was no child. She had dreamt it. It was not true.

She was drenched in sweat. She tried to shake her head, to rid herself of that terrifying image. 'Oh,' she groaned into the darkness. What on earth was the matter with her? This was much more than a bad dream. Just how many glasses of champagne had she drunk?

She reached out to pull the bell alongside her bed. Her quivering hand gripped the cord for a second, but then she let it fall back on to the bedcover. She could not summon Benton. Not yet. Not until she had restored some order to her spiralling thoughts. If Benton arrived now, with her incessant questions, she would drive Angel insane.

Angel let her aching body subside on to the pillows and groaned again as the pain rose to a crescendo, filling her head and all her limbs. Movement made it worse, it seemed. She lay very, very still. The pain subsided a little.

The nightmare seemed to crowd in on her, even though she had not dared to close her eyes again. Now the man was there—the unknown foreigner who called himself Max—and she could feel the touch of his hands on her body. Had he taken her while she lay senseless? John Frederick would have done so.

She closed her eyes then, as tightly as she could, trying to push away that terrifying thought. No! Max was not John Frederick. Max was loving and gentle. He would not have done such a thing. It could not be! It was only a dream…a nightmare. It was not true. It could not be true!

A nasty little voice in the back of her mind whispered that even nightmares could come true—and that she might even now be carrying Max's child.

She had been such a fool. Although she had been unwell for days—she recognised that only too clearly now—she had stubbornly insisted on attending that ridotto. Her fever had been mounting all evening but, instead of going safely home to bed, she—a woman who hardly ever drank wine—had downed glass after glass of champagne as if it were lemonade. No wonder she had behaved in such a stupid, immoral fashion. Between them, the fever and the alcohol had overcome all her inhibitions.

She must now face up to what she had done. She could tell no one, not even Benton. But she must be honest with herself.

She had flirted shamelessly with a complete stranger. She had agreed to go apart with him…had even suggested it herself. And she had allowed him to seduce her. She had been a willing partner in her own downfall.

No, that was not true! She had tried to stop him.

Almost, she wanted to laugh at the absurdity of her own protestations. She, of all people, should have known when it was too late to stop a man. She had never succeeding in stopping her husband. Why should a stranger, driven by his lust, behave any differently?

Because he was not a ravening beast like John Frederick. Max had cared enough for her reputation to ensure she was fully clothed—and masked—before he left her. Max would not have taken her against her will. He would not.

Angel shivered. She felt suddenly very cold. She pulled the bedcovers more closely round her, and curled up into a ball.

Max. Would she ever see him again? Could she recognise him if she did?

The image that had seemed so clear just a few moments earlier was beginning to fade. He was the tallest man she had ever met. He had a slight foreign accent. And he had a voice as rich as honey. That was all she knew, apart from his name. In her dream, she had seen his face, overlaid with her husband's, but in reality…she had no idea what Max looked like. His face had been painted. And he had refused to remove his mask.

If she was wrong about Max, if she was indeed carrying his child—she offered up a fervent prayer that it was not so—she would have to shoulder the burden alone. Baroness Rosevale would be ruined. She would bear a bastard. To an unknown father.

A stab of pain ripped through her body. She told herself it was the fever, just the fever. But it felt like an old familiar pain—the effect of her husband's lust on her body. She curled even tighter, kneading her belly with both hands. Silently, she prayed.

When Angel woke again it was still dark, but Benton was beside her bed, gently bathing her face with lavender water. Angel could barely raise her eyelids. Her whole body ached as if it had been beaten with hammers.

Benton smiled broadly, put down her cloth and lifted a cup to Angel's lips. 'Thank God you are back with us! Try if you can drink a little now, m'lady.'

Angel discovered that her throat was parched. She tried to speak, but no words came out.

'You *must* drink something, m'lady,' Benton said, offering the cup again.

Gratefully, Angel sipped. It was barley water. It tasted

like nectar. She sipped twice more. 'I don't understand—' she began.

Benton shook her head in concern and said, 'It is better if you do not try to talk yet. Wait until you have regained your strength a little.'

Angel frowned. What was Benton talking about?

'You have been very ill, m'lady. You came home with a raging fever. You have lain here for five days. We feared… Yesterday, we thought we would lose you.'

Angel blinked hard and sank back on her pillows. She felt so very weak…

'There have been dozens of callers, m'lady. Mr Rose-vale—the French gentleman—has called almost every day.' Benton nodded in the direction of a vase of spring flowers, just visible in the gloom. 'And he brought fresh flowers every time he came. Are they not lovely?'

'Take them away,' Angel said sharply, in a voice she barely recognised. Weak though she was, she could remember every second of her encounter with Pierre. She wanted nothing from him.

Benton looked puzzled for a moment, but she did as she was bid. When she returned to the bedside, she said, 'Her ladyship will wish to know that you are awake. Shall I fetch her to you?'

'No!' Angel almost groaned at the thought. She could not face her aunt's penetrating questions. Not now, when she felt so very weak.

'I…I told her ladyship that your fever had mounted quite suddenly, m'lady,' Benton said quietly. 'She did not seem surprised. Said she had seen it coming. I… She did not ask about anything else and I…I did not tell her that you had been out.'

'Oh.' Angel allowed herself a sigh of relief. It did not

matter that Benton heard it. The abigail would never betray her mistress's secrets.

There were worse secrets, however. Secrets that could not be voiced. Angel shuddered violently as she remembered what had happened to her and her innermost fear that she could be carrying Max's child. It had been the fever talking. It must have been.

Benton pulled the bedcovers around her mistress. 'You must rest now, m'lady.' She nodded to the chair by the bed. 'I will be here if you need me.'

Angel gave in and closed her eyes. It had been the fever. She was ill. She could not be pregnant. Max would not have done such a thing to her.

She repeated those words over and over, like a litany, until she fell into a troubled sleep.

In her dreams, there was a babe at her breast.

Chapter Ten

'It is well nigh three months since Ross left, and *still* no word from him.'

'Be reasonable, Max. Even the government has difficulty in finding out what is going on in France. Bonaparte—'

'Bonaparte has us all running round in circles.' Yet again, he drove his fingers through his hair. It was now thoroughly untidy. 'And as for the government's information… How are we to believe any of it? Did not our Embassy in Paris send word that no one was supporting the little tyrant? And then, two days later, it reported that he had entered Paris without a single shot being fired? They—'

'Max, that was weeks ago.' Louisa put her hand gently over his. 'I know how much you are concerned about Ross. And I know how much you want to join the Duke. But you yourself have said it is not possible. And we both know that you are right. As for Ross…I refuse to worry. He has as many lives as a cat. You told me so yourself.'

He pushed her hand away and began to pace. 'Even a cat may run out of lives in three months, Louisa. Especially alone in enemy territory!'

She rose and stood in his path. When he stopped in front of her, she took both his hands. 'Max, my dear, this is not like you. It is simply the result of inaction. You need to be doing something…but there is nothing you can do. Nothing.' She crossed to the side table and poured two glasses of wine. 'Here. Let us sit down and discuss matters calmly. There may be something that we have not considered. And if we apply a little logic, we may yet discover it.'

He made a noise that was somewhere between a laugh and a groan, but he took the seat she indicated.

'How does your cousin go on? Have you seen her?'

'I… She is recovered, I believe. Recovering. I called as soon as I heard of her illness, of course, but I have not seen her. She was receiving no one.'

Louisa took a deep breath. 'Is it wise to leave the field to the Frenchman, Max? She must be receiving by now, surely? It is weeks since the ridotto.'

'The Frenchman has not been received either, though he calls almost every day. With flowers.' Max could not hide his distaste. 'The man is playing a part, I think. Doing simply what is expected of him. My agents tell me he spends much of his time, and almost all his blunt, in trying to secure news of his sister.'

'How very singular. Is she not hidden away in some tiny village in the south? She can be in no danger, surely?'

'That depends. If Ross has found her, he will be trying to bring her to England…whether she is willing or not.'

'I see.' She gazed thoughtfully at her wineglass. 'Do you think the Frenchman suspects?'

'About Ross? No. I see no reason why he should do so. He knows nothing of Ross.'

'Strange, then, that he should be so anxious, is it not?'

Max nodded. He had been thinking exactly the same

thing. The more he learned of his rival, the more suspicious he became. There was something wrong about the man who called himself Pierre Rosevale. He was not to be trusted with anything, or anyone.

Max put his glass down sharply and rose to his feet. There *was* something he could do, after all. 'I may not be able to help Ross, Louisa, but I can certainly help to defend my cousin against this pretender. I have not the least doubt that he is a blackguard. I think it is time that I paid another call on the dear Baroness. Just to inquire after her health, you understand.'

Louisa smiled as she rose from her chair. 'I am sure that would be very wise, my dear,' she said, reaching up to kiss his cheek. 'And, forgive me, but may I suggest that you take a look in the glass before you go? You are…not quite your normal well-groomed self.'

Max glanced across at the mirror and groaned aloud. 'How very tactful you are, Louisa. And how right. I see that I must change my dress *and* do something about my disreputable appearance before I call on the noble Baroness. I promise I shall not disgrace you.'

Angel studied her face in the glass. She looked positively hagged. There were dark circles beneath her eyes, and her cheeks were shrunken. She would not have imagined it was possible to be quite so ill; or that it could take so many weeks to recover.

Recover? She no longer had a raging fever, but that was the full extent of her recovery. Otherwise, she was little better than before. In fact, she was on the verge of ruin, for she was now sure, almost sure, that she was carrying her unknown lover's child. She had believed in Max. But she had been wrong. He had betrayed her.

She had prayed for her courses to return. Every day, she

had prayed. And every day, she had been disappointed. She remembered everything she had learned from the hateful midwife about the other signs of pregnancy. As far as Angel could tell, she had them all…just as before. Her breasts seemed to be tender, her waist seemed to be thickening, and, these last few days, she had begun to experience a feeling of nausea, especially in the mornings.

Soon, Benton would notice what was happening to her mistress. And then, Angel's secret would be discovered.

Oh, why had she been such a fool? Angelina Rosevale, a woman who hated and feared intimacy with men, had allowed—no, encouraged—an unknown man to make love to her. Her fever, her intoxication…nothing excused what she had done. If she was carrying Max's child, if she succeeded in carrying it to term, she would be ruined, but she would have no one to blame but herself. In truth, Max had done only what Angel had wanted him to do…

She dreamt about him almost every night. In her dreams, she lay in his arms and rejoiced in his loving, in the touch of his hands on her willing body. In her dreams, she could see his face. But always, in the morning, it was veiled once more, hidden in the recesses of her mind. In the mornings, she was left with no more than an impression of loving strength, and of dark blue eyes that roved over her face as if searching for more and more ways to bring the flush of passion to her cheeks.

Angel pushed her hair back from her forehead and examined her face once more. Max had called her beautiful, all those weeks ago. If he could see her now, he would not use such a description. Apart from the colour of her hair, everything had changed. She looked, and felt, like a woman suffering.

And she was suffering.

Angel rose from her dressing table and began to pace

about the room. She had no desire to view the ruin of her face any longer. She needed to decide what to do.

She could take advice from no one. And, if she truly was increasing, she had very little time. Soon, it would be impossible to hide her condition from her household and her secret would become food for the gossips. Her only hope would be to find herself a husband before her pregnancy began to show. But where were the candidates? Even the London fortune-hunters would be reluctant to agree to marry in such haste, no matter how rich the bride. They would be bound to suspect the truth. The husband should, of course, be Max, the tall, foreign man who had seduced her. But...

Angel swallowed hard. There was no chance of that. None whatsoever. Max, it appeared, had completely vanished from London Society. There was no salvation by that route. She must look elsewhere for a husband.

Her glance lighted on the vase of flowers by the window. Pierre Rosevale still called on her at least every other day. And he always brought flowers. Angel was heartily sick of the sight and scent of them. She was always polite to him, especially when Lady Charlotte was present, but she no longer cared whether or not Pierre was the rightful heir to the earldom. She knew, beyond any shadow of a doubt, that he cared only for Julie, his sister. It was disgusting.

However, Pierre *was* unmarried; and Pierre *had* been attracted to Angel. He might possibly be persuaded to become a candidate for her hand, if only to secure her wealth. And he might agree to a hasty wedding.

Angel shook her head. What was she thinking of? She despised Pierre. How could she possibly be contemplating marriage to him? She knew what marriage was.

But she also knew she had no choice. She had to find a

husband within the next few weeks or she would be ruined, and her babe would be born a bastard. She owed the child a name. If Pierre was the only candidate for her hand, she would have to take him—and then learn to live with the consequences of her own folly.

Max bowed formally and glanced round the opulent drawing room. Though nominally 'at home', the Baroness was nowhere to be seen.

'Good afternoon, Cousin.' Lady Charlotte took a step forward to greet him, but did not extend her hand. She simply dropped a tiny curtsy. Clearly, she had decided to play the *grande dame*.

Max was irritated, but not at all surprised. Her antipathy to him was written clearly across her wrinkled features. As far as he knew, she had no cause for it, except that he came from the cadet branch of the family, the branch to which both Augustus and Mary Rosevale had belonged.

Deliberately, Max assumed an equally haughty expression and stared down his nose at the old lady. If she could rest on her aristocratic lineage, so would he. 'Good afternoon to you, ma'am. I had hoped to pay my respects to Lady Rosevale. I understand she is recovered but…' Letting the words hang in the air, he slowly surveyed the room.

Lady Charlotte looked quickly down at the Aubusson carpet. 'You are… My niece has…is…recovering, sir. I am sure she will be gratified to learn that you were kind enough to call.'

Max strode forward into the room. He was not about to be given his *congé* in such a fashion. 'Lady Rosevale *is* well enough to receive visitors, I collect?' he said, nodding in the direction of the ladies who were sitting on the sofas near the fire. The visitors had been chattering animatedly until his name was announced. Now they were all silent, watching the encounter between their hostess and the new arrival. Like sentries on the *qui vive* for intruders, Max thought, the tabbies were listening intently, ready to pick up the tiniest morsel of gossip. Well, he would not permit them to report that the Earl of Penrose had been vanquished by one elderly lady. 'I have no doubt that my cousin will receive *me*.' He threw the words down like a challenge.

Lady Charlotte still would not meet his eyes. 'No doubt.' The old lady repeated his words mechanically. 'Perhaps you will take some tea while you wait, Cousin?' She indicated a vacant place.

The very last thing Max wanted was to be forced to exchange polite nothings with Lady Charlotte's cronies. 'You are too kind, ma'am,' he replied smoothly. 'Unfortunately, I have another appointment shortly, and so I must decline your hospitality.' He forced himself to smile down at her. 'If you would be so good as to direct me to where I may find Lady Rosevale...?' He had the old lady cornered now, surely?

'I... My niece is taking the air, sir. She is under strict instructions to walk in the fresh air at least once or twice a day. I do not doubt she will return soon. But if you cannot wait...'

Clever. But not clever enough. 'I do have a particular reason for wishing to speak to Lady Rosevale today, ma'am. If you would be good enough to tell me where she is to be found, I shall go and join her.'

Her eyes narrowed. She knew that she was beaten; and she hated it. 'My niece is walking in the gardens, sir. I must ask you to remember that she is still very weak. The doctor has said that she must not be upset in any way.'

Max bowed. 'I shall have every care for Lady Rosevale's wellbeing, ma'am. You need have no concern on that score. Good day to you, ma'am. And to you, ladies.' He bowed again in the general direction of the fireplace and strode out on to the landing and down the stairs to the huge marble hallway. It was strange that he had not seen the Baroness when he arrived. He had walked across Berkeley Square through the gardens. There had been several people taking the air, but he would have sworn that his silver-haired cousin was not among them.

'Would your lordship not prefer to go through the house?'

Max had been making for the front door. The old butler seemed to be surprised. 'I was about to go into the gardens. I had understood that Lady Rosevale was walking there,' Max said carefully.

The butler allowed himself a tiny, superior smile. 'I fear there has been some slight...misunderstanding, my lord. Lady Rosevale is walking in the private garden behind the house. Would your lordship wish to be shown the way?'

'Yes. Yes, thank you, er...?'

'Willett, my lord.'

'Thank you, Willett.' Max dropped a coin into the butler's ready palm.

'This way, if you please, my lord,' said the old man, starting down the corridor. Then he glanced back over his shoulder, his sharp old eyes gleaming avariciously, and stopped. 'Your lordship may wish to be aware that her ladyship is taking the air in the company of her cousin, Monsieur Pierre Rosevale. He has been...most attentive during her ladyship's illness.'

The old man was very suspicious of the Frenchman. That was perfectly obvious from the way he pronounced the foreign name. Max extracted another, larger coin from his pocket and held it between finger and thumb. 'And do they often walk in the garden together, Willett?'

'Yesterday was the first time, my lord. Her ladyship was not strong enough to leave the house until then.'

Max rubbed his thumb over the surface of the coin and frowned down at it.

'But he has called every day since her ladyship was well enough to come down to the drawing room. Almost a week it is now, my lord.'

'Thank you, Willett.' Max allowed the coin to fall into the butler's hand. 'And now, perhaps you would show me the door to the garden?'

The butler nodded and started down the corridor once more. The coins had miraculously disappeared.

Angel took another deep breath and tucked her hand more closely under Pierre's arm. This was not going well. So far, her subtle approach had been a total failure. She would have to broach the subject more directly. But what could she possibly say? A lady could not baldly ask a man to marry her. It was impossible.

The longer she danced around the subject with Pierre, the more clearly she understood that, unprompted, he was never going to propose to her. He might stand in need of her help to pursue his claim, and of her wealth to search out the evidence to support it, but he did not seem to think he needed to put a ring on her finger in order to secure either. He seemed to be content to rely on Angel's—or rather, Lady Charlotte's—family loyalty.

'I fear that we shall not receive any news from Paris while Bonaparte is in control. I…that is, my aunt is most concerned that it is taking so long to gather the evidence for your claim.'

'I share her concern, Cousin.'

'It must be very difficult for you to be plain Mr Rose-vale, with no real…standing in Society. I could perhaps help you, but… Oh dear, this is so very difficult.'

Pierre stopped and turned Angel to face him. He was frowning. Even so, he still looked absurdly handsome. 'My dear cousin, you must not concern yourself about my future. Not when you are barely recovered from such a terrible illness.' He touched a hand to her hair and dropped a gentle kiss on her cheek. 'You should think on happier topics. Look about you.' He gestured towards the emerging beauty of the garden. 'It is spring. Everything is bursting with new life.'

Angel gulped. Could there be a hidden meaning to his words?

'I have no doubt that Wellington will triumph over the usurper,' Pierre continued. 'You yourself told me that your tireless Duke has never yet been defeated. It is merely a matter of time, I am sure. And then you will send for Julie…as you promised.'

'The Duke will not meet Bonaparte until he is ready,' Angel said gravely. 'He has never been defeated because he always fights on ground of his own choosing.' Seeing the look of inquiry in Pierre's eyes, she pressed home her point. 'It may be weeks, months, even, before battle is joined. And in the meantime, your position becomes increasingly precarious.'

'No. Why should it? I have the support of the Baroness Rosevale, and of the Lady Charlotte Clare.'

'That is…where the difficulty lies, I fear. You see… I must tell you, Cousin, that since your claim is unproved—and so strongly disputed by my Cousin Frederick, besides—it is becoming increasingly difficult for me to meet you, and support you, as I have been doing. You…you must remember that I am a young woman still and…and even though I am a widow, I may not do as I please.'

Pierre stared at her with narrowed eyes. He said nothing. Was he remembering that she had done exactly as she pleased at the ridotto?

'If I continue to meet you, and to walk and talk with you as I have been wont to do, my reputation could suffer. The gossips will say that I merely pretend you are my cousin in order to meet you alone. They will say that I…that we… It would be different if I were married. Indeed, I have been thinking of little else these last few days. Since my illness, you understand. If I had died…' She took a deep breath. 'As head of the Rosevale family, it is my duty to marry. And, as a woman, I need to marry while I am still young enough to—' She stopped, horrified at what she had so nearly said. It was worse than improper.

Pierre lifted her hand to his lips. 'My dear cousin…my very dear cousin, I am gratified that you should choose to confide in me. You are quite correct. I understand your concerns, and I applaud your sentiments. I agree that it is the first duty of the holder of any title to marry and to secure the succession. I would advise you to marry as soon as may be. I myself shall do the same. As soon as my claim has been proved. But, for me, nothing can be decided until then.' He kissed her hand again. 'Naturally, I appreciate the difficulties that *you* are facing on a personal level. A lady of your delicate sensibilities… I would do nothing—nothing—to embarrass you, my dear lady. If you wish it, I shall cease to call upon you.'

Angel ground her teeth. This was all going wrong!

'Good afternoon, Cousin.'

That hard voice, so infuriatingly familiar, came from behind her, on the path back to the house. Angel whirled round. Cousin Frederick was strolling nonchalantly towards her. There was a hint of a smile at the corner of his mouth. Her heart began to beat in double time. How long had he been there? Had he been close enough to hear what was said? She had thought her predicament could not possibly get any worse, but she had forgotten about the Earl of Penrose and his vindictive nature. He had absolutely no reason to feel kindly disposed towards her; and he would certainly wish to do everything in his power to undermine Pierre's position.

Cousin Frederick eyed Pierre with undisguised distaste. Then he turned back to Angel, ignoring the Frenchman completely. It was a studied insult.

Angel bridled. Pierre might be poor—he might even be an impostor—but he was most certainly a gentleman. He should be acknowledged as such. The Earl's manners were deplorable.

'I think, sir, that you have met my cousin, Monsieur Pierre Rosevale?' she said acidly.

The Earl's eyes narrowed at her words. Then he half-turned to Pierre and executed a tiny, impudent bow. 'We are slightly acquainted, ma'am,' he said, his voice even harder than before.

Pierre coloured, but stood his ground.

'I came to enquire after your health, Cousin,' the Earl said blandly. 'I trust you are now fully recovered?'

He was looking her up and down, gauging how much her illness had damaged her looks. Angel sensed that he was also assessing her weaknesses. She prayed that he could not see the tell-tale changes in her body.

'You *are* fully recovered, I hope, Cousin?'

Angel reached for the lifeline of good manners. 'I thank you, Cousin, I am…much improved. I am not yet permitted to go beyond the bounds of my own garden, however. As you see.'

'I am glad to hear it, ma'am. Your family—' the Earl threw a scornful look in Pierre's direction '—will be re-assured to learn that you are taking every care.'

He reached out and forcibly withdrew Angel's hand from Pierre's arm. She was too astonished to protest, even when the Earl placed her fingers on his sleeve. Pierre looked thunderstruck.

'You will excuse us, sir,' the Earl said pointedly. 'The Baroness and I have certain family matters to discuss.' As Pierre started forward, the Earl smiled coldly at him and raised a hand. 'Pray do not trouble yourself, sir. I shall ensure that no harm comes to my cousin. We shall take another turn around the garden. And then I shall return Lady Rosevale to the safety of the house.' He nodded to Pierre. 'Good day to you, sir.'

The Earl put his gloved fingers over Angel's and steered her down the path. Pierre was left where he stood, with a comical expression of astonishment on his face.

Angel was too bewildered to react to the absurdity of it all. She saw that Pierre had been made to look a fool, but all she felt was a desperate urge to flee from her black-browed cousin and his discussion of 'family matters'. No doubt he intended to take her to task once more. That was easy enough for a man of such dominating physical presence. Cousin Frederick towered over her. He was the tallest man she had ever met. Except for Max. Max had been a good two inches taller, at least, but Max, though equally powerful, was not intimidating. And Max did not have a voice harsh enough to make her quake in her shoes.

A crack in the paving took her unawares. She stumbled slightly, but she had not reckoned on the strength of his arm or the speed of his reactions. He caught her up and steadied her until she had regained her balance. Her composure, however, vanished completely. An odd tremor ran down her spine. She hardly dared to look at him.

'If you are recovered, ma'am, shall we go on?'

He now had her arm tucked very securely within his own. It was impossible to escape. Angel managed a nod.

'Excellent.'

He walked her slowly down the path, never once looking behind them to see whether Pierre was still watching. Cousin Frederick seemed to be absolutely certain that he had won the day. What an arrogant man he was!

Angel hazarded a quick glance over her shoulder. Pierre was nowhere to be seen. She should have known it would be so. She had been left alone, and defenceless, with Cousin Frederick. And, judging by his black frown, he was now preparing to ring a peal over her.

Chapter Eleven

Max was shocked at the change in her. Her face was drawn, her beautiful complexion almost lifeless. Even her glorious hair was dulled. When he had saved her from falling, he had grabbed her by the arms, only to discover that she was little more than skin and bone. She must truly have been gravely ill after the ridotto. To Max, it was clear that her aunt, and her doctors, were failing in their duty to promote her recovery.

The Frenchman had been assiduous in his attentions, according to the butler. Max did not doubt it. He had seen the results with his own eyes. The villain had even had the temerity to kiss the Baroness in full view of her own house. Max realised he was clenching his fists. It would have been so very satisfying to use them on the man, the sort of man who looked ready to buckle under the first blow.

He walked her slowly down the garden. Neither spoke. Max noticed that she was leaning quite heavily on his arm. She must be very weak indeed.

With difficulty, he forced himself to ignore the closeness of her body. He must focus on her ill health. For that, he must be to blame, at least in some measure. He tried to remember exactly what had passed between them on the night of the ridotto. She had complained, several times, about the heat. No doubt that had been her rising fever. She had drunk a great many glasses of champagne. That had been stupid…and also out of character, he now decided. She was not used to alcohol. It would probably have given her a dreadful hangover, to add to her fever, but was otherwise pretty harmless. As to the rest of their encounter…

Max found his memories of the ridotto were unusually hazy. With his mistresses, he had always been resolutely in control. But with the Baroness, he could remember only the beginning…and the end. He had been furiously angry and had set out to teach her a lesson. He had wanted to show her the risks she ran by being alone with a man, that she could easily be subdued by sheer physical strength. He had intended to frighten her, not to seduce her. But, somehow, once he had kissed her luscious mouth, the seduction had become…mutual. It was only her sudden resistance, at the last, that had brought him to his senses.

He was thoroughly ashamed of his behaviour that night. He had allowed his ungovernable temper, and then his lust, to dictate his actions. They had not been the actions of a gentleman. He suspected that only the Baroness's deep swoon—and the need to protect her reputation—had saved her from his wrath after she had repulsed him. He shook his head ruefully. Probably nothing was as dangerous for a woman as a man's thwarted lust. He had thought she was a wanton, and foxed, to boot. She had stood in need of his protection, but he had been so furious he had not seen it.

He owed her an apology, but it could never be made, for she did not know the identity of her would-be seducer; and it would be folly to tell her the truth. Better to help with the problems she had *now*. The most pressing of those was the villainous Frenchman. Judging by his behaviour a little earlier, he had designs on the lady's person. He was a penniless *émigré*; she was a rich aristocrat. The man was surely seeking to persuade her to marry him.

There must be a way of preventing it. Max silently promised himself that he would find that way, even if desperate remedies proved to be necessary.

'Cousin Frederick…'

Max clenched his jaw. How he hated that name!

'Cousin Frederick, I must ask what you plan to do about the dispute over the earldom. I collect that was the "family business" you wished to discuss with me?' Her gaze was still fixed on the path, but her voice held no trace of weakness.

He tried not to allow his impatience to show. She was a fool to let herself to be duped by that impostor, but it would not do to tell her so. He paused thoughtfully for a moment, before saying, 'What would *you* have me do about the dispute, Cousin?'

She looked up in surprise. 'Why, I…I would have you relinquish the title, until such time as the proofs have been examined and the rightful Earl of Penrose has been identified.'

'I have no need to offer proofs, ma'am,' Max said curtly. 'No one questions my birth. Not even you.' He glared down at her, daring her to gainsay him.

Her gaze wavered for only a second. 'You are correct, sir, but on that point only. Your place in the line of succession has not been proved beyond doubt, as we are both aware.'

'I see. You believe that that smooth-tongued Frenchman is your uncle's legitimate heir, do you?'

'I…that is, I—'

'I would have credited you with more sense, ma'am,' he added bitterly.

That had certainly lit a spark in her! She glowered at him. 'Your manners are not likely to win my support to your cause, Cousin.'

Max was surprised that she could show such spirit, weak as she was. She was a remarkable woman, but he must never let her suspect that he thought so. He had to keep the upper hand. He chose to say nothing.

'I will tell you frankly, sir, that I do not favour either cause. As head of the Rosevale family—' she uttered the words with conscious pride '—I have a duty to see that justice is done to both claimants.'

Max found himself nodding in agreement. That was very fair.

'Even you,' she added, pursing her lips.

Now that was the outside of enough! He only just succeeded in swallowing the curse that rose to his lips. How dare she?

She seemed to think nothing was amiss. 'In fairness, I should tell you, Cousin, that my aunt, Lady Charlotte Clare, is absolutely convinced that Pierre is my Uncle Julian's heir. Lady Charlotte remained in contact with my uncle for some time after he went to France. She has letters. She also has a portrait of Uncle Julian's wife, Amalie d'Eury. The likeness between Amalie and Pierre is remarkable.'

'But that is all you have, is it not? I'll warrant your aunt's letters make no mention of the birth of a legitimate son.' Max realised, too late, that he had made his words sound like an accusation of bad faith.

She flushed. It could have been anger...or embarrassment. 'The correspondence ceased shortly after the beginning of the Revolution in France. That was before Pierre and his sister were born. So—no, there is no mention of either of them in the letters.' She glared up at him. 'Are you satisfied now, Cousin?'

'For the moment. I thank you for your candour.'

'Oh, this is intolerable,' Angel cried. 'I will thank *you*, sir, to bring me back to the house. And then to take your leave.'

Max was tempted to laugh. It had been an easy victory. Too easy? He would give further thought to that once he was safely away from this nest of female vipers.

Pleading a headache, Angel went at once to her bed-chamber. She could not possibly face Aunt Charlotte and her cronies with their constant questions and sly innuen-dos.

She had failed with Pierre. And she had failed with Cousin Frederick. Pierre would not contemplate marriage until his claim had been proved. And Frederick would not stand aside to allow Pierre's claim. Pierre had been her last hope. Now, she had no hope at all.

She sank on to the *chaise-longue* and dropped her head into her hands. She would have to find somewhere to hide until she knew for certain…until the babe was born. And then—

'Shall I fetch your ladyship a tisane?'

'What? Oh, yes. No. Wait, Benton. I…I have no need of a tisane. I do not have the headache. It was simply that I wished to be alone…'

Benton nodded in sympathy. 'I knew it was too soon for you to be receiving, m'lady. You are not nearly strong enough yet. And those ladies—begging y'r pardon, m'lady—but they would talk anyone into the headache.'

Angel managed a small smile. Benton was absolutely right.

'I suggest that you rest before dinner, m'lady. It will help your appetite. You are not eating enough to keep a sparrow alive.'

Benton was right there, too. No doubt she was being kept informed by the other servants. There were no secrets in a house like this... Except one, for a little longer...

'You really must eat, m'lady, or you will never be well. Look how thin you are become. And your courses, too –' Benton stopped, thinking. 'Well, I suppose that is not such a terrible loss, considering how ill they make you.'

Just at that moment, Angel would have endured almost any pain to know that she was not carrying Max's child.

'Now, m'lady...' Benton removed Angel's shoes and swung her feet up on to the *chaise-longue*. Then she draped a light shawl over her and made up the fire. 'There. That's better. If I leave you for an hour or so, there will still be plenty of time to dress your hair before dinner. I can bring you a glass of wine, too. My first mistress, God rest her soul, swore by a glass of Burgundy. Said as it was the best restorative ever made.'

Angel closed her eyes against Benton's chatter and nodded slightly. Let Benton think what she liked about the life-giving benefits of Burgundy. But, please, let her leave!

Eventually, the door clicked softly. There was no longer any sound in the room, bar the occasional crackle from the fire. Angel sighed and relaxed into the *chaise-longue*. She had decisions to make—fearful decisions—but she was too tired to think straight. She needed to rest, to recover from that encounter with her exasperating cousin. What was it about Cousin Frederick? Every time they met, they quarrelled. He seemed to hate her. He certainly seemed to take pleasure in berating her.

On this last occasion, he had had cause. She had gone much too far in suggesting that he should relinquish his title. He had been insulted. And no wonder. He had every right to insist that Pierre prove his claim…if he could.

Angel's instincts told her that Pierre would never succeed in ousting Frederick from the earldom. And that Frederick, in spite of his foul temper, was a worthy incumbent.

What on earth had made her think that? She had no idea. Her mind must be addled.

Max loosed a string of soldier's curses at the closing door. How could the agents have been so utterly incompetent as to lose Pierre Rosevale? Of course the Frenchman had suspected he was being watched. He was not a complete fool.

He was not a fool at all. It was now the best part of a week since that encounter in Berkeley Square. Pierre Rosevale had walked calmly out of the Baroness's house. And then he had vanished, right under the noses of Max's agents. The men had searched for four days. And then they had sidled into Max's house, to report that they had lost their quarry.

Max swore again. Then he poured himself a glass of brandy and tossed it off. It did not help.

He would have to find another way of protecting the Baroness from the predatory Frenchman. Max had assumed—wrongly—that it would be easy to persuade him of the need to stop pursuing Lady Rosevale. A few threats, a promise of money…

Confound it! What was he supposed to do now?

He was very much afraid that the Frenchman had gone to ground in order to arrange a clandestine wedding. The blackguard could reappear, with the lady at his side, and simply announce that they were already man and wife. Then there would be nothing that anyone could do.

Max slammed his empty glass on to the desk and began

to pace up and down the study. There must be a way! There must be something—

It was so very simple that he laughed aloud. As long as Lady Rosevale was single, she was at risk from the Frenchman, who was desperate to win her hand and would probably go to any lengths to secure her. He might even force her into it. Max was nauseated at the very idea, but he had to admit it was possible. If the Baroness continued to frequent unsuitable events such as that ridotto, she would be easy prey. She could be abducted without difficulty, and held until her reputation was ruined. If that happened, she would be grateful to any man who would offer for her, even the Frenchman.

She was at risk as long as she was single. So it was high time that she remarried.

Max poured himself another brandy and considered the available candidates. Ross would have been an excellent choice, but there was no knowing how soon he would return to England. The others… Damn them, they were all gamblers, or womanisers, or just wastrels who would squander as much of the Rosevale money as they could get their hands on, while treating the lady abominably. He could not permit that. He did not wish to see her spirit cowed.

He could marry her himself, of course.

Good God! What had put such a mad idea into his head? They would murder each other within a week…if she did not drive him to Bedlam first. It was all Ross's doing. He had sown the seed before he left and now, from hundreds of miles away, his influence seemed to be just as strong. Ross had said that Max should marry the Baroness, that Max would thereby get his hands on his inheritance all the sooner.

And Ross had said that, if the lady was not willing, she could always be abducted.

Max threw himself down into his leather chair with a harsh laugh. It was utter madness. The Frenchman might be capable of such perfidy, but Max was not. Max could never force any woman into marriage, and as for an abduction... Impossible.

The logical solution was to seek an interview with the Baroness and to explain, coolly and rationally, the danger she was in. She was an intelligent woman. She would not dismiss Max's arguments out of hand. She would weigh them, and she would see that he was right. Once she understood, he would be able to rely on her to keep the Frenchman at a distance.

He pulled out a sheet of paper and quickly wrote a note to the Baroness, requesting that she favour him with a private interview at her earliest convenience. He hinted that he had information of great moment to impart, information that concerned her directly. Curiosity alone would lead her to agree. He signed the letter with a flourish. He was rather pleased with the effect.

Having despatched the note by hand, he swallowed the last of his brandy and set off for Louisa's house. There, at least, he would not be greeted by a termagant.

Angel was still fuming. That arrogant—! How dare he do such a thing? She picked up Cousin Frederick's scribbled note and read it again. He was more than arrogant. He deserved to be horsewhipped. Grimly, she ripped the paper into tiny pieces.

By now, he would certainly have received her reply. She smiled with satisfaction. She was proud of her efforts there. She was particularly pleased that she had refrained from replying in hot blood. The measured disdain of her reply would be much more effective than the angry note she had been minded to send off two days ago.

She pulled on her gloves and straightened her hat. For one blessed moment, she had forgotten the dilemma that faced her.

She shook her head at her reflection. At least she no longer looked quite so hagged. Benton had been right about the importance of trying to eat well. Angel's cheeks had filled out a little and her hair no longer looked so dull.

Tomorrow, she must start to make plans for returning to Rosevale Abbey. And find a means of persuading Aunt Charlotte to remain in London. The polite world would learn that Lady Rosevale was not recovered enough from her recent illness to face the rigours of the Season and was withdrawing to her country estate for the sake of her health. The tabbies would discuss her for a day or two, and then move on to juicier gossip.

Meanwhile, Angel would be safely at home, searching out a place to hide until her confinement was over. She did not dare to think beyond that. She had tried to tell herself that she might not be increasing after all, that she was mistaken about the signs…but after so many weeks, she knew the truth. And, deep in her heart, she wanted Max's child…she wanted to be a mother, rather than a barren husk. Even a bastard child…even though she would be ruined—

The door opened to admit Benton. 'The carriage is at the door, m'lady, as you instructed.'

Angel began to make her way out to the stairs.

'Would it not be better if I accompanied you, m'lady?' Benton said anxiously. 'It would take but a moment for me to fetch my cloak and bonnet. I can't be easy in my mind that you are going out alone. Not when you are barely risen from your sickbed.'

'Thank you, Benton, but the answer is no,' Angel said firmly. 'I am not going far and I am much recovered these last few days. You need have no fears on that score. I shall be back in good time for dinner.' Seeing the look of real concern on the abigail's face, Angel smiled and said, 'Tonight I will allow you to choose my gown. It is time I wore one of Célestine's more fanciful creations. And my faithful abigail shall create a hair style to suit. Will that content you, Benton?'

Benton beamed. 'Oh, m'lady, at last! I am so glad to see you are almost your old self again. I promise that, by the time I have finished, you will look like a princess!'

Angel smiled at the abigail's enthusiasm. Let her enjoy her triumph, for it would be short-lived. 'I shall be back in about an hour and I will wish to take a bath before dinner. Your miracles, Benton, must wait until that is done.'

Max found it difficult to resist the impulse to tear her impudent note into shreds. She had wasted two days before replying to his request for an interview. And now this! Arrogant, top-lofty...

With extravagant care, Max refolded the note and stowed it in the hidden inside pocket of his coat. It would be as well to keep it about him, for he planned to see his hot-tempered cousin in the very near future, whether she willed it or no. The summons was bound to come soon.

He poured himself a glass of madeira and tossed it off, before throwing himself into his favourite leather armchair. He cursed under his breath. It was thoroughly frustrating to have to wait for her to make a move. He was effectively imprisoned in his own four walls, waiting...

The problem was that frustration did nothing at all for his temper, at least where the haughty Baroness was concerned. If only Ross were here. His light-hearted banter had always been able to divert Max's mind, no matter how black his mood.

This time Max would have to divert himself.

He set himself to thinking positive thoughts about his cousin. It was not so very difficult after all, not when he bent his mind to her beauty and her astonishing response to him at the ridotto. Yes, she had been well on the way to being foxed, as well as feverish, but her reactions had been real. She had wanted him as much as he had wanted her. Perhaps they had both been caught unawares by the flame of passion that ignited when they touched?

Leaning back into the leather, with his eyes closed, Max could almost taste her. Violets. And an innocent awakening.

Innocent? What on earth had put that idea into his brain? She was a widow, had been married for several years... She could not be innocent.

Yet her response to his seduction had been strange, as if she were experiencing passion for the first time...as if she were uncertain of what would happen next, of what she would feel. And then, without warning, she had repulsed him and fallen into a deep swoon. That was the strangest thing of all.

In the space of a few seconds, she had gone from overwhelming passion to—

Could it have been fear? Max was horrified at that new thought. He had never—

The door opened. 'My lord, the lady has left Berkeley Square.'

At last! Max jumped to his feet and strode to the door.

Angel remained standing by the grave, head bowed. She had been away longer than she had intended. Benton would start to fret if her mistress did not return home soon. And yet…

Angel leant forward and traced the inscription with a gloved finger. *Sophia Elizabeth, beloved wife of James Milton, born 1790, died 1812.* Angel clasped her fingers together and tried to pray for her dearest friend. She had died so young—in an attempt to give her husband a longed-for child. Poor Sophia. She had been such a sweet girl, so full of life and laughter, but she had died here in London where Angel could not come to her. For Angel had been imprisoned in the country, obliged to mourn a husband whom she had neither loved nor respected.

She knelt to rearrange the flowers she had brought. 'Thank you, Sophia,' she whispered, 'for all the love and friendship you gave me when we were girls together. Forgive me for failing you at the last. It was not by my choice. And, if you can see me now, please help me to find the strength to go through the ordeal ahead. For you had a husband who loved you, while I…I have no one. And I am afraid.' She bent her head over her clasped hands and closed her eyes.

She did not hear the footsteps on the soft grass. She did not sense that there was someone beside her until a shadow fell on her, blocking out the warmth of the spring sunshine.

Startled, she jumped to her feet, to find herself seized by the shoulders and roughly shaken by her impossible cousin, the Earl of Penrose. He thrust her away, but he still looked to be absolutely incensed at her. She thought he might resume his attack at any moment. And they were alone in this deserted burial ground. She could call for help, but it would be a waste of breath. She was well out of earshot of anyone in the chapel or on the road beyond.

'Precisely what did you mean by that idiotic note you

sent me last evening?' There was fury in every word he spoke. He was almost shouting at her.

Angel bridled in her turn. 'My note meant exactly what it said, sir—that I see no reason to grant you an interview or to listen to your absurd allegations against my cousin, Pierre Rosevale.'

He shook his head and ran his fingers through his thick hair, in an oddly boyish gesture. 'You are a fool, woman,' he said. 'Your so-called cousin is a blackguard and a fortune-hunter. He seeks only to control you and your wealth. Cannot you see the danger you are in? He does not need to woo you, you know. He need only carry you off for long enough to ruin your reputation and then you would be more than ready to put his ring on your finger.'

Angel was too shocked to reply. Besides, Frederick was much too angry to allow her to say a single word before he had finished ranting at her. He barely seemed to pause to draw breath.

'And look at you. Here, alone in these gardens, with not even a maid to protect you. Anyone might carry you off. You are a rich prize, you know, Cousin. You should not allow such a ripe plum to fall into unworthy hands.'

She was now just as angry as he. 'And you, sir, are so much more worthy than all the other men in London, I collect?' Her tone was withering. 'I am to beware of being abducted by my Cousin Pierre, or any other man in London, but *you*, apparently, are above such things. Are you *quite* sure that there is not a closed carriage and a fast team of horses waiting in the lee of the chapel? You clearly followed me here. Pierre may covet my fortune, but so do most of the other purse-pinched gentlemen in London. By all accounts, the Earl of Penrose is one of them.'

'Are you suggesting, madam, that I have come here to abduct you…to marry you for your money?'

She could not hold his hard gaze, but she would not retreat. 'If not that, sir, then why are you here?' she shot back.

'Good God, woman, I came to warn you. Are you so prejudiced against me and my family that you cannot recognise goodwill when you meet it?'

Angel forced herself to laugh in his face. 'From you, Cousin? I think not.'

He was now white with anger. 'Any man who is fool enough to marry you, madam, will strike a very bad bargain. If he had any sense, he would have you locked up.'

'Enough of this, sir! You go much too far! We have nothing more to say to each other.' She pulled away from him and started towards the exit, but in two strides he was beside her once more and had taken her by the arm, forcing her to stop.

He took a deep breath, as if he were trying to regain control. 'I give you two choices, madam. Either you give me your word that you will not marry Pierre Rosevale, no matter what he may do to you; or I will take steps to ensure that you are in no position to marry anyone. Will you give me your word? Or are you determined on this folly of yours?'

'I will thank you to let go of my arm, sir.' She spat the words at him, but he made no move to free her. It was the last straw. 'As things stand, Cousin, you are my heir. You have everything to gain from preventing my marriage. To anyone. If I were to marry Pierre, and have a child, you would have nothing but an empty title.'

'I have no concerns about my inheritance, Cousin. You are barren. A barren woman cannot produce an heir.'

'Ah, but you are wrong, sir. I am *not* barren. And now that I am with—' She stopped, horrified. There was a look of blank astonishment on his face. Oh, merciful heavens, she had betrayed her secret in that rush of angry words—to the one man who was her true enemy. She tried to push past him, to get to the gate before her tears of frustration overflowed.

He caught her arm again. 'So that is the way of it. You are with child. And you will marry Pierre Rosevale. Yes, of course you will. Believe me, ma'am, you will live to regret it.'

'No, sir.' She kept her face stubbornly turned towards the exit so that he could not read her despairing expression. 'I may live to regret my actions, but they will not include marriage to Pierre Rosevale. He cannot contemplate marriage until his claim is resolved. While you remain Earl of Penrose, I must look elsewhere for a husband or I shall be…' She faltered. She could not say the terrible words. Wrenching her arm from his grip, she ran for the chapel and the narrow lane beyond, leading out to the turnpike road where her carriage was waiting.

He did not pursue her. Reaching the corner of the chapel, she stopped to catch her breath and saw that he was standing motionless near Sophia's grave. She should be grateful for any victory, however small. She had shocked the Earl so much that he was rooted to the spot.

Angel walked quickly round the corner into the shadow of the chapel of ease and fumbled for a handkerchief to dry her eyes. Would her groom notice that she had been weeping? Perhaps. She would have to drop a hint, somehow, that she had been deeply affected by the sight of Sophia's grave.

As to the rest, she dare not think about how she had betrayed herself. She had thought her situation was as bad as it could possibly be. But now she had put herself into the power of Frederick, Earl of Penrose, a man who had every reason to seek her ruin.

Chapter Twelve

Max could not decide which of them made him more furious, the woman for playing the doxy, or the man for accepting what she offered and then abandoning her, once he had planted his bastard in her belly. Clearly she had not fainted away when she lay with her precious Pierre. Or else the villain had continued, regardless. Either way, it was a thoroughly sordid episode.

Max could almost laugh at the absurdity of it all. He had been prepared to suggest that Ross should marry the woman. Or even that he himself might do so. She was eminently desirable, but she was not a fit wife for a man of honour. Max was lucky to have discovered the truth in time.

What was the truth? The Frenchman was handsome and charming, no doubt of it. He certainly had the knack of attracting the ladies; and the Baroness had succumbed. What was it that Ross had said about her? That she had led a sheltered life even after her marriage and had never gone much into Society. In other words, she was a pigeon ripe for the plucking, and easy prey for a practised seducer like Pierre Rosevale.

Yet it made no sense. Why had the man refused to marry

her? Why did he insist on waiting until his claim had been settled? The earldom was hardly a real prize; there was no fortune attached to it. The Rosevale fortune came with the lady herself and, now that she was carrying a potential heir, the Frenchman had every reason to secure her. As the father of the heir to the Rosevale Barony, he would control the estates until his child came of age.

Why did the earldom stand in the way of their marriage? It seemed to be nonsense, just a weak excuse to confuse a wronged woman.

In any case, it did not matter whether or not the man's reason was valid. If Pierre Rosevale was responsible for the Baroness's condition, the villain must be made to marry her and give the child a name. The Baroness had neither father nor brothers to protect her honour. It therefore fell to Max, her closest relative, to force the Frenchman to behave like a gentleman.

Max was rather hoping that the Frenchman would continue to resist. It was a pity that it was impossible to call him out. Still, Max would get real satisfaction from ruining the popinjay's looks. The damage could not be permanent, unfortunately. A bridegroom had to be unmarked for his wedding day.

Max began to pace the room. It was all very well to make such grandiose plans, but Pierre Rosevale had disappeared. There could be no marriage if the man was not found, and quickly, before the Baroness's condition became apparent to the world.

Poor woman. It was no wonder that she had railed at Max. She must be distraught. She was pregnant and unmarried. Her lover had refused to stand by her and had gone into hiding. She was alone, and she desperately needed a husband to give her child a name. What on earth was she planning to do?

She could not marry just *anyone*. She was the Baroness Rosevale. But then again, perhaps she thought that *any* husband was preferable to the disgrace of bearing a child out of wedlock. She might think so, but Max did not. He must make sure she married a man of standing. If the price was Max's title, he was prepared to pay it. Let the upstart Frenchman have the earldom. It had brought Max nothing but trouble, in any case. He would gladly revert to being plain Captain Rosevale.

Max's army training reasserted itself then. It was time for action, not words. The immediate answer to his cousin's problem was marriage—forced, if necessary—to the father of her child, which meant that Pierre Rosevale had to be found. Max's agents had failed there once already. Well, they would have to redouble their efforts this time. He would offer them a handsome reward for finding the man quickly.

He himself could not remain idle. He would join the hunt. If he were very lucky, he might be the one to find Pierre Rosevale, somewhere among London's dark alleyways. He certainly hoped so. It could prove to be a very satisfying encounter.

It had taken four days and much more blunt than Max could afford, but he had his quarry at last. The man had been discovered in Dover, of all places. According to Max's agents, the Frenchman had been trying to glean information about what was happening in Toulon. Blackguard though he was, Pierre Rosevale seemed to care about his sister. And now, he was waiting in Max's study, guarded by two burly agents. There would be no escape this time.

Deliberately, Max flung open the study door and marched in, like an officer arriving to inspect his troops.

He fully intended to intimidate the Frenchman in this interview. It was vital to get to the truth.

His man was standing by the fireplace, flanked by the two agents, with his hands securely tied behind his back. Clearly, the agents were taking no chances.

Max looked the Frenchman up and down. He was rather grubby. His linen was crumpled and he had not shaved for at least a day, perhaps two. His vaunted looks had been reduced to the commonplace.

'Untie him.'

The agents hastened to obey Max's sharp order. While they cut the cords, their prisoner assumed an expression of acute boredom, but once his hands were free, he leant back against the fireplace and lazily rubbed his wrists. He refused to meet Max's eye.

'You may go down to the kitchen for a meal.' Max gestured in the direction of the door, but the agents made no move to leave. 'You will be paid later. Wait downstairs until I send for you.' He stood motionless until the door had closed on the two men.

Max took a pace forward. 'Welcome to my house, *monsieur*. I am delighted to have the honour of your company at last. You have been—shall we say? —somewhat elusive of late.'

'I will have no truck with you, sir. You are no gentleman. I take it you plan to kill me now, in order to retain your title?'

'You have been attending too many melodramas since your arrival in England, I fear. I shall defend my position against your worthless claim in open court, if I have to. But there are other crimes that I will not tolerate. They must be settled here and now. For those, sir, payment is due.'

'I have committed no crime. You have no right to hold me here. I insist that you allow me to leave this place.'

Max strode over to the door, locked it and dropped the key into his waistcoat pocket. Then he strolled over to his desk and calmly sat down behind it. 'You have just confirmed what I have long suspected,' he said quietly. 'You have no honour. An honourable man would never get a lady with child and then abandon her, as you have done.'

'I have done no such thing!'

'Lady Rosevale is carrying a child. You cannot deny you are the father.'

'*Mon Dieu! Quel mensonge!* It is a black lie!'

'You dare to deny that you lay with her?'

'Of course I do! Besides—' He stopped short and clamped his lips tightly together.

'Besides?' Max said silkily.

The Frenchman coloured and looked away. He was not about to say anything more.

Max banged his fist on the desk and flung himself out of his chair. In two strides, he was on his adversary and had grabbed him by the collar, lifting him off his feet. 'Let us suppose, just for the sake of argument, that I believe you. If you wish to have any hope of saving your skin, I suggest you tell me who is responsible for her condition.'

Silence.

'Well?' Max tightened his grip a notch or two. The man could hardly breathe.

'Let me go and I will tell you,' the Frenchman gasped, clawing at Max's hands in an effort to prevent himself from choking.

Max opened his fists and let the man drop. Then he stood over him, threateningly.

'I have never lain with my cousin. I would not do such

a thing. I…I did not know that she had lain with anyone, far less conceived a child.' He paused, rubbing his throat.

'Get on with it,' Max snapped.

'I do not see how… There was so little time before she fell ill and she was accompanied by her aunt wherever she went. Except…except once. The night before her fever. I took her to a masquerade. It was not a fit place for a lady, but she insisted. She said it might be the only night of freedom she would have in London. Then she drank too much champagne and we…we quarrelled. She refused to have anything more to do with me. I think she may have returned to the ballroom.'

Max raised an eyebrow.

'She must have met someone there. That is where your culprit lies.'

Max laughed at the bitter irony of it. 'And what is his name, pray?'

'I do not know. I am guessing only. I saw nothing, you must understand. And everyone at the ridotto was masked.'

'You expect me to believe that my cousin, the noble Baroness Rosevale, would so forget her station that she would couple with a complete stranger at a ridotto?' Max tried to put incredulity into his voice.

'If she truly is *enceinte* there is no other explanation.'

Pierre was telling the truth, Max decided. He had been visibly shocked to learn of the Baroness's behaviour. But there must be another explanation. She must have met someone else…somehow. Whoever it had been, she still needed a husband. Why not Pierre? He was of noble birth, but poor. He could not afford to be fastidious about the child.

'Your cousin is a very wealthy woman. If you married her, your position would be secure. I do not understand why any man would refuse her…especially one in your position.'

'I am in no position to offer marriage to anyone,' Pierre said flatly.

'You mean, not until you are acknowledged the Earl of Penrose?' Max asked witheringly.

'Nothing can be resolved until Julie and I are reunited.'

'Your *sister*?'

'Nothing can be resolved until Julie and I are reunited,' Pierre said again, turning away abruptly. It seemed that he would not, or could not, say another word.

Max shook his head in frustration. Pierre refused the marriage, not because of the coming child, but because of his sister? He was a very odd cove indeed. However, Pierre was the least of his concerns now. Max had Ross on his side and he was sure that Ross would, by now, have found the missing Julie. Ross could be relied upon to bring the woman—and any evidence there was to be had—back to England with all speed. Even in Bonaparte's France, Ross would find a way.

In the meantime, Max must turn his attention to the pressing problem of the Baroness and her urgent need for a husband. Max was now satisfied that Pierre was not her secret lover, but the mystery remained. There was only one source of information left. The lady herself.

'I should much rather accompany you, Angel.'

'No, Aunt Charlotte. There really is no need. I am going home to recuperate. I shall go on much better in the fresh air, with good food from my own farm and long walks to restore my strength. I do not plan to entertain, so I have no need of a chaperon.'

'But you will be alone—'

'Dear Aunt, I am no longer a green girl who needs to

be guarded at every turn. I am twenty-five years old, remember, besides being a widow and mistress of my own estates.' Seeing the concern on her aunt's face, she added, 'I shall be perfectly safe on my own land but, if it will content you, I promise never to go out walking alone. Benton shall accompany me, or one of the footmen.' She paused and managed a brief smile. 'On reflection, a footman would probably be best. He will not amble along the way Benton always does.'

'But who will you talk to over dinner, or in the evenings?'

Angel's smile broadened at the blissful idea of silence at those times. 'Never fear, Aunt, I am sure I shall learn to enjoy my own company. I shall have my books and my music. I shall miss you, of course,' she added hastily, 'but that is no reason to deny you the pleasures of London. You have spent too many months keeping company with me. I know you must have yearned for the society of your London friends when we were buried at the Abbey. I cannot remove you from them now.'

There was a wistful smile around Lady Charlotte's mouth, but still she did not give up. 'It would take me only an hour or so to pack, my dear, and then we could go together. I cannot be easy in my mind if I let you journey alone, all the way to the Abbey.'

'Pray, be easy, dear Aunt. Benton accompanies me, and four male servants. We shall travel only in daylight. I shall not be in the slightest danger. Were you thinking that you would be able to defend me, where a coachman and three strong grooms could not?'

Aunt Charlotte coloured a little. 'No…but there are other risks for a lady travelling alone…'

Angel knew only too well the risks facing a lady alone, but it was now much, much too late to erect defences against them. Lady Charlotte would find out the truth eventually but, for the present, Angel needed to be alone at the Abbey so that she could plan for her confinement. Her aunt must be persuaded to remain in London.

'I shall have Benton with me at all times, Aunt. You need have no worries on that score. And now—' she bent to place a fond kiss on Lady Charlotte's wrinkled cheek '—I really must leave.' She pulled on her gloves. 'I must not keep the horses standing any longer. Goodbye, dear Aunt Charlotte. Enjoy your freedom in London. I should be at the Abbey by late tomorrow, and I promise I shall write to you as soon as I arrive. And every day after, if you like, until the end of the Season. Will that content you?'

Lady Charlotte smiled a little mistily. 'Oh, very well, child. But I warn you, if you fail to write every day, I shall post down to the Abbey to find out what is amiss, whether you will it or no.'

With that, Angel had to be content. She hurried out to her carriage before Lady Charlotte could think up even more reasons why Angel should not be alone at Rosevale Abbey.

The journey, normally so easy in summer, was a nightmare. The first day had been bad enough, but the next was worse. By the time they had had their first change of horses, Angel was feeling decidedly unwell. So far, her nausea had never turned into actual sickness, but as the miles passed, she was becoming increasingly sure that, today, she would not be able to control her wayward insides.

Benton's nonsensical chatter did not help. 'Enough, Benton,' Angel snapped at last, losing patience with the abigail. 'I should like to sleep now.'

'But your ladyship will never be able to sleep with all these bumps and ruts, and—'

'I said, that is enough, Benton,' Angel repeated, with menace in her voice. The abigail subsided. Angel closed her eyes and tried for sleep. It did not come. Benton had been right about the jolting of the carriage. This part of the road seemed to be particularly uneven. Angel swallowed hard. Unless she found a remedy of some kind, she was going to be sick.

She opened her eyes and sat up, reaching for her reticule. These days she went nowhere without her vinaigrette. She held it to her nose and sniffed hard. Oh, heavens, that was worse! She—

Benton's reactions were lightning-fast. From nowhere, she produced a handkerchief and held it to Angel's lips, while, with her free hand, she pulled the check string to stop the carriage. Angel groaned as it lurched to an abrupt halt. Heedless of where they might be, she threw open the carriage door and retched on to the ground below. Then she fell into her place once more and let her head sink backwards until it was supported by the cushioned seat. She clasped her hands over her stomach, trying to ease the spasms, and groaned again. Why had she ever embarked on this journey?

Benton was on her feet, with one hand on the open door to support her weight as she leant out. 'Drive on to the posting house at Speen Hill, John, but slowly this time. You have made her ladyship ill by driving so fast over this dreadful road. You should know better!' She pulled the door closed, resumed her seat and began to search around in her voluminous travelling bag. 'Here it is!'

Angel eyed the abigail suspiciously, but she need not have worried. It was only lavender water. Benton sprinkled some on to a clean handkerchief and gently stroked An-

gel's hot face. It was wonderfully cool and refreshing.
'Thank you, Benton. I…I do not know what came over
me—'

'Hmph! It is all John Coachman's fault, driving so fast
on such a road. I was beginning to feel a little queasy
myself, m'lady.' She stroked again. 'However, you will
soon be better. The Castle Inn is less than two miles from
here, I seem to recall. You will be able to rest there until
you are recovered. We could even stay the night if your
ladyship wishes. It will not matter if you are a day late
arriving at the Abbey.'

Angel managed a nod. Just at the moment, anything was
preferable to the swaying of a carriage. And the thought
of a warm bed and crisp sheets was unbelievably attractive.

It was just light when Angel awoke. She lay in the unfamiliar bed, gazing up at the canopy and wondering where
she was.

Then she remembered. She had disgraced herself on the
public highway. And she had felt so weak afterwards that
she had refused to go on. They were at the posting house,
and she had been put to bed with a posset of the landlady's
devising.

She sat up very gingerly, waiting for the normal wave
of morning nausea. Surprisingly, it did not come. She
sighed with relief and reached for the wrapper that lay
across the end of the bed. Then she rose and threw open
the curtains and the window beyond. The sky was still
traced with pink from the dawn, with wisps of apricot-
coloured clouds near the horizon. Overhead, the colour
was so dark as to be almost purple. It was ravishing. It
was much too early for anyone to be about. The only noise
was the swell of birdsong. Angel leaned her elbows on the
sill and drank her fill. The beauty calmed her. She breathed

deeply, relishing the scent of spring blossom. It was good to be alive…in spite of everything.

She would dress and go out into the garden so that she could touch the blossom and feel the dew on her fingers. There was no need to summon Benton. There was a simple travelling gown in her portmanteau that she could don without help. Such a beautiful morning demanded silent— and solitary—enjoyment.

It took only a few minutes to splash her face with cold water from the basin and button the heavy, dark green gown over her chemise, though it felt a little odd to be without her stays. She could do nothing with her hair, of course, so she simply tied it back with a ribbon. Then she slipped her feet into her shoes and swung her thick travelling cloak around her shoulders. With the hood over her bright hair, it covered her from head to foot and was warm enough to ward off the early morning chill.

She was just about to leave the room when she remembered. It was better not to take chances. She retrieved her reticule with her smelling salts and hooked it over her arm.

Two doors down the corridor from Angel's chamber, a male guest was snoring loudly. Angel grinned into the half-darkness. The snoring would cover any noise she might make as she crept down the stairs. In the passageway below, she stopped to listen for movement, but there was none. She made her way to the massive oak door and carefully drew the bolts. They had been well oiled—so as not to disturb sleeping guests, she supposed—and offered no resistance.

She pulled back the door and stepped out into the fresh morning air, breathing it deep into her lungs and throwing back her cloak and hood so that the slight breeze could ripple across her skin. Twenty yards or so from the inn, behind a low hedge, the garden was bursting with blossom.

She could just hear the sound of lambs in a distant field. She smiled a greeting to the world around her and started for the garden, raising her arms to the sky and humming softly. She knew now that, whatever happened, she would have a life that was worth living. And she would live it to the full. She had longed for a child. Now Max had given her one. His loving had been a blessing.

When she reached the hedge, her eye was caught by a patch of pure yellow primroses, nestling among the roots— such an unsullied colour, and such pristine petals. She bent down and began to pick one or two, so that she could tie them into a posy to carry on her journey. They had such delicate beauty.

She was so engrossed that she heard nothing. All she knew was that a man, perhaps two men, came up behind her and threw the folds of her cloak over her head. She could not see. Strong arms wrapped the cloth around her body. Her arms were trapped. It was impossible for her to free herself. She shouted for help. Once. Again. But her voice was swallowed up in the cloak. Still, she refused to give in. She would struggle to the uttermost of her strength. No man would find it easy to abduct her.

She kicked out. Her reward was a satisfying grunt of pain from one of her assailants. A rough voice cursed her roundly. Her captor—one of them, at least—was a common man. Strong arms lifted her feet from the ground. They were carrying her off! Who was taking her? And where? Wild images chased round in her brain. Had not Frederick warned her that she could be a target for abduction? But Pierre would not do such a thing to her, would he? She could not be sure.

It could as easily be Frederick himself. Had he not threatened to prevent her from marrying again? A man like

Frederick was capable of anything, even abduction…or worse. If Frederick was the culprit, she was lost.

She struggled even harder to get a hand free of the cloak. She met only folds and more folds. Still, she would not give up the fight. With an oath, the man flung her over his shoulder, knocking the wind out of her in the process. The next moment, he was almost running across the inn yard, as if her writhing body weighed nothing at all.

'Thank Gawd,' he said. 'Let's get her into the coach before she does any more damage. Swelp me, she's kicked my shin black and blue.'

A second voice laughed. Angel heard the sound of a carriage door opening. 'Your passenger, y'r honour,' said the second voice. 'I should warn you. She kicks like a mule.' With that, Angel's struggling body was dumped unceremoniously into the coach and the door was slammed behind her. Before she could even draw breath, the vehicle started to move and gather speed. She was being carried off by an unseen man, a man who undoubtedly had designs on her person. Behind them, the Castle Inn slept. It would be hours before any of her servants discovered that she was gone.

Angel found she was suddenly more angry than afraid. She continued to fight with the voluminous cloak that was threatening to suffocate her until, at last, she managed to make enough room to draw a full breath. She could still see nothing. But she knew that her abductor was here in the carriage with her. 'You villain!' she screamed at her unknown captor. 'You will hang for this! This is an outrage!'

'No, this is an abduction.'

Chapter Thirteen

The rich, honeyed voice had come from the furthest corner of the carriage. The voice, and the accent, were unmistakable.

Angel finally succeeded in freeing herself from the all-enveloping cloak. She could see again. And her ears had not deceived her. 'Max!' she gasped. 'Oh, Max!' She was so relieved that she had a sudden desperate urge to throw herself into his arms and let her tears flow.

'I am abducting you,' he said again, quite softly. 'I hope you do not object too much? Unfortunately, I am not in a position to allow you any say in the matter.'

The urge to weep vanished in a trice. She was not such a weakling. It was obvious that she had no need to be afraid of Max. He was undoubtedly a gentleman, with the manners of a gentleman…even when he was seducing her. The memory of *that* sent a ripple of sensation through her, part fear, part…part something she could not fathom. She had never expected to see him again. This was Max, the father of her child, a child she now desired with a full heart… If she stretched out her hand, she could touch him.

She stared across at him. In his wig and mask and face paint, he looked quite ludicrous, even in the dim light of the carriage. Her stomach turned over as a seed of suspicion began to grow, fed by the strangeness of her situation. What did he want with her now? And what did he need to conceal? What did he really look like under his disguise? Was he totally repulsive? A strangely familiar tremor ran down her spine.

'Do not be afraid, Rose,' he said, in that wonderful voice, which was like a caress on her skin. 'I cannot let you go, of course, but, apart from that, I promise—on my honour—that nothing will happen without your agreement.' He caught her gaze and held it. 'Nothing,' he said again. 'You need not fear me.'

She believed him. But it was all so bizarre that she wanted to laugh. What was the point of abducting a woman if you gave her a veto over everything that might then happen? And it was all too late, in any case. She was already carrying Max's child.

He did not know! The realisation hit her almost like a blow. A wave of panic engulfed her at the thought of giving him such unpalatable news. She gazed at the mysterious, masked figure, wondering if she could find the courage. Somehow.

No, it was impossible. She knew what he sounded like. He spoke in her dreams, night after night. She knew that he could kiss her almost into oblivion and set her body on fire. But she knew nothing else. She could not simply announce to a masked stranger that he had got her with child. It was absurd! It was ludicrous! It would suggest that she expected him to throw himself on one knee and propose marriage on the spot. He was more likely to spurn her as an unfortunate encumbrance if he learned the truth.

But why then had he abducted her? A bleak whisper in the back of her mind told her that Max had followed her to seize her for his own pleasure and would discard her as soon as she bored him. Then he would vanish again, as completely as he had done after the ridotto. If that were his intention, she could do nothing to prevent it. She should be terrified at the prospect of being so completely in any man's power. But, strangely, she was not. Not with Max. She knew what to expect. She was not afraid.

She raised her chin. She refused to let him think she feared him. 'Where are you taking me, sir?'

'Do not be afraid, Rosa. You will be accorded all courtesy.'

She sat up rather straighter and glared at him. 'I am not afraid, sir,' she said, rather sharply. 'I was merely enquiring about our destination. A simple answer will suffice.'

He laughed, a deep mellow sound. It warmed her heart. 'I congratulate you, my lady. Most women would have had a fit of the vapours by now, but you...' He smiled engagingly at her. 'You, Rosa, face abduction with perfect composure. You even have the courage to subject your abductor to sharp questioning. Remarkable. You have more mettle than many men.'

Angel felt she was blushing. At her abductor! The situation was utterly preposterous. What was it about this man?

At that moment, he reached across the swaying carriage to take one of her hands in his. The shock of his touch raced up her arm and all through her body, making her limbs tingle and her blood fizz. She had the answer to her question.

And when he raised her hand to his lips for a fleeting kiss, she was lost. A single touch, and she was almost melting, longing to be enfolded in his arms. She could not think clearly at all. She felt suddenly as if all her being were concentrated in that tiny island of sensation where his lips brushed her skin.

Max murmured something inaudible. Then he turned her hand over and placed a lingering kiss on her palm.

It was too much. Angel closed her eyes with a groan as the sensation flooded through her.

Max dropped her hand as if it were a hot coal. What on earth did he think he was about?

With a muttered word of apology, he sat back abruptly in his seat and tried to concentrate on practical matters for the rest of the journey. Luckily, they did not have far to go and Ramsey had set a cracking pace. But what a fool he was! Why could he not keep his hands off her? It would be his undoing. Besides, she had been dreadfully ill and was not yet fully recovered. And she was carrying a child, into the bargain. It was a wonder that she had not swooned as soon as she realised what was happening to her.

He must treat her as a guest…an honoured guest. 'You must be cold, Rose,' he said at last. 'Here.' He laid a fur rug across her knees, but found himself assailed by the temptation to bury his fingers in the silver silk of her unbound hair. With an oath, he flung himself into the furthest corner of the carriage and stared unseeingly out of the window.

He could feel her gaze on him, but she said not a word. It was very strange. She had shown such courage. Yet now, she was—

No, he must not presume to guess at what she thought, or felt. Besides, he would know the truth soon enough. They had the whole day ahead of them…and the night, too, if need be.

The night… His body began to heat at the thought of her as she had been on the night of the ridotto—beautiful, passionate, responsive… She could be so again, he was sure. He had only to take her into his arms and kiss her and then she would—

He could not take advantage of her in that way. His object was to discover the truth about the father of her child, not to ravish her for his own pleasure. Besides, he had promised her on his honour that nothing would happen—nothing—unless she wished it to happen. He would not break his word to her, no matter how much his body might clamour for release. He realised now that he had been a fool to believe that he could control his responses where she was concerned. He had told himself he was acting out of pure altruism, and family loyalty. Now that he had touched her again, he knew it was not true.

He resolved to keep his distance in future. It was the only possible solution. If he touched her, he might forget everything, even honour, for that same torrent of desire would engulf him. If he touched her, he would lose the power to resist.

A low moan suggested that she was in some distress. She was holding a hand to her mouth. He ought to help her, but he did not dare. He pushed himself further into the corner of the carriage and tried to school his features into blank indifference.

'Oh,' she groaned, 'if only the carriage did not lurch so.' She reached for her reticule, which had tumbled to the floor, and extracted a tiny box. She opened it and held it to her nose, inhaling deeply.

'Are you unwell, Rose?'

She swallowed hard. 'A moment's weakness only,' she said. 'I am quite recovered now.'

Max could not help smiling. So she had learned something from their encounter at the ridotto. 'When we first met,' he said in a conversational tone, 'you had neglected to bring your smelling salts. I am glad to see that you have now adopted the wiser course of carrying them with you at all times.'

She looked up at him without moving the vinaigrette from her nose. 'How do you know that?' she asked. She seemed genuinely puzzled.

'You were…in a deep swoon, my lady. I assumed that you would have a vinaigrette or some such, but I could not find one. I searched your reticule. And your pockets, too.'

'Oh!' She was blushing delightfully. Max fancied she must be imagining the scene as he searched through her discarded garments while she lay inert, and almost naked, on the bench.

'That is why I left you. I had to find some way of bringing you out of your swoon. But, by the time I returned, you were gone.'

'I…I…'

'I must congratulate you on your resourcefulness, my lady. Not only did you find the way out of the conservatory, you also managed to escape without being recognised by anyone.'

She had fixed her eyes on the tiny box in her hand. She was gripping it tightly, as if she were trying to crush it. 'You restored my mask.'

He nodded.

'And my gown.' Her blush was even deeper now.

He nodded again. 'My lady, I could not undo what had passed between us, but I truly wished to save you from further harm. I had even locked the door so that you would not be discovered before I could return.'

She looked up at him then, through her lashes. He fancied her eyes were glistening. 'You came back after all?' she whispered.

A bolt of desire shot through him. And he had not even touched her. He looked away. He did not know what to say to her.

The carriage was slowing, providing a merciful diversion. He glanced out of the window to see that they were turning into the drive to Ross's small, secluded house. Sergeant Ramsey had made excellent time. With luck, Max's various messages would have reached the house long since, and all would be prepared for their arrival. He experienced a slight flicker of guilt. It was unlikely that Ross would approve of what Max was doing, of course, but Ross was in no position to object. It was Ross's own fault for offering Max the run of his property during his absence. Max could always apologise…later.

It was a blessed relief when the carriage drew up at last. Sergeant Ramsey jumped down to open the door and let down the steps. 'Will it please you to descend, my Lady Rose?' he said, straight-faced, offering his hand to help her down.

She pulled her cloak around her and stepped elegantly out of the carriage. 'Thank you,' she said, pausing to look about her.

'You, too, Cap'n.'

Max threw his man a black look. 'I am not yet so infirm that I need to be helped down out of a carriage, Ramsey.'

'No, Cap'n,' Ramsey replied, without attempting to hide a grin. He made for the front door, which opened to reveal another grizzled manservant. 'Morning, laddie,' Ramsey said gaily. 'Everything in order, is it?' The two disappeared into the house.

Angel watched the exchange with interest. Then she turned back to Max. His appearance was even more bizarre in the full light of day. 'Captain,' she said thoughtfully. 'Would that be army or navy, I wonder?'

Max shook his head slightly. 'Another unsolved mystery for you, I am afraid, my lady.'

'Oh, I don't know. With a little logic…it should be possible to work it out. Now…' She narrowed her eyes and looked closely at him. 'Normally, it would be easy enough to tell. A naval captain would have skin as tough and brown as leather. Who knows? Perhaps under that paint you are as brown as a nut. But…I do not think so. Your hands— No, it is too late to thrust them into your pockets, Max, for I have seen them. Your hands are not a sailor's hands. An army captain, then. Am I right?'

She smiled up at him, tantalisingly.

'We are not here to play games, madam,' he said gruffly. 'Will it please you to go into the house?'

'Do I have a choice in the matter?'

'Of course. You may enter the house, where a chamber awaits you so that you may recover from the ordeal of being…forcibly removed from your household. Or you may remain where you are. The choice is yours. I should perhaps point out, however, that there are no other dwellings for miles and you will find it impossible to suborn my servants to help you escape.' He glanced up at the sky. 'You might also have noticed that it is about to come on to rain.'

'Oh, you are impossible!' She stamped her foot.

'Undoubtedly,' he said.

Ramsey reappeared in the doorway and nodded reassuringly towards his master. 'Breakfast will be served in half an hour, my lady.'

Her stomach rumbled so loudly that both the men heard it. Max laughed. 'I think her ladyship will be more than ready for it,' he said, throwing her a speaking look.

'Oh, very well.' She picked up her skirts and marched up the steps and into the house.

Angel walked slowly down the stairs. She had washed her face and tidied her person as best she could, using the brush and comb that had been thoughtfully provided in the bedchamber. She had avoided looking at the large bed. It was still morning. That would come, if it came at all, much later.

Ramsey was waiting in the little hallway to lead her into a cosy breakfast parlour, overlooking a rather overgrown garden at the rear of the house. The rain shower had been very short and now the sun was trying to part the heavy clouds. A sudden shaft of sunlight cut across the breakfast table, reflecting off the sugar basin. The smell of food made her stomach rumble again. No wonder. She had eaten nothing since leaving London on the previous day. She was quite ravenous.

Ramsey had taken his station by the sideboard. Max was standing by the table, ready to pull out her chair. 'Will it please you sit, my lady?'

'Thank you. I must admit that I am exceedingly hungry. What have you there, Ramsey?'

The old soldier beamed at her use of his name. 'Buttered eggs, if you likes 'em, m'lady, and devilled kidneys. Also a fine ham. And coffee.'

'Wonderful.' Angel decided that devilled kidneys, however tempting, might put too much strain on her rebellious stomach. 'Buttered eggs, if you please, and a slice of ham. Is there some bread, too?'

'Fresh rolls, m'lady, baked this morning. And new butter.'

Angel looked at Ramsey, and then at Max, in astonishment. Who on earth was responsible for this feast in a house that was miles from anywhere? 'I am overwhelmed,' she said.

'I should not say anything too complimentary until you have tasted what they have to offer,' Max said. 'Ramsey and Fraser can cook, after a fashion, but the results are somewhat…unpredictable.'

Ramsey cleared his throat ostentatiously, but Max ignored him.

Angel preferred to devote all her attention to her food. It was delicious. The rolls were as crisp and light as any her own cook could have produced. Angel ate her fill, but her abductor said not a single word throughout the meal. She took a final sip of her coffee and looked across at him. 'You are a harsh master, sir. I should be delighted to have a manservant who could prepare such a breakfast.' She smiled over her shoulder. 'Thank you, Ramsey. That was wonderful.'

'You may bring us another pot of coffee, Ramsey, and then be about your business. Lady Rose and I have private matters to discuss.'

'Have we?' asked Angel, once the door had closed on the servant.

'Yes.' He drained his cup, stood up and crossed to the window. He was still staring out when Ramsey returned with the coffee.

'Thank you, Ramsey,' Angel said. Max had not even turned round. It was useless to hope that he might acknowledge his servant's efforts.

The door closed once more and silence reigned. Angel poured herself another cup of coffee and slowly drank it. Max had not moved. Oh, the man was impossible!

'Max,' she began in desperation, 'why are you dressed like that? And masked, too?'

'You would not have recognised me, otherwise.' He was still looking out at the garden.

'I…I suppose not. But now that I have, will you not remove your mask?'

'The answer, my lady, is no, the same as before. No. It is better—for both of us—that I do not.'

So much for her friendly overtures to her abductor! He was almost as bad as Cousin Frederick! 'Then it is better—for both of us—that I retire until you are prepared to talk to me in a civilised manner. Good day, sir!' She set down her cup with a snap, rose from her chair and marched across to the door, flinging it open before he had time to move. Then, head held high, she walked smartly up the stairs to the bedchamber that had been allotted to her.

It had only one door. Surprisingly, there was a key in the lock. She turned it.

She was alone. And, for the moment, she was safe.

Angel stirred unwillingly. She did not want to wake up. She had been having such an enjoyable dream and—

Someone was knocking at the door.

She forced herself to open her eyes. Only then did she remember where she was…and with whom. Her heart began to beat rapidly. How long had she been asleep? She had thought only to rest for a little while but—she looked across to the window—the light seemed to be fading. It must be getting desperately late.

Her servants would have discovered her absence hours ago. What would they have done? What would she herself do in such a situation?

'My lady.' It was Ramsey's voice.

Angel heaved a sigh of relief. She knew she could not face Max.

'My lady, the Captain sent me to ask if you needed anything. He…er…he thought you might like a tray of tea.'

'Why, yes. Thank you, I should like that very much.'

'You shall have it in a pig's whisper, m'lady.' She heard his footsteps going down the stairs.

Tea! Yes, that would certainly restore her spirits. But first, she must restore herself. She could do nothing about the state of her travelling gown, unfortunately, which was sadly creased. She should have removed it before lying down on the bed, but without a wrapper or dressing gown, she had felt too…vulnerable to remove her clothes, even behind a locked door. It was all Max's fault, in any case, so he had no cause to criticise the state of her dress!

She sat down at the dressing table and began brushing her tangled hair. It was rather difficult to deal with the back. There was altogether too much of it and she could not see what she was doing. Benton would have made swift work of it, but Benton was not here.

Where was she? Would she have gone to find the local magistrate to report her mistress missing? What a scandal that would start! Angel quailed at the thought. But Benton would be failing in her duty if she did nothing at all.

Another knock at the door. 'Tea, m'lady.'

Angel finished retying her hair ribbon and unlocked the door. It was opened from the other side. 'Thank you, Ramsey— You!'

Max closed the door with his shoulder and carried the tea tray across to the table by the window. 'You ordered tea. I have brought it. Cream and sugar, m'lady?'

Words failed her. She turned her back on him and cursed silently. Now what was she to do? She had invited her abductor into her only sanctuary.

She heard the sound of tea being poured and then the clink of a spoon as it was stirred.

'May I suggest you drink your tea while it is hot?'

She was sure she could detect a thread of laughter in his voice. The confounded man was enjoying himself. And no wonder. She had had the upper hand and then, stupidly, she had let him regain it. She must start all over again.

She walked casually across the room and took her seat. 'Thank you so much for your concern.' She picked up her cup and sipped. 'Ugh. Too much sugar.'

'That, m'lady, is really your own fault. However, I will gladly pour you a fresh cup.'

Angel saw that, although there were two cups on the tray, he had poured only one. Now he was proposing to use his own empty cup for her. 'You do not wish for tea, sir?'

'Not at present. I had thought that we might… er…discuss our business companionably over the teacups, but you are obviously of a different mind. I have no desire to inflict my company on you if you do not wish for it.'

'Oh.' She had not expected that.

'Do you wish me to leave you now?'

'Yes. No. Oh, I— I do not understand any of this. You abduct me, but you promise to do me no harm. You speak of mutual business, but we can have no mutual business. We are total strangers. You—'

'*Total* strangers, ma'am?'

Oh, heavens, what had made her say that? Her choice of words could not have been worse. She suspected that she was blushing to the roots of her hair.

'You look quite delightful when you blush, you know, Rose. You are well named.'

'I am not,' she cried. 'My name is not Rose.'

He raised an eyebrow. 'Then perhaps you will tell me what it is, so that I may know how to address you?'

She took a deep breath to regain a measure of composure. 'No. It is better—for both of us—if I do not.'

His eyes widened behind the mask. After a second, he

bowed to her. '*Touché*. You learn quickly, my lady. And I suppose I deserved that.'

'And what do I deserve? What have I done to merit the disgrace you are bringing upon me? I have been in your company since dawn and now it will soon be dark. My servants will be distraught. I imagine the magistrate will have been alerted by now, and men will be scouring the countryside for—'

'No. No one is searching for you.'

'What? They must be. They—'

'I assure you that they are not.' He picked up the teapot and calmly filled the empty cup. 'Your abigail received a note from you before breakfast this morning. You told her that you had gone out for an early walk and had chanced to meet an old friend who invited you to spend the day, and the evening, with her.'

'Benton will never swallow such a Banbury tale. And she knows my hand. She will—'

He coughed. 'I should perhaps have mentioned that, in addition to his talents in the kitchen, Fraser has... er...remarkable skills with a pen. Your abigail will suspect nothing.'

'But—'

'To continue my tale...or rather your tale. You felt you could not refuse the invitation because your friend has...er...fallen on hard times and would take it as an insult. You are naturally not prepared to inflict the cost of feeding your servants on your friend, and so they are to remain at the Castle Inn until you return this evening.' He smiled coolly and offered her the sugar basin. 'Or perhaps...in the morning.'

Chapter Fourteen

There was another knock on the bedchamber door. Angel tried to ignore the way her heart was thumping in her chest at the thought of spending the night with Max. She did her best to assume an expression of boredom. 'More tea, I collect?' she drawled.

Max said nothing, merely unwinding his incredible length from the chair and strolling across to open the door. 'Thank you, Ramsey,' he said curtly to his manservant. 'You may put it on her ladyship's bed.'

Angel gasped and jumped to her feet. It was her own travelling valise. 'How on earth did that come to be here?' she cried.

Max smiled down at her, in such a superior way that she longed to strike him. 'Your abigail knows perfectly well how you were dressed when you left the inn this morning. The messenger who carried your note naturally requested a portmanteau containing everything you might need for your stay with your friend. Your abigail would certainly have smelled a rat if he had not done so.'

'Oh, you—!'

Max made her an extravagant leg, fully in keeping with his ridiculous costume. 'Do not trouble to thank me, my lady. I shall leave you now to see to your toilet. You have plenty of time to change. Dinner will be served in one hour. Pray do not keep me waiting.'

Worse than Cousin Frederick! Angel seized the hairbrush and threw it, but it was too late. It bounced harmlessly off the closed door. Her only consolation was that her aim had been true.

Max pulled out his watch and checked the time yet again. She was now almost half an hour late. Confound the woman, how long did she need to make herself presentable for a simple dinner? It was not as if she were meeting the Queen. He began to pace up and down the room. He would give her ten more minutes, and then…then he would go and fetch her, whatever state she was in.

The pacing was strangely soothing. It allowed him to focus on practical issues, such as trying to prepare plausible answers to the questions she was bound to raise. She was an intelligent woman but, so far at least, she had missed some obvious weaknesses in the story he had spun for her. She had not asked how he had traced her in order to carry out the abduction in the first place. Nor had she spotted the flaws in his account of the forged note to her servant. Her abigail would never have accepted any instructions signed 'Rose'. And, in any case, how would the unknown Captain Max have procured a copy of 'Rose's' handwriting in order to forge the note?

He patted the pocket containing the note the Baroness had sent him when she had so rudely rejected his request for an interview with her. He was glad that he had not destroyed it after all. It had proved extremely useful.

Yes, if she stopped to think about it, she would quickly conclude that Max knew exactly who she was…and a great deal about her, besides. Perhaps that was why she had not yet appeared? Perhaps she had already worked out his identity? Max sincerely hoped not. Her hatred of her 'Cousin Frederick' seemed to be boundless. If she connected Max and Frederick, there would be no chance at all of persuading her to confess the name of her secret lover.

After tonight there would be no more lies, however. He was determined on that. Once she had confessed to him, he would promise to help her to find a husband. He would try to trace the real culprit and force him to the altar. If that proved impossible in the time, Max would find some way of saving her reputation. He would let her see that her hated Cousin Frederick did not really exist and that he, Max, was not her enemy in any way.

He checked his watch again. Her time was up! He straightened his mask and made for the stairs, his anger mounting with every step. When he reached her bedchamber, he hammered on her door. If necessary, he would force his way in.

Force was not needed. She opened the door herself.

'Good God! What are you about? I gave you a full hour to make yourself ready for dinner, but you have not even begun.'

She glowered at him, but said nothing. She simply turned her back and walked over to the window where she sat down, looking out into the darkness.

'So you decline my hospitality, do you? And you have not the courtesy to speak even a word? I must tell you, madam, that my patience is not inexhaustible.'

'Your patience is non-existent,' she said in a low voice.

'My patience has been sorely tried by your lack of manners. Ramsey and Fraser have taken enormous pains to prepare a dinner fit for your…delicate constitution. But you are content to sit here sulking, so that their efforts go for naught. You may have a legitimate complaint against me, madam—'

She laughed ungraciously.

'But you have no cause to inflict your appalling temper on them.'

She sprang up then and faced him. 'I am of course beholden to you, sir, for your measured advice about how I should conduct myself. You are so *very* well qualified to offer it, are you not? After all, you always behave as a model of propriety. You would never dream of seducing a lady, or abducting her, or lying to her about who you really are, or—'

'I am not alone in refusing to divulge my real identity,' Max said sharply.

'But you have absolutely no idea of a lady's needs! You preen yourself on having done all that I could possibly require, do you not, sir? Well, you have failed... lamentably.'

'Nonsense.' He gestured towards the bed where she had unpacked the contents of her valise. 'You have everything you could possibly want. Even you can wear only one evening gown at a time.'

'And how, pray, am I supposed to do up my laces so that I may put it on?'

Max was taken aback for a second. Then he noticed the stays lying alongside her evening gown and almost laughed at his own stupidity. He had arrogantly listed all the flaws that she had overlooked; but it had never occurred to him to wonder whether he was capable of similar mistakes. It was obvious now. She had dressed without help that morning, in order to steal out of the inn to taste the dawn. She must be wearing almost nothing underneath her gown. If he had dared to touch her again, he would have known.

He looked her slowly up and down. She was blushing fierily. Even in a dark, crumpled gown, she looked absolutely delicious. 'My apologies, my lady,' he said, unable to suppress a fleeting grin, 'I should have remembered that a lady cannot wear a low-cut gown without being laced into her stays. Shall I send for Ramsey to act as your lady's maid?'

'Of course not!'

'I can assure you that Ramsey is old enough—and experienced enough—to be able to fulfil the role more than competently.'

She gave a very unladylike snort of disbelief.

'Alternatively…' he allowed himself a long, slow smile at the prospect '…I could perform the task myself.' He reached across and picked up the corset, letting it dangle by its laces from his fingers. It was an outrageous thing to do, and yet he could not resist it. Nor could he resist adding, with an appreciative glance at her lush breasts, 'I myself am…not without experience.'

She gave a gasp of suppressed rage and launched herself at him.

'No, Rose,' he said calmly, possessing himself of her wrists and pulling her body hard against him so that she had no room to kick, 'that is not how a lady of refinement should behave.'

'Let me go,' she whispered—but she leant in to him as she said the words. And her eyes had closed.

It was too late, for both of them. 'I think not,' he said and began to kiss her hungrily.

Her response seemed to be even more passionate than at the ridotto. The moment he released her wrists, she flung her arms round his neck, trying to pull their bodies even closer. She moaned deep in her throat when his lips fastened on hers. He did not need to coax her lips apart; she was already eager for him. The kiss went on and on.

At last, he ran one hand down the front of her gown, seeking her soft breast. Even through the heavy fabric, he could feel how her nipple peaked against his touch. That was not enough. He had to touch her skin. His hand went to the buttons of her gown, but they were tiny and his fingers were suddenly huge and clumsy. He groaned his frustration into her willing mouth.

'Max,' she breathed.

It was the most sensuous sound he had ever heard. Without conscious thought, he gripped the bodice of her gown and ripped the fastenings asunder. The front of the gown parted. Underneath, she was wearing nothing but a thin chemise.

He groaned and closed his eyes against the sight of her. He must not do this. She was carrying another man's child.

'Max?' She sounded uncertain, anxious.

'Forgive me,' he said hoarsely, putting her away from him, but allowing his hands to rest still on the smooth skin of her shoulders. He could not bring himself to let her go completely. Not yet. 'I promised you I would do you no more harm, but…' Abruptly, he removed his hands and indicated the gown that now hung from her shoulders, ruined.

She made a half-hearted attempt to cover herself. Even her breasts were tinged by a flush of embarrassment. After a moment, she turned her back on him and moved towards the pile of clothing on the bed.

'You have no option but to make use of Ramsey's services now, I am afraid. Pray believe I am truly sorry to have distressed you so. I will send him to you at once.'

'No,' she said firmly. 'There is no need. For the moment, I am perfectly satisfied with the assistance I have.'

Angel did not stop to think about what she was about to do. She did not dare. She knew that her courage might fail her.

Keeping her back towards him, she allowed the torn gown to fall to the floor. Then she picked up her stays and placed them around her body, over her chemise. 'Will you lace me up, please?' she said quietly, trying to stop her voice from trembling. 'I am afraid I am already late for dinner. My host will be growing impatient.'

He let out his breath in a long gust overlaid with uncertain laughter. It seemed that he was going to play out his allotted role in this little charade of hers. She refused to think where it might lead.

His fingers trembled a little at first, but once the stays were drawn together across her back, his touch became very deft. 'Is that tight enough for you, madam?' he said, pulling hard.

She could barely draw breath. 'Perfectly, thank you,' she gasped.

He ignored her and loosened the laces a little. 'You are a very poor liar, my lady,' he said. 'And besides, your impatient host would certainly have you able to eat...and to breathe.'

There was no answer to that. She reached for her gown. It was of dark blue silk, very plain, apart from a ruched ribbon edging to the low neckline and some delicate self-coloured embroidery near the hem. Still keeping her back to him, she stepped into it, slipped her arms through the long gauze sleeves and pulled the neckline into place on her shoulders. 'If you please,' she said quietly.

Perhaps wisely, he began to tackle the fastenings from

the waist downwards. Having finished with the skirt, he paused and took a deep breath before he began to fasten the buttons and loops from the waistline to her bare neck. He fumbled more than once.

'As a lady's maid, Max, you fall rather short of the highest class.'

'Do I?' He brushed her hair aside and began to fasten the topmost button, allowing his fingers to stray over her naked skin. She sensed that it was quite deliberate. A shiver ran through her. She was quite as aware of him as he was of her. And she was incapable of concealing her reactions.

'Mmm. Beautiful,' he whispered, running the back of his finger along the edge of the neckline, from shoulder to shoulder.

She shivered again, waiting for him to continue his exploration. Her breasts were beginning to ache for him, but he seemed determined to touch only her back.

He picked up the weight of her hair and arranged it carefully over her shoulders, patting the ribbon into place. 'My talents do not run to hairdressing, I fear, m'lady. Will it please you to look now?' He stepped away from her.

She could no longer hide from him. She turned at last to find that he was watching her with obvious admiration. No mirror was necessary. A sudden blast of heat filled her body at the thought that Max might still think her beautiful. He, too, looked a little warm, she decided, but his eyes were now sparkling wickedly behind that infernal mask. He was back in control of his reactions, even if Angel was not.

He offered his arm. 'Will it please you to come down to dinner, my lady? It would be a pity to waste such delectable fare.'

* * *

Max led her out of the room and down the stairs to the hallway. Her light touch on his sleeve was threatening to burn its way through to his flesh. He hardly dared to look at her, recognising that her effect on him was likely to undermine all his resolutions. He must remain true to his purpose. He was to discover the name of her lover, not to become one of that number himself.

He had all but betrayed himself. He had taken such pains to disguise his appearance, but then he had almost allowed his voice to give him away. So much for his pride in his own self-control. One touch on her peach-bloom skin and his foreign accent had slipped. Had she noticed? At one point, he had begun to sound remarkably like Cousin Frederick. His only hope was that she was so bemused by what was happening to her body that his change of tone had not registered with her. But he must not make that mistake again. This meal would be a trial. He must not allow his control to slip. He was not Frederick, the cousin she hated, but Max, the masked seducer.

Seducer? That was certainly not his intention, but, if he needed to play the part in order to persuade her to reveal her secret, then he would do so. Every other attempt to get to the truth had certainly failed.

He ushered her down the hallway to Ross's dining room. It was larger than the parlour, but still small enough for their meal to be intimate. It was better not to return to the breakfast parlour where they had quarrelled. In new surroundings, they could start afresh.

Ramsey bowed them into the room. There was a distinctly martial glint in his eye, Max noted. The man was no doubt spoiling for a fight in order to defend the lady's honour. Little did he know that she had none! Max tried to plant that idea in the forefront of his own mind, but then he looked across the table and her radiant beauty entrapped him all over again. Her colour was slightly heightened. His fingers itched to touch her naked breasts above the low-cut neckline of her gown. Her skin seemed to be shimmering with the delicate pink of dawn clouds. As if conscious of his scrutiny, she coloured even more and fixed her gaze on the table.

Ramsey brought the dishes from the sideboard and set them out. Max noted, with the small part of his brain that was still functioning, that a single dish had been left behind. 'You have forgotten one, Ramsey,' he said firmly.

'Ah…no, Cap'n. That is not fit to eat now. It is fish. And it is spoiled.'

'Oh, dear.' The Baroness put her hand to her lips. 'And it is my fault.' She surveyed the array of dishes. 'This is wonderful, Ramsey. You and Fraser have worked miracles. I am so sorry that some of your hard work has been spoiled because of my lateness.'

'M'lady—' Ramsey began.

'Thank you, Ramsey,' Max said sharply. 'We shall serve ourselves. You may return to the kitchen. I will ring if I need you.'

Ramsey shot to attention. But he threw Max a very challenging look, none the less. He had clearly taken the lady's side in this skirmish. 'The second course will be ready as soon as you wish, sir, m'lady,' he said, with emphasis, 'and—' At Max's warning look, Ramsey stopped short.

'Thank you, Ramsey,' Max said again, nodding towards the door. This time, the manservant could not delay any longer. He bowed himself out.

'I thought, my lady,' Max began, in his best seducer's voice, 'that you would be more comfortable without an audience. It is important that you eat. You have had nothing since breakfast.'

She looked up at him. 'And nothing for twenty-four

hours before that,' she said simply. 'I was…unwell upon the road. Without that, I should have been safe at the Abbey by now and—' She stopped. She was frowning. 'How is it, Max, that you knew where to find me when it came to this bizarre abduction of yours?'

He smiled and poured champagne into her glass. 'I suggest you drink it, my lady,' he said softly.

For a second she looked cross, but then she raised the flute to her lips and sipped.

'Good,' he said. 'This one question I will answer, though I know it will give birth to a host of others. And those, I shall not answer. Not tonight.'

She shook her head slightly. She seemed puzzled.

'The answer to your first question is simple enough. I followed you from London.'

'But how did you know where—?'

Max gave her a slightly crooked smile. 'One answer only, my lady. And I have already given it to you. Tomorrow, you shall have as many more as you desire. You have my word on that.'

'You will remove your mask?'

He nodded.

'And the rest of your disguise, too?'

He nodded again. 'If you wish to see the man beneath the mask, your wish will be granted.' He thought she looked a little dazed. 'And now you must eat. Will you take a little of this fricassee?'

At first she only picked at the food he set before her, but Fraser had excelled himself, in spite of the delay to their meal. The dishes were outstanding—light, tasty, and appetising. After a few tentative mouthfuls, she began to eat more heartily. Max congratulated himself on that, at least. A pregnant woman needed to eat for the sake of the child she carried.

He refilled their glasses. Somehow, over these last weeks, she had acquired a taste for champagne. At the ridotto, it had had a remarkable effect on her inhibitions. With luck, it would now loosen her tongue.

'If you have finished, my lady, I will ring for the second course.'

'Yes, thank you, I—'

She was blushing again under his scrutiny. But he had not even touched her! The champagne must be working more rapidly than he had imagined it could.

Ramsey appeared so quickly in response to the bell that Max suspected the man had not been in the kitchen at all. Max frowned at him and said, 'You may clear these dishes, Ramsey, and bring in the second course. Then you and Fraser may take yourselves off. I shall not need you again tonight.'

The sergeant glowered at him, but knew better than to argue. He turned his attention to the lady instead.

'Thank you, Ramsey,' she said, smiling up at his grizzled countenance. 'That was delicious. My compliments to the cook…or cooks.' Ramsey sketched a rather awkward bow, before busying himself with the task of clearing the plates.

Max ignored the undercurrents and crossed to the sideboard to open a second bottle of champagne.

The second course seemed to pass even more slowly than the first. Max was becoming acutely conscious of the way her unbound hair gleamed in the candlelight. Every time she moved to raise a fork to her lips or to reach for her glass, the reflections on her hair shifted alluringly. That single ribbon was crying out to be undone so that the full weight of her hair would be loose on her bare shoulders. And it would look even more beautiful against a pillow.

That image was definitely a mistake! He was already

uncomfortable enough in his laughable costume, without allowing the nearness of her body to fire his lust. He took a long swallow of his wine, trying to remind himself of his purpose. He must ensure she was relaxed enough to lower her defences. She needed to be just a little foxed. He topped up her glass, ruthlessly trying to suppress the reactions of his wayward body.

With a sigh, she pushed her plate away and reached for her wine. 'That was truly delicious,' she said and sipped. She smiled suddenly. 'You know, Max, I was used to think that I disliked the taste of champagne. But now...' She sipped again. 'It is your fault, I think.'

Max returned her smile. The moment had surely arrived.

He found he did not know what to say!

He leaned back in his chair and cast his eyes up to the ceiling. He was a fool! He should have thought of this! Cousin Frederick could tax her about the lover who had made her pregnant, but Max the seducer could not. Max the seducer had never been told that she was with child.

He resolved on an oblique approach. In truth, it was all he had. 'Tell me, my lady, how is it that you came to be at the ridotto in the first place? You were alone when I found you, but I'll warrant you did not arrive there unescorted. Had you sent your lover to the right about?'

She reddened.

He wondered whether it was anger, or embarrassment.

'I have had no such lover, sir,' she said in a very low voice. She was now staring down at the table in front of her. 'You—' her voice was barely above a whisper, but it held a thread of immense bitterness '—you are the cause of my current predicament.' She raised her head and looked at him. He would almost have sworn that her eyes were glistening with tears. Her expression was anguished.

'But men do not care for such things.' She pushed back her chair and rose to her feet, turning for the door.

For the first time, Max felt guilty. She was right to blame him for taking advantage of her when she was foxed. He had not cared about her predicament and neither had the man, or men, who came after him.

He caught her arm, but she would not turn back to face him. 'I care a great deal about what happens to you, my Lady Rose.' Without releasing his hold, he came round the table to stand close behind her. 'No harm shall come to you because of my actions,' he said softly. 'And I shall do everything in my power to protect you from any man who would do you injury.'

She said nothing.

'Rose?'

'Please do not address me by that name,' she whispered. 'My name is…my name is Angel.'

'Angel…' He should have known. Her name was Angel. Of course it was. He put his hands on her shoulders and turned her round to face him. There were traces of tears on her cheeks. She was blinking hard in an effort to hold them back. He raised her hands and kissed them, first one and then the other. 'My Lady Angel,' he murmured. 'Much more beautiful than the rose.'

'Oh, Max…'

He placed a hand on her cheek, rubbing away the tear-stains with his thumb. 'No harm will come to you, my Lady Angel. You have my word.'

Her eyes widened. She looked lost and, at the same time, so very desirable. Max could no longer control his need for her. He pulled her into his arms and began to kiss her with something akin to desperation. He was dying of thirst and she offered him, not water, but the nectar of the gods.

* * *

Angel had never tasted anything like this. Max's kisses were much more intoxicating than any amount of champagne. She felt as though she could have floated up into the air, like thistledown, had it not been for his strong arms anchoring her into their embrace.

She did not want this kiss to end. Max treated her with a tenderness she had never before experienced, even when he seemed to be demanding that she respond to him. She soon found that she, too, could be demanding. With this man, she had been set free. She tried to say his name, but the sound was lost in a long moan in her throat. She had not known she was capable of such a reaction.

He broke the kiss so abruptly that she almost fell. He was short of breath and, behind the mask, his eyes were unfocused. She must have knocked his wig a little askew, for she could see his own dark hair above his forehead.

'Max…' She reached out a hand to him, but he stepped back so that her fingers met only thin air.

'That was unforgivable,' he said. He put his hand up as if to run his fingers through his hair and grimaced when they met the coarse wig instead. He straightened it, muttering an oath that she could not catch. 'I gave you my word…' He shook his head. 'I can only apologise, Lady Angel, and remove myself from your sight.' He bowed and started for the door, keeping as much distance as possible between their bodies.

'Wait, Max.'

He stopped, but he did not turn back to her.

Angel took a deep breath. If she said the wrong thing now, he would leave…and, in spite of all the terrible fears that haunted her memory, she did not want Max to leave. She felt… No, she *knew* that Max did not want to use her as her husband had. He desired her, but he wanted her to desire him just as much. Max wanted to be in control, so that Angel need not be. But, every time they kissed, his control snapped. They both knew what he was capable of, what he had actually done at the ridotto. She was certain that he regretted it keenly. So he had sworn, on his honour, that it would not happen again. Now, he was afraid that he was about to break his word. He was afraid of what he might do.

How did she know all this? That was a mystery to her but, gazing at his hunched shoulders, she was certain it was true. He had given her a veto over anything that might happen. She could insist, at any time, that he leave her…but she could also insist that he remain.

She picked up her skirts and walked nonchalantly past him to the door. There, she turned back to him and smiled her company smile. 'It is late, sir, and I think it would be best if I retired. Will you be so good as to escort me to my chamber?' She stood there, pointedly waiting for him to open the door for her.

She thought she detected a hint of uncertainty in his demeanour as he pulled the door open and stood back to let her pass through. Trying to hide a smile, Angel tucked her arm through his. 'You are too kind, sir,' she said politely. They proceeded along the hallway and up the staircase in total silence. Angel could feel the tension in his body. Her own body was coiled like a spring, being wound tighter and tighter.

It is my choice, she told herself. If I ask him to stop, he will do so. If I ask him to leave, he will go. But I want him to stay. Tonight, I want to experience— Oh, I do not know what I may experience but I feel that, with Max, something wonderful is awaiting me. I do not care who he may be, or how he may look under that costume. He is the father of my child, after all, and I am in some way bound to him. Can it be so wrong that I want to be with him now? It may be the only chance I ever have.

Max dropped her arm the moment they reached her door. He bowed again. 'Good night, my Lady Angel. Sleep well.'

She looked up at him through her lashes. 'You are forgetting one or two important things, I fear. I shall get no sleep at all, dressed as I am. And I have no lady's maid to help me.' She reached for the handle and opened the door. Then she calmly walked into the room and crossed to the dressing table. 'I am afraid that I must rely on your good offices to unlace me,' she said simply. She did not intend that he should have any choice in the matter.

She stood absolutely still, waiting. She refused to turn round until she was sure he would not retreat. Even when she heard the click of the latch, she did not turn.

'Angel.' His voice was low and strained.

She glanced over her shoulder and smiled brightly at him. In the relative gloom of the bedchamber, she could not see his eyes behind the dark mask. 'Come, master abigail, let us see if your talents are better suited to unlacing.'

He groaned aloud. 'Beware, madam. I am not made of wood.'

'No, indeed,' she said quickly. 'Judging by the way you laced me up, your fingers are made of…of…' She felt his hand on her hair, pushing it aside so that he could undo her gown. She forgot what she had been about to say. Her brittle façade had shattered with the first hint of his warm breath on the back of her neck.

He began with the ribbon in her hair. Slowly, very slowly, he pulled one long end so that the bow came undone. With a low murmur of approval, he untied the knot, gently freeing the strands that might be damaged, and raising his hand high above her head to pull the ribbon free.

For a moment, he allowed it to trail from his fingers, catching the light as it twisted back and forth, and then he loosed it. It dropped on to her breast and shivered across her skin, before drifting to the floor.

Angel closed her eyes on the sensation. The coiled spring that was her body tensed yet more.

She waited. Something else must happen soon. But there was no movement behind her and she was unable to force her body to turn round. She was sure—almost—that he was still there, although she could no longer detect the sound of his breathing. Then she felt the pressure of his fingers straining the tight bodice of her gown as he began to undo the fastenings. And she was glad.

This time, he was slow, and painstaking. Every single loop was carefully undone before he passed on to the next. This time, he never once touched her skin. This time, nothing was ripped. Max was back in control.

'There,' he said, undoing the last button on her gown and holding the bodice together so that it remained on her shoulders. 'If you will just hold your gown in place decently, my lady, I will loosen your laces. Then I will leave you to make ready for bed.'

Angel was tempted to let the gown drop to the floor. If she did nothing to stop him, he would be gone from her in a matter of moments.

'If you please, my lady.' His voice was cold. He was still holding the back of the gown, waiting for Angel to take over.

Angel sighed and put her hands to her shoulders.

'Thank you.' He began to undo her laces. Soon, the stays would part and there would be only the thin chemise between his fingers and the skin of her back. Angel was quite sure he had determined not to touch her. Surreptitiously, she took a deep breath, trying to expand her ribcage so that his task would become more difficult.

'An abigail clearly needs the patience of a saint,' he muttered in irritation. He was struggling to unpick the knot.

'An abigail should avoid using knots that cannot be undone,' Angel retorted.

There was a sharp intake of breath. 'Be careful, my lady, or you may find you have to sleep in your stays.'

She ignored his warning. 'If the knot is too tight, I suggest you cut it. I am sure you can lay hands on some scissors…or a knife.'

'Do not tempt me,' he said harshly, still working on the knot.

Angel felt the sudden freedom as it came undone. She could no longer hold her breath. Her ribcage collapsed and the stays drooped.

He stepped back from her abruptly. 'I will say goodnight now, my lady. I am sure you will be able to manage, without any more help from me. Sleep well.'

She spun round, still holding the gown to her shoulders. She could not bring herself to let it go. It would seem so dreadfully…wanton. 'I…I am grateful to you, sir. I should not have thought that any man could perform such a service without trying to…take advantage of the situation. Yet you—'

'I have given you my word, my lady. You will be safe here, in your own chamber, behind a locked door. You will be left alone. To sleep.' He bowed, preparing to leave her.

Oh, he was obstinate. Why the sudden qualms? And why now? He had had no such scruples at the ridotto. 'I shall not lock my door. I have no desire to be alone.' The words were out. She could not recall them. She took a deep breath and said, 'I want you to come to me, Max.'

He was silent. It seemed to be an age before he spoke. 'Are you sure?' His voice was very low. He was avoiding her eyes.

'Yes,' she said immediately. 'Yes, I am sure. But…'

'What is it, my lady?'

'Please, Max…without the mask. I want – I need to see you as you really are.'

He hesitated. Then, at length, he nodded. 'Since you are so sure, my Lady Angel, it shall be as you wish.'

Chapter Fifteen

Max pulled off his wig and threw it angrily to the floor of his chamber. He was furious with himself. He had lost control. Again. What was it about that woman?

She blamed him for what had happened to her. Oh, he had perhaps introduced her to the delights of dalliance, but it was her own fault that she was increasing. She must have known the risks, when she decided to take a lover to her bed. Unless… What if someone had forced her?

He swore vehemently. What an impossible coil! He had promised to share the bed of a pregnant woman. And still he did not know the identity of her lover. What's more, he had promised to remove his mask! He was an utter fool!

He kicked off his ridiculous buckled shoes with a groan. How on earth had his forefathers tolerated such discomfort? The satin coat and waistcoat followed, along with the mask. He drove his hands through his hair and went across to the washstand. At least he could remove this confounded paint!

The cold water was a shock. He stopped, looking at himself in the glass. This was no way to prepare. Whenever he touched her, he lost control. If he was to have any chance of discovering the truth, he must make preparations now, while he was still alone, still coherent. He had promised, but…

He smiled bitterly at his reflection and went to retrieve the mask.

Angel was sitting on the edge of the bed, shrouded in her wrapper from neck to ankle. Her gaze was fixed on the dying embers of the fire. She was twisting her fingers together, trying to control her shaking. Now that she was alone, she could not understand why she had even considered such a thing. She was a virtuous widow…and she had brazenly invited a nameless man to share her bed.

A widow could not be both virtuous and pregnant.

At the sound of the opening door, she clutched her wrapper more tightly to her. He had not bothered to knock. For a fallen woman, it was clearly not deemed necessary.

He was carrying a single candle. And he was still wearing his mask!

She gasped. She would never have expected him to break his word.

He threw her a strange look and proceeded to extinguish all the other candles in the room. Then he strode past her shivering form to draw the curtains around the bed. Only the side where she sat remained open. He came to stand before her, candlestick in hand. 'You are shivering, my lady. It is no wonder. You are cold and your feet are bare. May I suggest you get into bed?' He raised his free hand to draw the remaining bedcurtain.

Angel swallowed. She had invited him. She could not break her promise now, even though he was clearly intent on breaking his. She moved the bedcovers aside and pushed her body between the sheets. They were cold. No one had come to warm the bed. Even with her wrapper, she shivered.

She forced herself to look at his looming figure. Odd—it seemed broader than before. He was wearing a dressing gown of some dark material. His hair shone black in the candlelight and hung loose to his collar. His face was covered by that infernal mask.

'Max,' she managed at last, 'you promised…'

He grinned at her. Or was it a grimace?

He took his hand from the bedcurtain and put it to the strings of his mask. It came undone immediately and fell away.

And in the same instant, he blew out the candle. All Angel saw, in the fleeting afterglow, was the vague shape of his face, and his dark eyes, gazing intently into hers.

He sat down on the bed with his back to her. Angel heard the little click when he put the candlestick on the bedside table. Then he lay down beside her and pulled the curtains closed. The mattress moved under his weight. Angel felt her body begin to roll towards him and grabbed the sheet to steady herself. As long as there was space between them…

He made no move towards her. Instead, he raised his arms and clasped his hands behind his head, making a strange silhouette. As Angel's eyes became more accustomed to the deep gloom, she discovered the cause. He was still wearing his dressing gown.

Without turning to her, he said, 'Do you wish me to leave, Angel?'

There. She had her chance. She had only to say… She closed her eyes and took three long, slow breaths. She was not afraid after all. 'You cheated me, Max.'

His rumble of laughter made the bed shake. 'I kept my side of the bargain, my lady. You should have been more specific in your demands. However, it is only a matter of time. In the morning, you may look your fill. For the moment, there are more important matters to occupy us...if that is still your desire.'

'I...'

'Angel.' His voice was serious, but that rich, honeyed quality was there still. 'Angel, the decision is yours. Nothing will happen unless you wish it.' He moved lazily, as if settling himself for sleep.

'Oh, heavens. I—' The space between them seemed immensely wide. 'Max—' Angel stretched her hand towards him. It encountered cool silk. And then it was lifted gently to his lips. She could feel him smile as he kissed her skin.

'You are cold.' He pulled gently on her arm, encouraging but not forcing. 'Come. Let me warm you.'

That voice was irresistible. He opened his arms to her and she went into them, willingly.

Max drew her close and rested his chin on her hair. With his free hand, he began to stroke her arm, slowly and surely warming her skin through the layers of fabric. 'Relax, Angel. You are safe. I will not hurt you.' When she said nothing, he dropped a light kiss on her hair and pulled her more closely into the comfort of his body.

She was warm already. Even her toes were tingling. She was lying with a man and he was simply holding her. It was a strange new sensation; and it was wonderful. She felt...cherished.

'Better?'

She wriggled closer. The knotted belt of her wrapper pushed uncomfortably against her hipbone.

'Would you like me to help you?' he asked softly.

She nodded against his chest. She could not speak.

He took his time. He was in no hurry now. He ran his fingers lightly across her cheek and tilted up her face for his kiss. Slowly. He must go slowly. He must have frightened her before. He must not do so again.

Gently, he kissed her brow and her temples, then the peach-bloom skin along her cheekbones. He could feel the heat of her blush against his lips. She made a tiny sound in her throat. Like a kitten. He smiled against her skin and moved to kiss her closed eyelids, lingering there. Her long lashes brushed against his lower lip, with the softness of a caress.

She moved closer still, raising her mouth to his.

Slowly. Her lips were too tempting. Too soon. He cupped her cheek, turning her head a little so that he could reach her temple once more, and then her neck. She moaned a protest. But it quickly became a murmur of pleasure when he began to nibble his way down the rim of her ear. He paused there and touched his tongue to the groove behind her earlobe. Her whole body started.

'Do you wish me to stop?'

She sank back against him. 'N…no. Don't stop.'

He kissed the corner of her jaw and continued his exploration down the side of her neck, feeling the rapid beat of her pulse against his lips. He longed to taste her skin there, but it was too soon. Only the lightest of touches would do. He must go slowly.

She whispered his name.

'Mmm?'

'Kiss me.'

'I am kissing you, Angel.'

She strained towards him. 'Properly. Please, Max.'

He smiled into the darkness and began to address himself to the line of her jaw. Her bone structure was beautiful.

'Max…'

'Soon, Angel. Soon.' He was determined to taste every inch of her skin before he touched her lips. Kissing Angel's mouth was like touching fire. The conflagration would consume him. He had learnt his lesson that first time, in that confounded greenhouse. This time, she was in his arms by her own choice. He must make her ready.

He must make her wait.

He touched his tongue to the point of her chin, and then kissed his way upwards, by infinitesimal degrees, almost to her bottom lip. There he stopped. Her head dropped back on to the pillow, arching her neck towards him. Her lips parted on a trembling sigh. Her glorious hair was spread across the pillow, becoming increasingly tangled as she tossed about in response to his measured onslaught. If only he could see it… He reached out to touch it with his fingers. Her skin was like a peach, but her hair… He lifted one of the heavy locks. This he could kiss. Now. He touched it to his lips. And tasted violets. He moaned in his turn.

'Oh, Max…'

He forced his body back under control. That was better. But it could not last much longer.

He began to stroke her arm, as he had done before he started kissing her. Before, he had stroked down to her hand, now he stroked upward to her shoulder, and her throat, where the heavy wrapper ended. At first, she purred with pleasure, but when he transferred his touch to her neck and then her ribcage, she murmured a protest, 'No, not like this.'

Max stopped immediately.

She moaned even more and began to tug urgently at the knot of her belt.

'Let me help you,' he said again, covering her fingers with his. She stilled in an instant under his touch.

Not yet. She was not yet ready. He stroked her breast lightly, just once, through the thick fabric and lifted his hand away. He moved his body so that his mouth was over hers, almost but not quite touching. He could sense the nearness of her parted lips. They were so very tantalising.

He resisted. He laid a hand on her knotted belt and said, 'Do you want me to undo this?'

Her head moved on the pillow but she said nothing.

'Angel, I will help you to disrobe if that is your wish. But you must tell me so.'

'Please, Max,' she whispered. 'Yes.'

He needed both hands at her waist to untie the belt. She must have been afraid, to have knotted it so tightly. And yet she had not repulsed him.

The belt came loose. Max made no attempt to remove her wrapper. She alone must decide upon that.

The decision came quickly and unmistakably. Angel put one arm round his neck and used the other to carry his hand to her breast, under the wrapper.

She was naked beneath it!

The shock send Max's heart racing and his blood pounding in his ears. Desire surged through him so strongly that he almost took her, there and then.

It was the purr of satisfaction that stopped him. She was softening, opening, but she was nowhere near ready for him. He had to wait. Even if his body was screaming for release, he had to wait.

He raised himself on one elbow, grateful for the momentary distraction. Touching her was almost driving him wild. He put a hand to the front of her wrapper, touching only the fabric. 'I imagine you would be more comfortable without this, Angel. Hmm?'

'Yes.' It was a tiny, purring whisper.

Max eased the wrapper from each of her shoulders in turn. Now she was lying on it, uncomfortably. 'If you lift a little, Angel, I can get rid of it for you.'

She did not lift her body as he expected. Instead, she

rolled on to him and put both arms round his neck. Max gasped for breath, grateful for the thin barrier of his own dressing gown. He could not afford to feel her naked body against him. Not yet.

He tried to divert his thoughts by concentrating on the wrapper. It was still trapped under her hip. On this occasion, he chose to forget good manners. They were too dangerous. He simply grabbed a fistful of the fabric and tugged the wrapper free.

She was shocked enough to protest briefly, but she did not remove her arms from his neck.

Max pushed the wrapper out through the bedcurtain and dropped it on to the floor, where his mask already lay. It seemed fitting.

Angel was now pressing the full length of her body against him. 'No, sweet,' he said, gently pushing her on to her back once more, 'not like that. Let me show you.'

He had promised himself every inch of her body, and now she was offering it to him. He started at her neck, and then began to move downwards, kissing and tasting. Her throat, her ribs, her flat stomach, her thighs, her calves, her ankles, the arches of her feet. He did not allow himself to touch her breasts, or to come near the core of her. His own body could not endure such intimate exploration. He would do it—yes—but only when she asked. Only when she understood where it would lead.

'Max—' she sounded as if she were pleading now '—Max, this is unbearable.'

'Do you want me to stop?' he said quietly.

'You know I do not, you wretch,' she groaned.

Max grinned and moved back up the bed to lie beside her. 'What do you want of me, Angel?'

She hid her face against his chest and growled as she encountered the silk dressing gown. Seizing the lapel, she said, 'To remove this, first of all. I want to be able to touch you, too, Max.'

He put his hand over hers and held it still. 'Angel, this is the last barrier between us. If I remove it, it will be on the understanding that I am going to make love to you, that we are going to be together, fully and sweetly. You can still stop this. Are you sure you want it gone?'

She pushed her fingers under the lapel to touch the skin of his chest. 'Yes,' she said.

'As you wish, my Lady Angel.' He lifted his body a little, shrugged out of the dressing gown and then pushed it out of the bed to join her wrapper.

Though they were both naked now, he was still determined to go slowly. He pushed her gently on to her back and began kissing her again, keeping a little distance between their bodies, even though he was now desperate to press his whole length against her. She had fainted, once, when he was about to enter her. He did not want to frighten her again.

He was still avoiding her lips and her breasts, but it seemed she was no longer prepared to let him set the rules. First, she forced his hand to her breast. It was lush and heavy, with the nipple standing proud against his palm.

'Kiss me, Max,' she begged, but when he moved his lips to hers, she shook her head. 'No, not here.' She put her fingers on his where they stroked her breast.

Max dropped a tiny kiss on the corner of her mouth and then slid down to her breast. He took the nipple in his mouth and sucked strongly, drawing a groan of pleasure from her. 'Am I hurting you?' he whispered wickedly, knowing very well what the answer would be.

'Don't stop,' she breathed.

He continued to suckle at one breast while caressing the other with finger and thumb. Her moans were beginning to rise to fever pitch. 'Angel, do you want more?' he said, trying to curb his own desire just a little longer.

'Oh, Max, I need you. I need you now. Please, Max.'

He did not lift his head from her breast but he stroked his free hand down her belly to the juncture of her thighs. He had to be sure she was ready. At the first touch of his fingers, she opened to him. He smoothed his palm over her curls and touched his finger to the core of her. She was hot, and wet. He stroked. Once. Twice. And again.

She cried out and convulsed against him. 'Oh, Max. Oh!'

He pulled her into his arms and held her until the shaking stopped. He forced himself to think of her, only her. His own needs must wait.

'Max?' she said at last, in a small, uncertain voice. 'What…what happened?'

'Was that the first time, sweet? Have you never felt that before?'

'No.' She sounded dazed.

Max felt suddenly privileged, and proud. 'Angel, that is what happens between a man and a woman, when they are together. When they make love. It can happen for us both…when I am inside you.'

'I… Oh… But I have never… Oh.'

'It happens only when there is tenderness, and trust, and lo— And longing to be together, Angel.' He began to touch her breast and her belly, stroking gently to arouse her all over again.

When he started to suckle once more, she forced his head away. 'No, Max. Not that way. I want us to be… together. Make love to me, Max, please.'

Max swallowed hard and closed his eyes. She had had one climax already. He must try to go slowly, for her sake.

He did not think he could.

He moved fully on top of her. She welcomed him, pulling him closer and opening her thighs to receive him. He began to kiss her lips, as he had been longing to do since he had first lain down beside her. 'Oh, Angel,' he breathed. She tasted of violets and honey.

She was ready for him. He eased into her warmth, just a little way, and stopped, afraid that she might freeze. But she was warm and welcoming.

'Don't stop,' she sighed. 'Please don't stop.'

It was too much. In one long stroke, he pushed very slowly into her, until he was fully sheathed. He tried to hold still then, to hold back, but it was impossible. He started to move within her. And at his first stroke, she shuddered to a climax around him.

The last remnants of Max's control broke. He drove into her once more and cried out as he, too, found an ecstatic release.

Angel lay quietly in the dark, listening to Max's slow breathing. Her whole body was glowing with the warmth of his loving. How could she ever have imagined that it could be like this? Max had been so gentle and tender...the first time. And then, later, he had teased her to explore his body as he had explored hers. She had discovered that a man, too, could be driven almost to distraction by failure to touch, failure to kiss.

She smiled into the darkness. His body was beautiful, especially when it was aroused. And she could torment him into losing control. The first time had been slow and gentle. The second time had been quick and almost fierce, leaving them both exhausted. Would there be a third time? What would it be like? Who was this man who affected her so powerfully that she had gladly accepted him?

He was asleep. Now was the time, perhaps, to find out

why he was so very determined to hide his face from her. She reached out to him.

'What are you doing, Angel?'

He was not asleep at all! 'Searching for scars,' she said as calmly as she could. She continued to trail the tips of her fingers over his face, testing every inch of his skin. She could not see him, so she would explore him instead. She so much wished to discover why he had insisted on that mask.

'Mmm. I am sorry to disappoint you. I do not think I have any more scars than the next man. But, pray, do not stop. Your touch is very…stimulating.' He breathed a kiss on to her skin as her hand skimmed across his mouth.

'Stimulating? What a very strange thing to say.'

A rumble of laughter shook his chest. 'Oh, Angel. For all those years of your marriage, you have so little under-standing of men. Are you truly unaware of what you are doing to me?'

Even in the darkness, she could feel herself blushing. 'I… We…'

She tried to pull away from him, but Max was not pre-pared to allow that. He took her back into his arms, cra-dling her against his chest and gently stroking her hair. 'It is not my place to comment on your marriage. Forgive me.'

Angel gradually relaxed under his hypnotic touch. She had never felt so…cherished, or so ready to trust. 'My…my husband, John Frederick—' She felt his sharp intake of breath as she spoke the hated name. It was an odd reaction, to be sure, but she had more important things on her mind, things she needed to say. 'John Frederick was chosen by my father,' she continued slowly. 'Papa knew he was upright and honest and could be trusted with my fortune. In all those things, my father's judgement was sound. But there were things Papa could not know... John Frederick was a younger son, you see. Although he was content to accept my wealth, he...his dignity was offended by the thought that I would inherit the Barony while he remained simply the Honourable John Frederick Worthington. He even tried to encourage Papa to marry a third time, in the hope that he might sire a son. Papa refused. And pointed out to John Frederick that the wealth and the title were inseparable. If I were no longer the heir, I would lose most of my fortune, too. John Frederick was furious. He could not rail at Papa, of course. So he took his anger out on me.'

Max pulled her closer, never ceasing that hypnotic stroking. His warmth pervaded her, surrounding her with comfort in the velvet darkness. 'Did he hurt you, Angel?' he asked softly.

'N...no. Not then. He did not even shout. But his cold fury was so intense that it terrified me. I was sure he hated me.'

Max nodded against her hair.

'That was when John Frederick began to chide me for my failure to conceive. He had to have a son, he said, to inherit the Barony. He—' she swallowed hard '—he never once said that *I* needed a child. It was always *his* child, *his* heir.'

Max made a sound in his throat. It was almost a growl.

'He would come to my bed every night when he was at home, whether I— He said it was my duty. Twice, I fainted because he...when he... It changed nothing. He said that it made no difference since I was just as un...unappetising when I was awake. After we had been married for three years, he brought a doctor to examine me.' Angel shuddered at the memory. 'And a midwife. I...I cannot tell you how it was.' She shuddered again.

'They said I was probably barren but there was just a chance that I was merely a shy breeder. The doctor prescribed a regimen.' Angel took a deep breath. 'No riding, no strenuous exercise of any kind, no wine, no rich food to heat the blood. And no social engagements to excite the mind. John Frederick added that last one himself,' she said bitterly.

'Your papa—?'

'Papa could not interfere between husband and wife. He was grieved at the little he knew of what was happening. But he could do nothing.'

Max put his lips to her brow. 'Angel, you do not have to tell me any more of this. It is too distressing for you.'

'No. No, I have never been able to tell anyone before. I have to tell it to someone—or it will consume me.'

He nodded against her hair. 'Exorcise your demons then, my sweet,' he whispered, holding her very close.

'John Frederick hired a midwife to keep watch on me, the same one who had been with the doctor when he— She was a terrifying woman. She had huge hands. And they were never clean. Her breath smelt of gin, even first thing in the morning. She made me swallow the most disgusting concoctions. And every time it…became clear that I had not conceived, she would berate me and advise John Frederick to remove even more of my meagre freedoms.

'And then it happened. The midwife said I had conceived at last. She waited two months—she wanted to be sure, she said—and then she told John Frederick. I was put to bed, like an invalid, and permitted to walk about my chamber for thirty minutes a day, no more. I felt like a prisoner. But I would have endured it all for the sake of a child.'

She swallowed hard. 'I lost the child. It…it almost broke my heart. And the midwife said it was my fault, that I would never carry a child to term, that I was as good as barren.

'When John Frederick learned of it, he seemed like to have a seizure, he was so furious. He came to my chamber and ordered everyone out, even the midwife. And then he beat me with…with his riding crop.'

'Oh, God! Angel—'

She put a finger to his lips. 'It was the only time, Max. And now—with you—I can see that he was not a complete monster.'

'You are too forgiving!'

'No, Max. He…he did not mean to beat me. And it did not last long. He seemed to come to his senses and to realise what he was doing. He threw down the crop and ran out. I did not care what he did, only that he went.

'They brought him back on a hurdle, the following day. He had galloped out to the furthest reaches of the estate in the pouring rain. His stallion had thrown him. He was not badly injured, but he had lain for hours in the open before they found him. The fever went to his lungs and… and he died.'

'Good riddance!'

Angel ran her hand across her face. 'Papa helped me to restore my life to something approaching normality. He was very kind.'

Max snorted in disbelief.

'No, Max, you are wrong. Papa had done what he truly believed was best for me. He could not know what would happen. And he was desperately grieved by the little he did discover—'

'You did not tell him the truth?'

'My father? How could I? I told no one. In the light of day, I could not have told even you. And besides, the truth would only have served to hurt him yet more. He helped me to regain the spirit that I thought had been driven out for good. I became almost my old self again. And he promised me that I should have time for myself before I needed to marry again. This time, he would find me a better husband. He said the final choice would be mine.' She took a deep breath. 'And then he died.'

Max put his hand to her cheek and caressed it. He thought he felt a tear on his fingers and lifted them to his lips. He tasted salt. 'Oh, my dear,' he said gently. He could think of no words of comfort to offer her. Her terrible suffering, borne with such steadfast courage. And now, when she no longer had a husband assaulting her every night, she had lain, perhaps only once, with an unnamed lover and conceived at last. It was a bitter irony.

He would not allow her to face public ruin. He would find this lover of hers and force him to the altar, at the point of a pistol if need be. And, if the lover could not be found, there was still Pierre. There must be ways of persuading him…

But what if Pierre were no better husband material than the despicable John Frederick? She must not be put through another such ordeal.

'Max.' She snuggled into his warmth, putting a hand to his face and stroking his cheek as he had done to her. He could feel his stubble against her palm. 'Thank you for your understanding, Max. It seems more bearable, somehow, now that someone else knows. I…' her voice sank to a whisper ' I am glad it was you, Max.'

She placed a tiny kiss on the point of his chin. The movement crushed her soft breasts against him so that he groaned. He had been overwhelmed with pity for her sufferings, but her touch rekindled the slow-burning embers of desire. He was in bed with a beautiful, passionate woman. And she was using her new-found experience to arouse him yet again.

She ran her fingers down the side of his chest to his hipbone and then began to feather them across his stomach. He caught his breath sharply, and then let it out on a low moan. 'Angel, do you know what you are doing to me?'

She hid her face against his chest. After a moment, she began to taste his skin with flickering touches of her tongue. Her fingers were moving down his belly.

'Angel—'

'I have always been told I am a quick learner,' she whispered wickedly, cupping him gently and then trailing her fingernails up his hard length until he groaned with need. 'Perhaps it is time for my next lesson?'

It was already light when Angel awoke again. She could feel the warmth of Max's naked body curled around her back and his steady breathing against her cheek. She closed her eyes again, savouring the wonderful feelings he aroused in her—faith and trust and sharing. She had not known that it was possible for a man to be so tender with a woman. She had not known…that any of it was possible. For this man, she would—

Max's hand moved to her breast and cupped it possessively, but the tempo of his breathing had not altered. He was still asleep. Now was her chance to feast her eyes on his face, to imprint it for ever on her memory. One day she would be able to tell her child about how his father had looked.

Very slowly, she stretched out her arm and parted the bed curtains, so that a little light penetrated. Then she eased herself out of his embrace and turned to look her fill.

'No! Oh, no!'

He started from sleep in the same moment that she threw herself from the bed, catching up a coverlet to hide her nakedness.

'No!' she screamed. 'No, no, no!'

Chapter Sixteen

This time there was no oblivion, though she longed for it. Every fibre of her body was shrieking against his betrayal. She wanted to rage at him but she could not. She had no words foul enough to describe what he had done.

She drew the coverlet more closely around her body and tried to recover the remnants of her dignity. She stared coldly at him. She would not allow him to think that he had the upper hand, even now.

He was totally shameless. He rose from the bed and stood facing her, making not the least attempt to cover his nakedness. 'No?' he asked silkily. He bent to retrieve his dressing gown. 'I do not recall that any such word passed your lips last night.' He stared at her, daring her to contradict him.

'Cover yourself, sir,' she snapped. 'Have you no shame?'

He smiled coldly, but he did shrug himself into his dressing gown, lazily belting it about his waist. 'There is nothing shameful, my Lady Angel, in what passed between us last night. Nothing.'

'No?' She was now shaking with fury at the full realisation of what he had done, and how he had done it. Her whole body burned with shame. She had trusted him with her innermost secrets, had welcomed him into her body and, all the time, he had been using her. 'What you have done is worse than shameful. It is despicable. And I—God help me—I am to bear a child by such a man?' She could not keep the agony out of her voice.

He took a step towards her. He looked thoroughly menacing. 'You are not carrying any child of mine. Look to your other lovers, my lady. You will not foist your bastard on to me.'

He was repudiating her, and his child. He was a monster. He was Cousin Frederick, her enemy, to his fingertips, but she would not crumple before his onslaught. She straightened her shoulders and raised her chin defiantly. The Baroness Rosevale would not be cowed. 'My bastard, as you are pleased to call it, Cousin, was sired on a greenhouse bench while I lay insensible. By *you*! Do you dare to deny it?'

'Yes,' he said baldly.

He was staring back at her. Every line of his body shouted haughty rejection of her accusation. He was wrong—he must be wrong—but he clearly believed what he had said. She shook her head despairingly. 'I have no other lover. No man but you has lain with me.' Then she turned her back on him. She could not bear to look at him one moment longer. It hurt too much. 'Please go,' she cried. 'Just go.'

Angel waited a long time for the sound of movement, but none came. Clearly, he did not intend to leave. Had he not humiliated her enough? She was ready to weep, but she refused to let him see such weakness. She whipped up her anger instead. 'You gave me your word you would do me no harm and I believed you. If only I had known it was you… You have ruined me…and taken pleasure in it, have you not, Frederick?'

'My name is Max. And I do not break my word. I will marry you, Angel.'

The shock of his words left her gasping for breath. She spun round to face him. He had not moved. He was staring at her still. His expression seemed to be a strange mixture of determination and relief. Relief? That was impossible. She must be imagining it.

She tried to speak, but could not even begin to address him. Frederick? Max? Who was this man?

He walked round the bed and placed a chair beside her. 'Sit down, Angel. You look as though you are about to faint.' He moved away so that the bed was between them once more. 'Sit down,' he said again. 'You need not be afraid. I will not come near you.'

Angel sat, pulling the coverlet up to her chin with both hands.

'You are confused.' He ran his fingers through his hair. 'So am I, I will admit. I am many things, but I am not a liar, Angel, nor am I a rapist.'

Angel gasped. All the remaining colour had drained from her face.

'If I had taken you in the way you allege, it would certainly have been rape. It did not happen. If you are carrying a child, Angel, it is not mine. And if there has been no one else… Angel, are you sure about your condition? Absolutely sure?'

Her eyes widened. Then she shook her head and covered her face with trembling hands. It was not a denial. It was sheer bewilderment.

Max's mind was racing, exploring and discarding explanations for her extraordinary accusations. She had been terrified of the marriage bed and of the pain she had experienced there. Everything she knew of pregnancy and childbearing had come from a vicious husband and a brutal midwife. He was certain she had consulted no one about her condition. No one knew. Except her hated Cousin Frederick. She had seemed so sure, but...

'Angel,' he said gently, 'look at me. I did not rape you. You are not carrying my child. Have you thought that you may be mistaken, that you may not be breeding at all?'

She dropped her hands from her face and gazed at him in blank astonishment.

Max tried to smile reassuringly at her. Then another thought struck him. 'I can assure you that you were not carrying my child. But it is possible, I suppose, that you now are.'

Angel considered her image in the glass. Would she pass muster with her servants? Her dress was neat enough— thanks to Ramsey's ability to act the part of lady's maid— but her face was ashen. She raised a hand to her cheek, trying to pinch some colour into her skin. Her fingers were still trembling.

She had succeeded in ejecting Cousin Frederick from her bedchamber, but he had not left the house. And he had sworn that *she* would not leave it either, until she had promised to marry him. He was a monster! She could never marry him!

Picking up her reticule, she cast a final glance around the room. That strange tremor ran through her again at the sight of the great bed where Max had—where Frederick had— She trembled again as her skin began to heat. Had her body known all along that they were one and the same? Had she really...?

Her pulse was beginning to race. She needed to get away from this place. She pulled open the door and made her way rapidly down the stairs to the hallway, where Ramsey was waiting. 'Is the carriage ready, Ramsey?'

'Not exactly, m'lady.' He would not meet her eyes.

'No, it is not,' said an unmistakably harsh voice. Frederick strode along the hall and stationed himself between Angel and the front door. 'Nor will it be, until our... business is resolved.'

Angel glared at him.

'Show her ladyship into the breakfast parlour, Ramsey, and then make yourself scarce.'

Angel bit back the retort that rose to her lips. She refused to dignify Frederick's appalling manners with any kind of response. Nor did she look at him. She straightened her back and followed Ramsey to the parlour.

'M'lady, shall I—?'

'Thank you, Ramsey,' she said firmly, rejecting his obvious concern. She knew she ought to be perfectly capable of dealing with his lordship. And his foul temper. She selected a chair near the window and took her seat, calmly arranging her skirts. Then she waited.

It was a full five minutes before he appeared. He strode into the room and stopped dead at the sight of her. 'Very good,' he said, with a reluctant nod. He did not apologise for keeping her waiting, or for preventing her departure. He simply launched into speech. 'Now, madam, I will have you listen to me. You may or may not be carrying my child, but you are certainly ruined, since you have spent the night with me. There is no solution except marriage. And the sooner, the better. I shall not permit you to leave here until I have your word on it.'

She stared up at him, making no attempt to hide her seething anger.

He ignored it. 'I am waiting, madam,' he said, leaning back against the closed door.

Two could play at that game. Angel forced herself to relax into her chair and nonchalantly began to search in her reticule for a handkerchief. 'Ah, here it is.' She began to dab at the back of her glove. 'Such a pity these gloves are marked,' she said calmly, concentrating on her task. She was determined to goad him into a display of fury. As long as he was in control, she would never get away from him.

He did not rise to the bait. He simply cocked his head on one side, watching her. 'Very good, Angel,' he said again. 'Unfortunately for you, I am too old a campaigner to be taken in by such a tactic.'

The tone of his voice made her look up. He sounded like Max. He sounded like the man she had longed to

'Angel, there is no need for this hostility. I am not your enemy, as you seem to believe. Marriage between us need not be so bad, surely?'

She swallowed hard. 'Marriage between us is unnecessary,' she retorted crisply. 'No one will know I have been alone with you. Unless you, or your servants, betray me.' She flung him a challenging look. 'My London household believes I am on my way to Rosevale Abbey; my household there will think nothing of my having been delayed a day or two upon the road. And you yourself were at pains to conceal my abduction from my servants at the Castle Inn. I shall simply return there and then continue my journey. My reputation will not suffer.' She rose from her chair and walked towards the door. 'Now, sir, if you please—'

He did not move. 'And if you *are* breeding…what then?' he said softly.

Angel closed her eyes. She did not want to think about

that. She did not understand her body at all. She had been so sure… But she knew precious little about childbearing. She accepted Max's word without question. So she had to admit that she must have been wrong about the signs. Yesterday, she had not been pregnant. And since it had been so very difficult for her to conceive, even when she was married, surely she could not be at risk today, after only a single night in Max's arms?

'Angel?' He tried to draw her towards him.

'Release me, sir,' she hissed, attempting to shake him off. 'I will not marry you. I hate you.'

'Do you? I think not.' He stepped towards her and took her into his arms, pulling her close before she had time to resist. And then he began to kiss her.

Angel knew she should fight him, even though he was so much stronger than she. She wanted to try. But the touch of his lips brought back memories of bliss that melted her bones. Last night, she had waited so long to feel his mouth on hers. This morning, nothing had changed. She could not hold out against his touch. It took every ounce of her strength not to kiss him back, and even there, she was weakening by the second.

He raised his head and looked into her face. His dark eyes were smiling down at her. Somewhere, deep in her soul, she had recognised those Rosevale eyes, even behind his mask. She had seen them in her dreams.

'Hate cannot feel like this,' he said softly and kissed her again.

She groaned. She could not help it. She was lost. Instead of pulling away, she leaned into him and returned his kiss in full measure.

It was Max who broke it, putting her from him. He shook his head and ran his fingers through his hair. 'No, you do not hate me,' he said huskily, 'nor I you. And marriage is the only solution. Give me your word on it, Angel.'

She could not look at him. She raised her hand to her lips as if to wipe away the taste of him, but the gesture was never completed. She sighed deeply. 'I will marry you, sir, if I am carrying your child. Not otherwise. On those terms—and on those terms only—I give you my word.'

'Angel—'

'And in the meantime, I shall return to Rosevale Abbey as if nothing untoward had happened.' She was regaining her self-control at last. 'I take it I may trust to your honour not to betray me?'

'You are being foolhardy, Angel. You—'

'No, I am following the only logical course. Now, if you would be so good as to give orders for the carriage, I will trouble you no longer.'

'I do not accept your terms. You will not leave here until I have your word—'

Angel glowered at him. 'I have given you my promise. I shall not go further. What, would you hold me prisoner here? Or drag me to the altar against my will? So much for your vaunted honour, Cousin Frederick! You have none!'

He paled at her scathing words. 'Enough, madam. There is nothing more to be said.' He wrenched the door open and stood aside to let her pass. 'I accept your word as given. I shall wait to hear from you.'

Angel was beginning to feel unwell again. It must be the rocking of the carriage. And she had the headache from answering all Benton's questions about where she had been and how she had come to encounter a friend so early in the day. The story Max had concocted was highly improbable, but Angel had had to continue with it. She had no choice in the matter.

Except to marry him.

She could not marry a man who had used and humiliated her. It would be like John Frederick, all over again! She would not put herself in the power of such a man!

Her conscience rebelled. She was being unfair. He was nothing like John Frederick.

Angel's mind was suddenly filled with images—not images that she had seen, for it had been dark, but images that she had felt in her soul. She knew how it felt to be touched, and caressed, and cherished. He *had* treated her with honour. Nothing had happened that she had not willed.

She put her hand to her aching head. She could not afford to remember such things. He was her enemy. She must banish him from her mind.

'Are you unwell, m'lady?'

Angel shook her head at the abigail. 'I have the headache a little, that is all.'

Benton glanced out of the window. 'We shall be at the Abbey in fifteen minutes, m'lady. I shall make you a tisane and then you can—'

The cramps were so strong that Angel cried out and bent double.

'M'lady?'

Angel put her hands to her belly against the well-remembered pain. 'Oh, heavens! Why now?'

Benton threw her a sympathetic look and let down the glass. 'I'll tell John Coachman to whip 'em up, shall I, m'lady?'

Angel nodded, gritting her teeth against the pain.

The abigail shouted her instruction and then set about easing her mistress's distress. 'Your courses always arrive at the worst possible time, do they not, m'lady?' she said, offering a handkerchief soaked in lavender water. 'But we'll have you tucked between the sheets in a trice. If only you had not stopped with your friend on the road… You would have been home long since.'

If only… Angel closed her eyes. She could see Max so clearly that he might have been before her. How quickly he had been proved right. She was not increasing after all.

Marriage between them was now out of the question.

Angel closed the drawing room door and came to join the old lady on the sofa. Lady Charlotte had been unusually kind and patient since her return from London. Normally, she fussed a great deal if Angel was in the least indisposed.

It suddenly occurred to Angel to wonder why her aunt had returned at all. Had she been commissioned to plead Pierre's case yet again? She refused to listen to any doubts on the subject of Pierre's claim. And she would never hear a word in his dispraise. Angel decided it was time to discover exactly what lay behind her aunt's staunch support of a man who might be an adventurer. 'Did you see Pierre again before you left London?'

Lady Charlotte coloured. 'I… Yes, he…he did call. The day before I left.'

'Has he any news?' Angel refused to mention Julie's name, even when Pierre was not present.

'Nothing to the point, no. The talk in London is of nothing but the Duke. They say there will be a battle this time. The French usurper has raised a huge army.'

'The Duke has never yet lost a battle, Aunt. I am sure there is no need for concern. What does Pierre say about it?'

'He is concerned for his sister, of course. And he is

impatient for the conflict to be over, so that his case may be proved.'

'You seem very sure, Aunt.'

'Of course, I am! Why, there can be no doubt of his claim. He—' She stopped suddenly and bit her lip.

'Aunt Charlotte, you know perfectly well that there is every reason to doubt his claim. He has produced no proof at all, other than his likeness to Uncle Julian's wife.'

The old lady was twisting her hands in her lap.

Angel took hold of them and forced them to be still. 'Aunt Charlotte, you are concealing something from me. Why are you so certain that Pierre is the heir?' She pressed the old lady's fingers meaningfully.

'Oh, dear.' Lady Charlotte was staring at her skirts. She was now bright red. 'He showed…he brought me proof, Angel. There can be no doubt that he is Julian's legitimate heir.'

'Why did you not show it to me?'

'I…I could not. It mentions…other things.'

'Other things?'

'Things that you do not need to know, Angel. I promise you, there is no doubt. You will trust my word, surely?' Lady Charlotte looked up. There was a spark of challenge in her eye.

A few months ago, Angel would not have dreamt of doubting her aunt. But she had been deceived by Pierre. And then by Frederick…Max. She would trust nothing but the evidence of her own eyes from now on. 'I am very sorry to distress you, dear Aunt, but this matter is too important. As head of the family, I am afraid I must insist on seeing these proofs. Where are they now? Does Pierre have them?'

'I have them,' Lady Charlotte said in a tiny voice.

Angel took a deep breath and dropped a kiss on the old

lady's wrinkled cheek. 'I think I shall ring for some tea. That will revive us both, will it not?'

Lady Charlotte looked up, startled.

'And while we are waiting for the tray, I will go and fetch your box.' She held out her hand imperiously. 'The key, Aunt, if you please.'

'And so I am summoned to Rosevale Abbey.'

'Without any explanation?'

Max strode across to the window and stared out. He knew perfectly well why he was summoned. The Baroness must know the truth of her condition by now. At least she had the courage to tell him to his face. She— Angel... Yes, Angel had courage. And more.

He shrugged his shoulders. 'Her letter gave no reason for her summons, Louisa,' he said carefully. He had trusted Louisa with so many of his secrets, but this one was... different. He could not divulge it to anyone, even the woman who had shared his bed for so long.

'Will you go?'

'Yes.'

Louisa said nothing.

Max was not surprised. Louisa never pried. She had not even asked why Max now visited her only as a friend. She deserved better than this from him. 'If only Ross had returned,' he said suddenly, and began to pace. 'It has been too long. Even he—'

'You are anxious about Ross because you have decided to join the Duke,' she said with a sad smile. 'I am right, am I not? You dare not leave until you know Ross is safe.'

'We are in the devil of a coil, Louisa, and I can do nothing until it is resolved. I have...responsibilities. I wish I did not. The Duke is in desperate need of veterans to join the colours—but I cannot go. Battle may be joined any day now and— Dammit, Louisa, I feel as if I am being slowly strangled by all this!'

She poured a glass of wine and brought it to him. 'You will wear out the carpet, my dear. Will you not sit down?'

He grimaced.

'Max, I can see how troubled you are. Will you permit me to advise you?'

He paused and then nodded.

'You are concerned for Ross's safety. And you cannot shirk the responsibilities of your position as Earl of Penrose.' When he nodded again, she continued, 'You need have no fears for Ross. I am convinced of it. As to the rest… You have told me, many and many a time, that you could have wished the title to Hades, that it has brought you nothing but trouble. If you chose to relinquish it— even to that Frenchman—it would be no dishonour. Truly, it would not.'

Max tossed off the wine. He could not be sure of anything at present. And he had responsibilities beyond the Earldom. Lifelong responsibilities, perhaps.

'I would advise you to make no decisions in haste. Go to see your Baroness. Listen to what she has to say. And then decide what you will do. Bonaparte has not left Paris. He needs time yet to marshal his forces to meet the Duke. You will still have a choice, Max.'

'How wise you are, my dear. And how restrained in offering your counsel to an angry bear. Thank you.' He kissed her swiftly on the cheek and made for the door. 'I shall do as you suggest. And when I return…I promise I will tell you of my decision, whatever it may be. Goodbye, my dear.'

The door closed behind him. Louisa stood in the middle

of the room, staring at the sudden emptiness around her. Finally, she sat down and put her head in her hands. He was gone. Whatever happened now, she knew that he was lost to her.

Chapter Seventeen

It was frustrating to be travelling in a closed carriage. Max would much have preferred to ride, or at least to drive himself. But Sergeant Ramsey was adamant that only a proper carriage was fitting for an Earl.

Max grinned to himself. Yes, he had given in to Ramsey's stiff-necked posturing, though the driving rain might possibly have had something to do with it, too. For his pains, Ramsey was sitting on the box, getting thoroughly wet. It seemed a fitting punishment.

The carriage turned into the posting inn for the last change. Max lounged back in his seat, leaving Ramsey and the groom to see to everything. Not long now. They would soon be arriving at Rosevale Abbey. And he would see her again.

Max swore aloud as his body began to heat. What was it about that woman? He had only to think of her and he began to lose control. And if he allowed his mind to dwell on her beauty, and on the way she had responded to him… He cursed again and pulled himself upright. This would not do! Good grief, he was no longer a callow youth! Why was he reacting as if he were?

Because Angel was different from any other woman he

had known. Logic told him, rather against his will, that he had been reacting oddly to her from their very first meeting. He had always been able to manage his temper in the presence of ladies. But not with Angel. With Angel, he flew into a rage every single time.

And so did she.

He forced himself to think slowly and clearly. She was a Rosevale, too. In terms of shortness of temper, they were much alike. Equally cursed. Did it follow that she was as strangely affected by his presence as he was by hers?

Was she?

He refused to pursue that avenue. He must think, instead, of what was likely to happen once he reached the Abbey. She had summoned him to tell him that she was carrying his child. Or that she was not. The latter was much more likely, all things considered. It had been only a few weeks since they had spent the night together. She could not possibly be sure that she was breeding. Not so soon. But she could certainly be sure that she was not.

Max found he was strangely disappointed. Madness! Did he want to be shackled for life to a harpy with a temper that went up like a rocket, without the least provocation? No man in his right mind would wish for such a wife. Besides, she hated him. She had said so, in no uncertain terms. She had agreed to marry him only in order to give her child a name. That was all.

He closed his eyes. The carriage was moving off again. The rain was drumming on the roof. Poor old Ramsey! He would be soaked. He would have to be taken to the Abbey kitchens to dry out. No doubt he would be given a hot meal there, too. If there was time, of course.

It might well be a very short interview. It was bound to be private, with no witnesses, so he would have an opportunity to—to what? What did he want to say to her, to do?

He refused to contemplate what he wanted to do. That was very intimate, very protracted, and not at all fit for a noble lady's drawing room. But he must know what he was going to say.

If she said there was no child… He felt a sinking in his stomach. It had to be sympathy for her. It could be nothing else. She longed for a child, and she had suffered so much to conceive one. Her reputation might be saved, but at the price of yet another proof of her failure as a woman. He must be understanding. He must *not* mention the fearful word 'barren'. He would be kind, and polite, and matter of fact. He would wish her good fortune. And then he would leave. Without touching her. That was the most important thing of all.

He forced himself back to the coming confrontation. If she told him she was breeding—unlikely, but just possible—he must assure her that their marriage could be celebrated forthwith and that he would be a much better husband than she feared. That they could learn together. That there was a spark between them which could be nurtured into a glowing fire, if they were both prepared to try. He could teach her about lovemaking, and about love— No. That was impossible. He knew nothing about love, nothing at all. And he certainly did not love Angel Rosevale. She was a termagant.

He repeated that to himself as he settled back into the corner. He might as well try to sleep. There was nothing else to be done on a journey as tedious as this. Besides, he might be setting off for the Continent soon. In the army, there would be precious little sleep to be had. And he, too, would be out in the rain with Ramsey. He smiled wryly at the memory of their shared discomforts. It always rained before the Duke's victories. He was famous for it. If it rained on Bonaparte, the British troops would take it as an omen. It might be needed, too. The Duke had never lost a battle, but he had never taken the field with such an ill-assorted bunch of raw recruits either. He needed every experienced man he could get. Including Max.

'The Earl of Penrose, my lady.'

At the sound of his name, Angel's heart lurched and began to race. A great wave of heat engulfed her.

He nodded to the butler and strode into the drawing room. Angel felt as if all the blood in her body was sinking to her feet as she rose to meet him. He looked…stern. Her pulse began to drum in her ears. She clasped her hands tightly together in an attempt to mask their trembling. She must not touch him…

'Good morning, Cousin,' she said, dropping him a tiny curtsy. 'It was good of you to come, especially in such appalling weather.' She found she could not even meet his eyes. His mere presence was too much for her senses. 'Will you not be seated? My aunt will join us in a moment.'

He straightened, surprised. Then his brow creased into a puzzled frown. 'Angel—'

She cut him short, with a gesture. 'I should prefer it if you did not use that name, sir. We are not on such terms that—'

'Are we not? I had thought that we were as close as it was possible to be, ma'am.'

She felt the flood of colour rising to her hairline. He had struck, unerringly, just where she was weakest. 'We were. To my…my regret. But that is in the past. There is no reason now—*no reason at all*—to resume such a relationship,' she said, laying stress on the words. She was regaining a measure of control. At last. She raised her head proudly and looked him in the eye. 'I should prefer to be on rather more formal terms in future, if you please.'

'I do not please,' he growled. 'But I will do as you ask.' He paused, assessing her. So that was to be the way of it. As far as he could tell, she was neither glad nor sorry that there was to be no child. His understanding was not required. 'Cousin,' he added coldly.

'Thank you.' She sat and motioned him to the chair opposite.

'Is there any point, ma'am? You have imparted your message. It hardly seems appropriate for us now to indulge in half an hour of small talk. You will clearly be delighted to have me out of your house. And I shall be more than happy to oblige you.' The words were as cutting as his tone was bitter. For some reason, he could not help himself.

'Oh!' She glanced round at the door, and then said quickly, in a low voice, 'The p...promise that I made you will not now be redeemed, it is true. But I asked you here for another reason. It is—' The door opened. 'Ah, here is my aunt,' she said loudly, rising from her seat.

Max bowed to the old lady. She seemed smaller than when he had last seen her.

'Aunt, you remember Cousin Frederick?'

Max noticed that she still pronounced the name with a degree of loathing, but he could sympathise now. He had been shocked to learn that Angel's brute of a husband was also called 'Frederick'. No wonder she could barely bring herself to say it. The name was a curse.

'I am well aware of who he is, Angel.' Lady Charlotte sounded coldly furious. 'I have never yet felt the need for an introduction, however.' She moved towards the fireplace and sat down on the sofa without so much as a nod in Max's direction. He might not have been in the room.

Angel looked embarrassed. This time she did not sit. 'I asked you for this meeting, Cousin, in order to discuss the question of the Earldom. I…we… It has come to my notice that proof does exist in support of my cousin Pierre's claim. There can no longer be any doubt, sir. Pierre is the rightful Earl of Penrose, and will become Marquis, too, of course. I wanted to tell you this, face to face, before the news became known.'

Max simply stared at her. It was the last thing he had expected.

'I must ask you, sir, to set about relinquishing the title to Pierre as soon as may be. I…I am sorry. It will be a distasteful business for you.'

Max was not to be so easily dismissed. 'If I am to be so rudely displaced, I think you must grant me sight of these proofs of yours. I do not doubt your word, of course, but…' He smiled coldly, letting the words hang in the air. The old lady was looking suddenly very uncomfortable.

'It is a letter, sir,' Angel said stoutly. 'From my uncle, Lord Julian Rosevale. In it, he commended his son to our care. It is beyond dispute.'

Max's smile broadened. 'I hesitate to mention such things, but are you sure that it is your uncle's hand? Such things can be forged, you know.'

Angel flushed bright red once more. Her eyes flashed with fury. The pulse in her throat was now beating so rapidly that Max was tempted to reach out a hand to calm it.

'There is no question of any such thing,' snapped Lady Charlotte from across the room. 'It is without doubt my brother's hand. What is more, he included mention of… private matters, matters known only to the two of us. No one else but Julian could possibly have written it.'

Max said nothing. He simply stood, waiting. He was not prepared to leave without sight of this vital letter.

Angel went across to where her aunt sat and put a consoling hand on her arm. 'He has the right, Aunt,' she said softly. 'I am sure you may trust his discretion.'

Lady Charlotte raised her head and turned to look stonily at Max.

Still, Max said nothing. He returned Lady Charlotte's stare and stretched out his hand.

'You, sir, are a—' The old lady did not finish the sentence. After a moment or two, she pulled a paper from her pocket and handed it to Angel.

'Thank you, my dear,' Angel whispered. Then she turned back to Max. 'Here is your proof. And I must ask you, on your honour, never to betray the other matters that the letter contains.'

Intrigued, Max took the letter and scanned it quickly. *'My dearest sister,'* it began, *'I write in haste. Amalie's father has already been taken, and I fear that they will soon come for me, and for Amalie, too. If you should receive this letter, Amalie and I will be dead. I ask you, as my last request, to give help and succour to my beloved child who comes to you with this letter. I ask it also in remembrance of Charles, who was my friend, and who was more than a friend to you. With my last breath, I swear to you that it was not I who betrayed your love. In memory of that love, I beg you, Charlotte, to take care of my child. Julian Rosevale.'*

Short, and very much to the point, Max decided. And the old lady had been trying to hide the fact that she had had a lover, someone named Charles. Why, it must have been nearly thirty years ago. No one would care about such an old scandal. What mattered was the rest of the letter, and there—

Max swore under his breath and threw the letter on to the low table nearest Lady Charlotte. 'Precisely how long have you known about this, madam?' he demanded.

'I—' Angel began.

'Pierre gave it to me on the day he arrived,' said the old lady flatly. 'I saw no need to disclose it to anyone else. My word—the word of a Rosevale—should have been enough, even for you.'

Max wanted to strangle her. She had had her blasted proof for months, since before Bonaparte's escape, and she had concealed it. His temper exploded. 'By God, madam,' he shouted, 'you have done your family and your country a grave disservice by your duplicity. Only this has held me here. And now I discover that it was for naught. God forgive you, for I shall not.'

He strode out of the room and down to the hallway, calling impatiently for his carriage. If the weather improved, they could be on their way to Brussels in forty-eight hours, perhaps less. Captain Max Rosevale might still be in time.

Angel was shocked to the core. She had seen Max angry, but never like this. And his furious outburst made no sense at all. What did it matter whether he was deprived of his title in February or in June?

Lady Charlotte retrieved the letter, folding it carefully before stowing it away in her pocket. 'Such language! Disgusting! But only to be expected from that branch of the family, I dare say.'

Angel was pacing the floor in renewed agitation. 'I do not understand,' she muttered, half to herself. 'What could he possibly mean by ''a disservice to your country''? What has that to do with Pierre's claim?'

'What matters now, my child, is that we give the good

news to Pierre as soon as possible. It is obvious that
Cousin Frederick will not try to maintain his claim any
longer. Pierre will soon be able to take his rightful place.'
She beamed at the prospect. 'I think I should return to
London, my dear, to be with him. He will need my sup-
port.'

Angel frowned, shaking her head. She cared not a fig
for Pierre. She had thought she was beginning to understand Max, but this…?

'Forgive me, Angel, but you *are* quite well now, are
you not? I will remain here if you need me, of course,
but—'

'You need have no fears on that score, Aunt. There is
nothing to keep you here at the Abbey.'

'Thank you, Angel. I shall start packing at once. Excuse
me, I must go upstairs. Now, where is that woman of
mine?' She started for the door.

Angel reached it first. 'I think it is high time that I took
charge of this matter of the inheritance, Aunt. There is no
knowing what Cousin Frederick may do if he finds Pierre
now.' She reached for the door handle. She knew exactly
what she had to do. 'We will both start back for London.
This very afternoon.'

With such a late start, there was no prospect of reaching
London before nightfall, but Angel insisted on the fastest
possible pace, none the less. Max had left in a towering
rage, and he had appeared to be talking nonsense. There
was no knowing what he might do when he was in such
a foul temper. What if Max sought out Pierre, challenged
him?

Angel closed her eyes against the terrifying picture of
Max lying dead on some soggy common. She might never

see him alive again, never hear the caressing tone of his voice—

Oh, dear God, she loved him! Why had she not seen it before? Why else did she think of nothing but him? She was in love with a man who hated her and who was gone to London to commit heaven knew what kind of crime. She must stop him!

She dropped her head into her hands. Oh, Max—

'Are you feeling unwell, Angel? I am not at all surprised, travelling at this furious pace. There is no need for it, surely?'

Shocked out of her brooding, Angel frowned at her aunt and then glanced at the sleeping abigail opposite. Benton would sleep through the trump of doom, but it was still unwise to discuss private business in her presence. Angel nodded towards the abigail and put a finger to her lips. 'I am well enough, Aunt. A little tired perhaps, that is all.'

'But we *will* stop soon?'

'We must continue as long as it is light, Aunt, if we wish to reach London in good time tomorrow. You did say you wished to see Pierre as soon as possible, did you not?'

'I… Oh, very well. Yes, I do wish to see Pierre. He will need my advice about how to go on, now that he—' She broke off in response to another warning frown. She looked decidedly mulish. After a slight pause, she asked airily, 'Were you planning to invite Pierre to move to Rosevale House now, my dear?'

Angel clenched her fists in an attempt to control her irritation. Aunt Charlotte never ceased to promote Pierre's cause, even when it was unwise to do so. Angel had absolutely no desire to invite Pierre to be a guest in her house. He was not…trustworthy. It seemed that he was indeed the rightful Earl of Penrose, but that did not make him a boon companion. 'I have not thought about it, Aunt,' she said in a quelling voice. 'Perhaps, when we are comfortably established in London once more…' She made a play of settling back in her seat. 'Benton seems to be able to sleep in spite of the swaying of the carriage. I think I shall endeavour to do the same.' She closed her eyes.

She did not sleep. She had not expected to. But at least Aunt Charlotte had been silenced. Angel could concentrate on her own thoughts, which did not extend to Aunt Charlotte's precious Pierre. At least… Angel experienced a sudden pang of guilt. She was being unfair. Her aunt had suffered at the loss of her younger brother. Indeed, the whole family had been devastated by the news of his execution. Though they had tried every possible avenue to save him, all had failed. And now his son had appeared. It must seem like a miracle to Aunt Charlotte. Especially when coupled with the news of her lover…

Angel would not have believed the tale if she had not heard it from her aunt's own lips. Prim, proper Aunt Charlotte, carrying on an illicit liaison with the Frenchman who carried the secret letters to and from her brother! But her secret had soon been betrayed; Angel's father had put a stop to the lovers' meetings. Aunt Charlotte had blamed Julian—no one else knew, she said—but Julian's deathbed letter swore it was not so. Pierre had apparently said the same, at his very first meeting with the old lady. He had learned from his servants that Augustus Rosevale had been spying on her. Augustus was the source of the betrayal. No wonder Aunt Charlotte had taken Pierre to her bosom at once. At a stroke, he had restored her faith in her younger brother and given her even more reason to nurse her hatred of all Max's family!

Max. The man Angel loved. The man who was about to become plain Mr Rosevale all over again. Would he meekly accept his change of status? Unlikely. There was nothing in the least meek about Max Rosevale. He was strong and decisive. He was remarkably stubborn. And when he was in a fit of temper, almost anything could happen.

Except with her. She was not afraid of his rages. They could be turned, oh, so easily, into passion. She remembered that fierce confrontation in the little breakfast parlour. Fury. And then passion. And then fury again. If only she could be alone with him. Once more. Just once. She would ensure that passion triumphed.

'Is that all clear?'

'Yes, m'lord.'

'You may cease m'lording me, Ramsey. It is plain Captain Rosevale from now on. No more of that high-flown nonsense, if you please.'

Sergeant Ramsey cleared his throat loudly.

Max ignored it. 'It is too late for me to visit my lawyer tonight. That will have to wait till tomorrow morning. But, for the rest, you had better make a start now. Get the horses away first, of course. We don't want to be cooling our heels on the dockside, waiting for them to arrive. I warn you that I shall want to leave London the moment my business is concluded, so don't fail me, Ramsey.'

'You can count on me, Cap'n.'

Max softened a little as he looked down at his old comrade. Max had been issuing orders for the best part of half an hour but Ramsey had not uttered the slightest protest. The man would probably have to work all night to ensure everything was prepared for their departure. He did not deserve to suffer under Max's temper.

'I know I am being unreasonable, Ramsey,' Max said, 'but there is no time for niceties. Bonaparte is mustering

a huge army. If we delay, we may be too late to join the
Duke.'

'You'll be going to Horse Guards first thing, sir?'

Max shook his head. 'There are too many interfering
idiots there. I'd never get away at all. No, I shall leave it
to my man of business to organise the purchase of my
commission. You and I will simply arrive in Brussels and
present ourselves for duty. Sir Thomas Picton has the Fifth
Division, I believe, so there should be no problem about
establishing our credentials. I should like to serve with him
again.'

'Old Tom Picton'll not refuse you, sir. He's too good a
general to turn away a seasoned campaigner.'

'Let us hope so. What I'm planning to do is irregular,
to say the least.'

Ramsey nodded.

'If they turn me down, I can always enlist.'

'Now that, begging your pardon, sir, is a load of nonsense. If you was to—'

'It won't come to that, I'm sure. Now, we'd best be off
about our business.'

'What if I need to find you tonight, sir? Will you be at
madame's?'

'I plan to call on *madame*, yes, but I shall not stay. You
can reach me at my club if need be. I shan't come back
to the house tonight.' He smiled. 'I know better than that.
You'll have a clear run, as usual.'

Ramsey smiled back. 'Very good, Cap'n.'

Max watched him go. Ramsey would organise everything, as he always had. The man was a marvel, provided
he was left alone to get on with things. Max had learned
long ago to give Ramsey his head at such times. Even so,
Max's timetable was next to impossible. There was only

the remotest chance of being out of London before noon next day.

It was good to be in action again, Max decided. He began to make a mental list of his own tasks. First, he must formally relinquish the Earldom, though he had not the slightest idea how that was to be done. Then, in addition to his commission and funds for his own needs, he must make financial provision for Louisa and for his servants. He must leave a letter of explanation for Ross. And he must make his will. There would be little enough to leave now, but all of it would go to Ross. There was no one else.

And now he must call on Louisa. That he did not relish. What was he to tell her? Not the whole truth, certainly. He would say that he was no longer the Earl of Penrose, of course, but he must try to avoid discussion of the Baroness. Louisa knew Max much too well. If he spoke of Angel now, Louisa might guess something of the truth. Max did not want that, for Louisa's sake as well as his own. He would do best to keep his visit short, and he would tell her he was leaving first thing in the morning. That was a lie, the first he had ever told her, but it was a necessary one. If she believed his plans were already settled, she would not be tempted to persuade him to change his mind.

No one could do that, not even Louisa.

Chapter Eighteen

With a sigh of relief, Angel allowed herself to be handed down from the carriage. If Angel was a little stiff, poor Aunt Charlotte must truly be suffering.

The old lady was much too proud to let any such weakness show. She mounted the steps to Rosevale House as if she had just returned from a quiet stroll. Her sharp tongue was not to be silenced, however. 'I hope you are now satisfied, Angel,' she said. 'We are back in London far earlier than normal, thanks to your insistence on setting off at daybreak. I declare, I was sure we should be overturned. Such a pace!'

'But we are safely arrived, Aunt,' Angel said soothingly. She felt more than a little guilty about having subjected her aunt to such a frightful journey.

The old lady snorted.

'And we still have part of the afternoon,' Angel continued. 'I shall send to Pierre at once, asking him to wait on us. You will be able to give him the news yourself.'

Lady Charlotte started for the stairs. 'I must bathe and change my dress before Pierre arrives. Such an important occasion requires us both to look our best. I shall wear my purple silk. And you, Angel?'

'I I have not decided, Aunt. But I promise not to disgrace the occasion.'

Lady Charlotte had only just disappeared to her bedchamber when the butler said quietly, 'Excuse me, but may I have a word with your ladyship?'

'What is it, Willett?'

'I have just been informed by the housekeeper that your ladyship had a visitor this morning, before I had arrived to take charge. She would not give her name, but she asked if you were expected in London soon. The housekeeper knew better than to disclose your ladyship's business to a stranger, of course. She said that Rosevale House was kept in constant readiness so that your ladyship could visit at a moment's notice.'

'Which is true, of course. I wonder who she was? Did she say she would call again, Willett?'

'Apparently so, m'lady.'

'I am not in the habit of receiving anonymous callers, but if she should call again, I wish to be informed immediately. And send a footman to Monsieur Pierre Rosevale's lodgings, if you please. He is to present my compliments and invite Monsieur Pierre to call on Lady Charlotte and myself at his earliest convenience.'

'May he say on what business, my lady?'

'No. But he may say that the matter is urgent.' Willett bowed and withdrew, without any visible sign of disappointment. Angel knew better. The butler was eager to know exactly what was going on. However, Angel had no intention of giving the servants any more food for gossip. They already knew that Max had stormed out of the Abbey. That was quite enough for now.

Max. He was the reason she was here. She must see him immediately, persuade him not to do anything rash. He might be in a rage still—and he had cause—but she would be able to calm him. She was sure of it. If she could just find a way of being alone with him, she had only to touch him… She needed to turn his fury into passion once more.

She hurried up to her chamber. She needed to bathe and change, but first she must send a note to Max, asking him to call on her. But how was it to be managed? He hated her. His first instinct would be to refuse. She flung off her bonnet and sat down at her writing table. Faced with the daunting blank paper, she found she could not write a blatant lie. Not to Max. After some thought, she settled for a version of the truth: that there were urgent matters relating to the transfer of the Earldom, matters that she must discuss with him before the day was out.

She quickly folded and sealed the note, and rose to pull the bell. She would send the message round to Max's house by hand. The footman would be instructed not to return to Berkeley Square until he had delivered the note to Max and received a reply. Angel would not breathe easily until she was sure that Max was safe. He must not challenge Pierre!

With the note safely despatched, Angel rang for hot water. She needed to change her dress, and today she must choose with care. She desperately wanted Max to admire her, as he had done when they were alone together. She must be sure she was looking her best.

Oh, heavens! Pierre would arrive soon. He certainly would not hesitate to answer Angel's summons. What if the rivals arrived together?

'Everything is ready, Cap'n. Just as you ordered. And the groom started for Harwich last night. The horses will be waiting there when we arrive.'

'If we ever do,' Max said bitterly. 'You have done sterling service, as usual, Ramsey. It is a pity that my lawyer was not fashioned from the same clay as you. Decisions are difficult, and quick decisions impossible, it seems. I fear there is now precious little chance of our leaving today. The papers will not be ready for my signature before this evening and, in the matter of the Earldom, perhaps not even then.' He began to pace.

'Begging your pardon, sir, but where was you planning to rack up for the night? Being as how I've shut up the house now.'

'What? Oh, that's of no moment, Ramsey. Let the house remain as it is. I can easily shift to find a bed. No, there are much more important things for you to do this afternoon. I had intended to purchase supplies in Ostend, but we might as well do it in London, since we are stranded here. It will save time once we're across the Channel.' Max dug into his pocket. 'I have prepared a list. Here.'

Ramsey ran his eye down the paper and nodded. 'I'll get this packed up, all right and tight, by the end of the day, Cap'n, and have it sent down to Harwich. Was you wanting me to hire a post-chaise?'

'I would, but I have no idea how soon we shall be able to leave. I should know more once I've seen the lawyers again. Report to me here at the club this evening, Ramsey. With luck, we may be able to start at first light. I take it you are ready to move as soon as I give the word?'

'Yes, sir. Apart from this list, o' course.'

'Excellent. At least there is one man in my service who may be relied upon. Thank you, Ramsey.' Max took some coins from his pocket. 'Here. Make sure you get yourself a good dinner and a decent bed. It may be the last you have for quite a while.'

'Aye, sir.' He grinned. 'It'll be just like the old times, won't it?'

'Yes, Ramsey. Exactly like.'

* * *

Angel was truly worried. It was now many hours since she had sent for Pierre, but he had not arrived. Messages had been left at all his usual haunts. Apparently, no one had seen him.

Worse, her note to Max had not been delivered at all. The footman had returned to report that Max's house was shut up. It appeared that he had left London. Would she ever see him again?

As the hours passed without news, Angel had begun to fear the worst. Perhaps there had been a duel after all? Perhaps Max was lying dead somewhere, and Pierre had fled? Or perhaps Max himself—? No. It was nonsense. Such things happened only in Gothic novels. Except that—

The door opened smoothly. 'Begging your ladyship's pardon…'

'Yes, Willett?' said Angel sharply. She was not in the mood to deal with petty domestic matters. Not now. It was almost time to retire for the night.

'There is a…visitor downstairs, asking to see your ladyship.'

'At this hour?'

'Your ladyship said you wished to be informed if she called again.'

'Oh. That visitor. Yes, of course. Did she give a name?'

'She will not give her name, m'lady, but…she says her business concerns the Earl.'

'Lord Penrose?'

'Er…she indicated that she wished to speak to you about the…er…the previous Earl…er…Mr Frederick Rosevale.'

'Oh. But—' Angel hesitated. So Willett knew exactly what had happened! Listening at doors, no doubt. But she really did not want him to guess that she was more than mildly concerned about Max. 'What have you done with this visitor, Willett?'

'She is waiting in your ladyship's bookroom.'

'Very well. Tell her that I shall join her directly.' Angel stepped up to the glass to check her appearance. She was deathly pale. Well, that could not be helped. She must see the woman, in case—

But who on earth was this mysterious woman? And what information did she have about Max? Angel's stomach turned over at the mere thought of him. It seemed an eternity since she had seen him, and even longer since she had felt his touch. She stopped, closing her eyes, remembering how his very nearness could make her skin tingle… Every night she dreamed of being with him. And every morning she awoke to find herself alone. It was torture to have a mind so full of him and yet to know that he was now lost to her.

She tried to force such indelicate thoughts to the back of her mind and made her way down to the bookroom, where Willett was waiting to open the door for her.

Angel's visitor was most certainly not a servant. She was a very striking woman, with lustrous black hair and huge brown eyes. She was modestly and attractively dressed, but not quite in the first stare of fashion.

She curtsied elegantly when Angel appeared. 'Lady Rosevale.' She spoke in a low, cultured voice. 'It is very good of you to receive me. Especially so late.'

'I will admit that I was intrigued by your message, Mrs…?'

'My name is of no moment, my lady.'

Angel bridled. 'I am not in the habit of dealing with unknowns.'

The dark lady smiled. She was very beautiful indeed when she smiled. And yet, there was a hint of sadness in her eyes that Angel had not at first noticed. 'I think you will wish to know, Lady Rosevale, that your cousin—he who was lately called the Earl of Penrose—has decided to return to the colours. He left for Brussels this morning.'

So that was where Max had gone! He had left without a word. No doubt this woman knew all about his departure, even though Angel did not. Had the woman come for some kind of revenge? If so, she would get short shrift. 'Why should that concern me, pray?' Angel said haughtily.

'It is not for me to say whether you should be concerned, my lady. I came to tell you only that Max is determined to be in the thick of the fighting. That he is in a mood to take any risks, however foolhardy. He has settled all his affairs in England. I think—no, I am almost sure that he does not expect to return.'

'Dear God,' breathed Angel, turning away to hide her consternation. 'What makes you think—? How do you come to know this?'

The dark lady paused. Then she said, 'I have known Max for a long time. And I have come to…understand him a little. He does not care a fig about the loss of his title, but he has lost something else, something infinitely more precious to him. I think he feels that his duty to his country…his honour…are all that remain to him.'

This woman must be Max's mistress! The realisation crowded out all other thought. Angel whirled round to inspect the woman more closely. She was beautiful. Refined. And so very composed. Max confided in her. Did he love her, too? Angel felt a sudden fierce stab of jealousy. This woman had known Max for a long time, years perhaps, whereas she, Angel, knew so little of him. If only—

The visitor was speaking urgently now. 'My lady, Max left London hours ago. If the weather is fair, he may take ship as early as tomorrow. No one can change his mind about rejoining the colours, I am sure, but if you would see him, talk to him, you might be able to ensure that he goes with an easy mind, and that he has some reason for coming back to us. To you.' She turned for the door.

'Will you not remain for a space, ma'am? I should like to ask—'

The dark lady shook her head. 'There is nothing more I can tell you. I must go now. No one must know that I have been here. It is not fitting.'

Angel was completely bewildered, but her good manners were automatic. 'I thank you for the warning, ma'am. I can understand that it has been difficult for you to come here. Painful, perhaps. I assure you that I am grateful. I shall try to use your information wisely.'

'That is all I could possibly ask. Thank you, my lady.' She paused in the act of opening the door. 'God bless you,' she said quietly, and was gone.

Angel sat down very suddenly and stared at the wall. Max had gone back to the army. If the visitor was to be believed, he was in a reckless mood. The loss of the Earldom could not have made him so, surely? It was not credible. Max was quick-tempered, certainly, but he was honourable, too. He would never behave in such a childish fashion.

No, it was not a question of the lost title. What had the mysterious lady said? Something about giving him a reason to come back. And Angel could provide it? Truly?

Angel's face was suddenly very hot. Her limbs felt weak. She tried to stand up, but her legs would not support her. Please God, do not let her give way to weakness now! She was about to lose the man she loved. She must go after him! There was no time to be lost. If she set off now, this very minute, she might reach Dover before he sailed.

She pushed herself to her feet at last and pulled the bell

to order her carriage. It was dark outside, and the rain was falling. Progress would be very slow, but she could not bear to wait till first light. She must go now. And she must pray for unfavourable winds at Dover.

'Penrose!'

Max ignored the call. He hated that name now, but London did not yet know it was no longer his to use. He would sign the necessary papers later this morning, and then the whole world would learn of it. He walked on, looking about for a hackney to take him to the City.

'I say! Penrose!' The voice was most insistent.

Max turned. He found himself confronted by Addley, a man whom he knew only slightly. They were members of the same club.

'Have you heard the news?' Addley sounded excited.

'No. What news?'

'There's been a battle. It's over. The Duke's been routed.'

'I don't believe it,' Max said immediately.

'Had it from Wellesley-Pole and he should know. Wellington's brother, don't you know.'

'I still don't believe it,' Max said again.

'Terrible defeat, apparently. Terrible. Carnage. Knew it would happen, of course, with a makeshift army like that. You were one of those who thought old Nosey was invincible, weren't you? Well, now you'll have to admit that—'

'Good day to you, Addley.' Max spun on his heel and hurried away before he succumbed to the temptation to plant the man a facer. Addley was a fool of the first order. He must have it wrong. There were plenty of those in London who would delight in traducing Wellington.

But William Wellesley-Pole was not one of them. He

was Wellington's older brother. Perhaps…perhaps it was true.

Max felt almost sick at the thought. It was not so much that he had failed in his duty to his country. Max would never forgive himself for that, but he knew that one single man could not change the course of a battle. Not unless that man was Wellington.

It was the thought of carnage. Max had seen carnage in the Peninsula. He had seen bloated bodies lying in fly-blown heaps. He had buried his friends. Carnage.

If it were true…

Max ran his fingers through his hair and swore fluently, ignoring the shocked reactions of the passers-by. What was he to do now? He should have been there, standing shoulder to shoulder with his comrades. He felt empty. He was a soldier without a battle to fight.

'Sir?' It was Ramsey, come to meet him as arranged. 'Sir, have you heard?'

Max forced himself to behave like a soldier, though the face he turned on Ramsey was bleak. 'Aye, Ramsey. I have heard. But I still don't believe it.'

'Sir?' Ramsey was clearly puzzled.

'According to Addley, Wellington has been routed.'

'It's a lie!' Ramsey exclaimed. 'It must be!'

'Aye, and so I thought. The source is good though—the Duke's own brother.'

'Still don't believe a word of it. Nor should you, sir. The Duke's never yet lost a battle.'

Max grimaced. 'I hope to God you are right, Ramsey.'

Ramsey nodded firmly. 'No doubt you'll discover that I am, sir. And in the meantime—'

'In the meantime?'

'The Baroness has been trying to find you, sir. Something desperate urgent, it seems. Been sending out messengers since yesterday.'

'What is the message? Do you know?'

'Not exactly, sir. Only that you was sought.'

Max let out a long breath. 'Then I had better pay a call on my noble cousin, I suppose. For the moment, at least, I have nothing better to do,' he added bitterly. With that, he started off in the direction of Berkeley Square, but when he reached the corner, he slowed and called over his shoulder, 'Meet me at the club in an hour, Ramsey.' Then he strode on without waiting for a response.

Angel. Angel wanted to see him. Urgently. Why? What could she possibly want with him now? They had parted on the worst possible terms.

He quickened his pace. There was no point in indulging in fruitless speculation. He would be at Rosevale House in a matter of minutes. And then he would find out exactly what she wanted.

He would not tell her about the rumours. He could not. She would be horrified to learn that the Duke had been defeated. He could not be the one to bring her such tidings. He would try to appear quite his normal self.

A bizarre thought struck him and he laughed rather unsteadily. How could he be his normal self on a day like today? His normal self was wont to rage at the poor woman. Today was a day for mourning, not for raging.

The front door opened even as he reached for the knocker. 'My lord! Sir!' The butler had heard the news, it appeared, but was still confused as to the correct mode of address.

'I am no longer Lord Penrose, Willett,' Max said calmly, stepping into the hall and taking off his hat. 'I understand that Lady Rosevale wishes to see me?'

'Yes, my lord. I mean, no, my lord. Or rather—' The man was twisting Max's hat in his hands.

'What the devil is the matter with you, Willett?' Max asked testily. 'And will you kindly stop trying to ruin my hat?'

The butler started and put the hat down abruptly. He opened his mouth, but no words came out.

Max became conscious of a commotion on the upper landing. Several voices, arguing heatedly. 'What is going on here, Willett? Tell me! Now!'

The butler's eyes were bulging, but Max's sharp order had had an effect. Willett managed to speak at last. 'Her ladyship, sir. She— Late last night, sir. She's gone!'

Chapter Nineteen

'Now, Lady Charlotte, perhaps you will have the goodness to explain what has happened.' Max did not attempt to humour the old lady. She had made no secret of the fact that she hated Max and all his family. She had agreed to speak to him now, but only because Angel had disappeared.

'I hardly know myself,' she said, in a slightly tremulous voice. 'I had retired for the night when the woman came.'

'What woman?'

Lady Charlotte glared at him, but must have decided to ignore his rudeness, for she said, 'She gave no name, I understand. It was very late when she arrived the second time. She was here for twenty minutes, perhaps less. After she left, Angel ordered the carriage and set off for Dover.'

'Dover? In the middle of the night? In the pouring rain?'

Lady Charlotte nodded.

'Did she tell you why she was going to Dover?'

'She told me nothing at all. I knew nothing until this morning. She left instructions that I was not to be disturbed.'

'Has she gone alone?'

Lady Charlotte bridled. 'My niece does understand the

dictates of propriety, sir. She would never undertake such a journey alone. She has her abigail with her, besides her coachman and two grooms.'

Max relaxed a fraction. Whatever Angel was doing, she should be in no danger with so many servants to protect her. But Dover? Why Dover? And why set out in the middle of the night, in the pouring rain? It was madness. 'The woman who called. What was she like? Old? Young? Not a lady, I collect?'

'No, not a lady. Ring for Willett. He let the woman in. He will be able to describe her to you.'

Max pulled the bell and stationed himself in front of the fire. 'I assume you have sent for the new Lord Penrose to assist you?'

Lady Charlotte coloured. 'He is nowhere to be found. I fancy—'

The door opened to admit the butler. The old servant now seemed to be a little more composed, for which Max was thankful. It might be possible to extract some useful information from him.

'You admitted a woman who asked to see your mistress but who gave no name. Describe her to me, Willett.'

'Er…yes, m'lord. She had called earlier in the day, before we arrived here. The housekeeper turned her away.'

'What did she *look* like, Willett?' Max said, in exasperation.

'Oh. Yes, sir.' The butler narrowed his eyes, remembering. 'She was quite young, of medium height for a lady, with very dark hair and large dark eyes. Her speech was educated. She was dressed in a dove grey gown—not silk, I think—and a matching bonnet with a pleated lining. Pink, it was. I noticed it particularly, because it became her so well.' He smiled to himself. 'She was a remarkably fine-looking young woman.'

Yes, of course she was! Max muttered a curse. Louisa! It could have been no other. What possible reason could Louisa have for calling on Angel? He would make it his business to find out and—

'Will you go after her?' Lady Charlotte was looking Max in the eye for the first time in his life. She was clearly anxious and, without Pierre, she could call on no one but Max. 'I fear that she may intend to set sail for the Continent.'

'Nonsense,' Max snapped. 'Why on earth should she do that?'

'I have no idea. But why else does one travel to Dover?'

Max had no answer to that. And in any case, he needed to focus on action. His choices were clear. He could seek out Louisa, in order to discover why Angel had gone to Dover. Or he could set off in pursuit of Angel, in hopes of arriving in Dover in time to prevent her from carrying out whatever rash plan she had concocted. There was not time to do both. Angel had too much of a head start on him. Even now, he might well come too late.

His decision was quickly made. 'Willett, send a man to order me a post-chaise and four. For Dover. Quickly now! I must be off as soon as may be.'

'Thank you,' breathed Lady Charlotte.

Max shook his head. 'I doubt that your niece will thank me, ma'am, for interfering with her plans. Whatever they may be.'

The journey seemed interminable, even though the overnight rain had not resumed. Max found himself wondering why he had ever set out at all. It was none of his affair that Angel had run off to Dover. Perhaps she had a lover there?

That thought was instantly dismissed. Angel had had

only one lover. Himself. He pushed that memory to the back of his mind. It was much too vivid for his comfort. Whatever Angel's motive for flight, it was not a lover. It must be something else. Pierre, perhaps? Yes, that was possible. Pierre was missing, too. While she had left Berkeley Square with only her servants, it would have been possible for her to collect Pierre somewhere en route. It seemed entirely plausible.

But it did not explain Louisa's visit. Nothing explained that.

Max glanced around at the passing scenery. They would stop at Sittingbourne soon, for a change of horses. He would take the opportunity to stretch this legs. Did he dare delay for a bite to eat? He had swallowed nothing save a cup of coffee all day. Max smiled wryly. He had intended to breakfast after his visit to the lawyer's office. That worthy would be far from pleased to find that all his hasty researches were being ignored. However, the man would be paid. And his work on the transfer of the Earldom would be needed in due course. Nothing had changed there. Except the degree of urgency.

By the time the chaise pulled in to the Red Lion Inn, Max had decided to call for something to eat. He would be on the road for some hours yet, and he could not afford to continue indefinitely without food. Besides, there might be no need at all for his journey. If Angel were merely conveying Pierre to Dover…

Max climbed down while the postilions were busy unharnessing the spent team. He beckoned to one of the ostlers. 'Have you seen a private carriage today, carrying a lady with silver-blonde hair?' When the ostler looked blankly at him, Max pulled out a half-crown and held it up to the light. The man's eyes grew round. 'A private carriage,' Max said again, and proceeded to describe Angel's carriage in minute detail. Ostlers tended to pay much more attention to horses and carriages than to their passengers.

The ostler shook his head. 'No, sir, we ain't had a carriage like that at the Red Lion. Not today. I'd 'ave remembered.' He held out his hand and Max dropped the coin into it.

With a sigh, Max made his way into the inn. The landlord was a large, rather red-faced man. His wife, he said, would be delighted to prepare some victuals for the gentleman. Perhaps a little game pie and new-baked bread, since the gentleman was not able to wait for a meal to be cooked fresh? And a tankard of home-brewed ale?

Max permitted himself precisely twenty minutes for the meal, excellent though it was. He found he could not stop thinking about Angel. The act of describing her to the ostler had made it impossible to banish her image from his mind. She was there. She would always be there. She seemed to be haunting him.

He threw some money on to the table and made his way out to the inn yard. The new team was ready. The postilions were lounging against the chaise, but snapped to attention as soon as he appeared. 'Right, let's see what kind of time you can make for this next stage,' Max said, patting his pocket. The post-boys nodded eagerly. The prospect of a handsome tip was always good for speed.

'Begging y'r pardon, sir.' It was the ostler.

'What is it now, my man?' Max was impatient to be on his way. He had tarried too long already.

'That carriage, sir.'

'What about it?'

'I seen it, sir.'

Max exploded. 'What do you mean, you've seen it? You told me, not half an hour ago, that you had not.'

The ostler recoiled a little from Max's fury. 'I...I...' he stammered.

'Out with it, man. When did you see it?'

''Bout ten minutes after you arrived, sir.'

'Where?'

The main pointed. 'There. Passing on the high road. Team looked pretty fresh.'

Max groaned. Somehow, he must have overtaken her on the road. He gave the ostler two more half-crowns and flung open the chaise door. 'Right, you two. I want you to overtake that carriage. You know what it looks like, so let's see what you can do. Well before Canterbury, if you please.'

'No, sir. No.'

'What now, ostler?' If the man was hoping for more money, he would be disappointed.

'Yon carriage weren't bound for Canterbury, sir. It was going back to London.'

'What?'

The ostler repeated what he had just said. The carriage was not bound for Dover, but for London. He was sure of that. And he was equally sure that it was the very carriage the gentleman had described.

Max drove his fingers through his hair. What the devil was the woman doing? Whatever it was, he had better go after her. He tipped the ostler generously and then gave the grinning postilions their new instructions. 'If you want to see these yellow boys,' he said sharply, producing a couple of guineas from his pocket, 'you would do well to stop grinning and make shift to overtake that carriage.'

Angel was in flat despair. She had been berating herself for hours. How could she have been so stupid? She knew that no one travelled to Ostend from Dover. She did know. Of course she knew.

She glanced across at Benton. The abigail was awake, for once, and looking rather apprehensive. It was no wonder. After the first hour of the return journey, Angel had threatened the woman with dismissal if she uttered another word.

Angel wished she might be alone. Silence, though welcome, was not enough. With Benton watching her, Angel could not permit her despair to show. She wanted to weep—and to scream with frustration. So much wasted time! And how the men on the dockside had delighted in informing her that she should have been in Harwich. But she would not give up. Not now. She knew that the chances were slim, but she *would* go to Harwich. She must at least try to see Max before he sailed. She would never forgive herself if she did not try.

She glanced out of the window at the sound of the yard of tin. Some other carriage was trying to give her the go-by. Her team must be tiring. Her coachman would probably stop in Rochester for a change.

Suddenly her carriage began to slow. What on earth…? After a moment, it came to a standstill. Benton moaned, her eyes huge with fear. No doubt the abigail had visions of highwaymen up ahead. Preposterous! In broad daylight on the Dover road?

The carriage door was thrown open so violently that, for a second, Angel almost believed in highwaymen, too.

'Lady Rosevale!'

It was Max! No, that was impossible. She must have imagined it.

'Lady Rosevale, would you be so good as to ask your abigail to get down? I have urgent business to discuss with you, and this carriage has not room for three persons.'

Benton looked from the open door to her mistress and back again. Then she shrank further into her corner.

'I said get down, woman!' Max repeated sharply. 'You are not being abandoned. You may travel in my chaise.'

The abigail scrambled to obey. As soon as she had gone, Max sprang into the carriage and took the place opposite Angel.

She could not take her eyes from his face. She had thought she had lost him, and now he had appeared, as if from nowhere, like a knight in a romance. She had a thousand questions, but she wanted only to look.

'My Lady Angel,' Max began in a rather hard voice, 'I am at a loss to understand your behaviour. Perhaps you would be kind enough to explain what you are doing on the Dover road? You *have* been to Dover, I collect?'

'Yes.'

'But why?'

There was no possible answer but the truth. 'I know that you are duty bound to return to the colours, Max, and I promise that I am not trying to stop you. I just wanted... I could not bear to think that you would go into battle without knowing that—' He was staring at her. She could not go on. She looked away.

There was a long silence. Max broke it at last. 'Without knowing what, Angel?' he asked gently.

'That you have...friends who wish you well and who will pray for your safe return.'

'Friends?' He took her hand and pressed it. 'Or just one special friend?'

She wished he had not taken her hand. It was burning. She knew she ought to say something, but her whole being was focused on his touch. She could not speak.

Max raised her hand to his lips and kissed it, watching

Angel's face all the while. Then he turned her hand over and placed a lingering kiss on her palm.

Angel closed her eyes and sighed with pleasure. She could not help herself.

The carriage swayed as Max moved to sit beside her. He was still holding her hand. 'Angel,' he said seriously, 'did you go to Dover for me?'

She nodded.

He put his hands on either side of her face and forced her to look at him. 'You beautiful idiot. What made you think I would be sailing from Dover?'

'I didn't think at all,' she said huskily. 'I just set out. I was so afraid that you would be gone.'

'I am here now. And I no longer have any reason to leave,' he said firmly. He began to kiss her. It was a long, searching, passionate kiss, a kiss of promises given and received. When they finally broke apart, Max looked shaken. 'You *will* marry me now,' he said. It was not a question.

Angel could not meet his eyes. She shook her head, waiting for his explosion of anger.

For once, it did not happen. 'Angel, I know that you love me,' he said slowly, as if he were addressing a simpleton. 'Do you deny it?'

She shook her head again.

'Good. We are making progress at last. And you do understand that I love you?'

A surge of joy ran through her. She risked a single glance up at him. From the way he was gazing at her, there could be no mistaking that he meant what he said. He loved her!

'I need an answer, Angel.'

'Yes,' she whispered.

'You, my Lady Angel, will drive me to distraction. We love each other. Why will you not agree to marry me?'

'Because I am barren.'

Max muttered a choice oath. But then the anger left him and he laughed aloud. 'My dearest love, you may not have it both ways. Last month, you were sure that you were breeding. This month, you are barren all over again.'

'But you need an heir.'

'Captain Max Rosevale can manage very well without an heir. There is nothing to inherit. I should say the same, even if I were still the Earl of Penrose. The one who needs an heir, my dear Lady Angel, is *you*. And I plan to take every available opportunity to give you one.'

Angel blushed rosily and hid her face.

Max ran a finger lightly down the side of her cheek and under her chin, forcing her to look up at him again. 'It is true, is it not, my love? Mmm? We may succeed...but, then again, we may not. The Rosevales are notoriously bad breeders. Your father sired only one child, as did mine. How my grandfather succeeded in siring more is a complete mystery. What matters here is that you and I should marry, because we love each other. God willing, we will have a child. If we do not, then Pierre will be your heir. If he outlives you, he will be able to add the Barony to his other titles. And I am sure he would be delighted to inherit your wealth.'

Angel grimaced. 'Perhaps Pierre is *not* what he claims. Nothing is completely certain, after all. *You* may be the Earl, Max.'

He put his arms round her waist, and pulled her hard against his body, kissing her until she was dizzy and gasping for breath. 'I do not give a fig for the title. The only title I want is to be Angelina Rosevale's husband. It matters not if I am called "Captain Rosevale" or "the Earl of Penrose".'

'Truly? Even though people will say that you married me only for my fortune?'

He leered wickedly at her for a moment and then looked away, a picture of guilt. 'Curse you, woman! You have found me out! I had been so sure you would not discover my fell intent, at least until I had you firmly in my power.' He gave a cackle worthy of Macbeth's witches. 'But even now, you shall not escape my clutches…!'

For several seconds, there was dead silence in the gloomy carriage. Then Angel burst out laughing and, with gentle fingers, forced him to look her in the face. His eyes were sparkling with unholy glee. He made a very unconvincing villain. 'You, sir, are a—' She stopped in midsentence. She could not think of the words to tell him what she thought of his trickery. She loved this man. She loved the way he teased her and made her laugh. She loved the way he could look at her, turning her insides to water with a single wry smile. She loved…she loved everything about him.

The glories of Rochester Castle were receding into the distance when they heard another blast on the yard of tin. A mail coach, probably, and filled with passengers who would be craning their necks to see inside Angel's carriage. Reluctantly, Max stopped kissing Angel. She gave a tiny mew of protest, until he drew her into the crook of his arm and began to stroke her hair. They were now too deep in the corner of the carriage to be seen by anyone.

Max was beginning to feel guilty about keeping silent. She was so full of joy that it seemed cruel to dash her down. But he would have to tell her before they reached

London. The whole city would be in mourning by the time they arrived.

'Max?'

'Mmm?'

'Are you leaving for Harwich today?'

Now was the moment. 'I…I shall not be leaving at all, my love. You see, I—'

'My lady! My lady! Look!' The coachman had hauled his horses to a stop and was gesturing excitedly with his whip at the chaise and four which was in the process of overtaking them. It contained a single officer in a blood-stained uniform. It also contained two French eagles, whose banners were fluttering out of the window.

'Victory!' cried Angel's grooms with a single voice.

The officer smiled wearily and nodded at them. And then the chaise accelerated forward on its dash to London and disappeared round a bend in the road.

'Victory!' Max repeated in an awed whisper. 'Thank God!'

Chapter Twenty

'You cannot marry Cousin Frederick, Angel. You said yourself that you would never do so. And now that he has lost the Earldom, he has nothing whatever to offer you. Why, the man is a fortune-hunter!'

Angel calmly took another sip of her morning coffee. She forced herself to smile at her aunt. 'I am not marrying Frederick Rosevale, Aunt, I am marrying Max. He is no fortune-hunter.'

Lady Charlotte snorted in disbelief. 'Why, he—'

'Aunt Charlotte, I must ask you to say no more on the subject,' Angel said firmly. 'I am going to marry Max whether you approve or not. I should not like there to be a rift between us, but...'

Lady Charlotte looked suddenly shocked. She opened her mouth as if to protest, but then she closed it again without saying a word.

The long case clock in the hall chimed ten.

'They are late,' Angel said. 'But I suppose that it is difficult with such crowds of people milling about. Such a victory! No wonder they are cheering.'

The door opened. 'The Earl of Penrose and Mr Rosevale,' Willett intoned.

Angel rose to welcome them both. 'The Earl and Mr Rosevale, indeed. Pray, which is which?'

Max grinned at her. She could see from his eyes that he was longing to kiss her. With Aunt Charlotte in the room, however, even a peck on the cheek was impossible.

'Pierre! At last!' cried Lady Charlotte, pointedly ignoring Max's presence. 'We have been scouring London for you.'

'I was out of town, I fear, ma'am. Such sad news! Oh, it is a great victory, but the losses are terrible. Thousands of dead, and thousands more injured.'

'Look,' Max said quietly to Angel, 'I have brought a copy of *The Times*. It contains the Duke's despatch in full. You will see that Picton died on the field and—'

The drawing room door was thrown open. 'Miss Rosevale,' Willett announced, 'and Captain Graham!'

For a second, there was complete silence. Then everyone spoke at once, exclaiming in surprise. The door closed behind a tall red-haired man with searching blue eyes. At his side, dressed in a dowdy travelling dress, was a beautiful fair-haired woman, who could almost have been Angel's twin.

Captain Graham held up a hand for silence and then bowed to Angel. 'Lady Rosevale, may I present Mademoiselle Julie Rosevale, only child of your uncle, Lord Julian Rosevale.'

Angel could not believe her ears. She looked across at Pierre. He was staring fixedly at Julie. He seemed to be oblivious of everyone else.

Max was beaming. He strode forward and clapped his friend on the shoulder. 'You've been a mighty long time getting here, Ross. What kept you?'

'In the circumstances, I think we made pretty good time,' Ross protested. 'It's almost impossible to pass. The streets are full of people, cheering and singing. And we were almost run down by one of those mail coaches, all hung with oak leaves, taking the news to the rest of the country.'

Max grinned at him. 'That wasn't what I meant, as you are very well aware.'

Ross nodded. 'It is a long story. And it was a long journey. We had to escape across the Pyrenees and make our way to Santander to find a ship. You know how difficult those trails are, Max.' Ross looked across at Julie, and then at Angel. 'Your cousin is a remarkable young woman, ma'am. She never once complained, in spite of hardships that would have daunted many men.'

'Pierre...?' said Angel. Pierre had not moved an inch. He was staring at Julie as if she were some kind of vision. Julie, too, stood transfixed, with high spots of colour on her cheeks.

Angel could see Captain Graham's jaw working. He had turned very pale under his tan. She offered her hand to him. 'May I thank you, sir, for bringing Julie safely to us? But, please, will someone explain? You said that Julie was my uncle's only child. But Pierre is Julie's brother, is he not?'

'No, I am not Julie's brother, nor am I your heir,' Pierre said, tearing his gaze away from Julie at last. 'I am Julie's cousin, Julien Pierre d'Eury.'

Lady Charlotte was on her feet in an instant. 'You villain!' she cried. 'You lied to me!'

Pierre flushed bright red. 'I apologise, *madame*. And to you also, Cousin,' he added, half-turning to Angel. 'You at least had no part in your father's despicable treatment of Lord Julian.'

'Nonsense!' cried Lady Charlotte. 'My brother—'

'Your brother, the Marquis, left Lord Julian to die, in

spite of repeated pleas for help. I believe that was despicable. And dishonourable.'

'He did no such thing!' protested Lady Charlotte. 'And no pleas for help ever reached us. Angel's father tried every possible avenue to find out where Julian was and to rescue him. But he failed to find any clue to Julian's whereabouts. When he learned of Julian's death, he was devastated. We all were.'

Pierre looked chagrined. At last, he said quietly, 'I regret the deception, but in the circumstances, I felt I had no choice. Since we could afford only one passage to England, it fell to me to come to confront the Marquis. I am sorry I allowed you to be misled about the letter, but it seemed the best course at the time. By pretending to be the heir, I drew any threat on to myself, rather than on to a vulnerable orphan girl. You must understand that we had been brought up to believe that your family had left Julie's father to the mercy of Madame Guillotine and that you would have been far from concerned to learn that Julie was dead, too. I came to London to defend her interests against someone I believed to be her implacable enemy. I was wrong in that belief. I see that now. But once the lie was out, it was impossible to take it back.' He drew himself up proudly. 'I do not regret what I did. I had to protect Julie.'

He crossed to Julie and took her hand. She had barely moved from the doorway, nor had she spoken a word. But when Pierre kissed her hand, she smiled. It was a smile full of sunshine. 'Once Julie's identity is formally acknowledged, we can be married at last,' he said.

Angel was almost sure she saw a spasm of pain shoot across Captain Graham's face, but when she looked again, he was smiling at Pierre and Julie. 'Your father's English lands came back to the Rosevale estate, Julie,' she said.

'They are not rich. But they are rightfully yours. I will ensure that they are restored to you.'

'Thank you, Cousin Angelina,' Julie said, speaking for herself at last. 'Pierre and I will be very much in your debt.'

'It is nothing. I am merely restoring property to its rightful owner. Which reminds me... Oh, dear!'

'What is it, Angel?' said Max, coming to stand protectively by her side.

She looked up at him with dancing eyes. 'Poor Max. I am afraid your moment of freedom has been cut short. Pierre is not the Earl of Rosevale after all. You are.'

Max closed his eyes for a second. Then he looked hard at Angel and said, 'You, Lady Rosevale, are in need of a lesson in manners.'

Angel laughed up at him. 'And you, my Lord Penrose, are the last person on earth capable of providing it. Would you not agree?'

He shook his head at her, but he was smiling, too.

Angel looked round at the assembled company. Even Aunt Charlotte seemed to have regained a measure of good humour. 'It may be a little early in the day,' Angel said, 'but I think I shall order champagne. We all have a great deal to celebrate.'

After hours of discussion and celebration, they were alone at last in the privacy of Angel's drawing room.

'Poor Captain Graham.'

'Ross? Why so?'

'Did you not notice how he looked at Julie, Max? He is in love with her, I am sure, but she does not return his regard. She will marry Pierre.'

Max frowned. 'If you are right, then I am heartily sorry for it. Ross has had no easy life. However, he is a man of strong character. I am sure he will learn to forget her. In time.'

Angel said nothing more on the subject. It was not her place, for she had only just met Ross Graham. Pierre, on the other hand... 'Poor Pierre. I think he hated the deception he had to practise on us.'

'Oh? What makes you say that?'

'Because he would never allow his claim to be formally asserted. He always gave me a reason for delay.'

'Possibly,' said Max after a moment. 'Or perhaps he— No matter. We will never know the truth...so we ought to try to think well of him.'

Angel nodded thoughtfully. 'Do you think Pierre and Julie will be happy together, Max?'

'Why not? They know each other very well. Much better than we do, for example. Which reminds me...'

Angel raised her eyebrows, wondering what was to come.

'Lady Charlotte,' Max said flatly. 'I do not think that your aunt's presence in this house will be...er...conducive to conjugal harmony, my love.'

Angel giggled. 'You mean she will cause us to fight even more than we do already?'

Max smiled back at her.

'I, too, have been thinking about Aunt Charlotte. She seems much taken with Pierre and Julie. I fancy she would make them a splendid house guest. Preferably a long way from London.'

'Minx.'

Angel bowed her head in acknowledgement of his compliment. Then her smile died. There was one more question to be asked. And she knew the answer would hurt.

'The woman—the lady who visited me. Who is she, Max?'

'Her name is Louisa.'

Angel's silence was eloquent.

'She is—she *was* my mistress.'

'Max—'

'You do not have to say it, Angel. I promise you that my relationship with Louisa is over. There is no need for us to speak of her again.'

'But—'

'No, Angel! That is enough, I said!' Suddenly, he was furious.

Angel jumped to her feet and seized him by the arm, forcing him to look at her. 'You, sir, have a temper like a fiend. There is no need to berate me, simply because you are feeling guilty.'

'Angel—' Max frowned menacingly.

'And, besides…you are wrong.'

She had surprised him. 'Explain,' he said curtly, but she made no move to comply. She could be as stubborn as any mule. 'If you please, my love,' he said, rather grudgingly.

She beamed at him. 'Thank you. That is…something of an improvement. May we sit down?'

He eyed her suspiciously, but helped her to a seat. 'You are plotting something, I think.'

'I?'

She was trying so hard to look affronted that he burst out laughing. All his anger had vanished in an instant. He was surely bewitched. 'Forgive me, Angel. I had no right to speak as I did.'

'True,' she said, returning his smile. 'And now, may I speak about Louisa?'

'I— Yes, if you must.'

'I have no desire to pry into what there may have been between you and Louisa. You have said that it is over, and I trust your word.'

'Then, why, in the name of—?'

'Max, she helped me. Without her, we… Max, you will not leave her destitute?'

'Under that prickly exterior, my Lady Angel, you have a soft and tender heart.' His voice was hoarse. He swallowed. 'Louisa is a beautiful woman. She will soon find another…protector.'

'But she deserves better of you, does she not?'

He paused, thinking. Then he nodded. 'Yes. Yes, she does. She was a respectable widow, once. If she had not been so beautiful, she could probably have found employment, somehow. As it was, her choice was starvation or…'

Angel touched her hand to his cheek. 'Can you not help her, Max? Let her be a respectable widow again. Heaven knows that the role is difficult enough, even when one has money.'

He turned his head enough to kiss her palm. 'I will gladly offer her an independence. It will be for her to decide whether to accept it.'

'She will not.'

'You cannot be sure of that.'

Angel shook her head in disbelief. 'Would you accept a payment for giving me up, Max?'

'Ah. I see what you mean. You are right, I suppose. Louisa may be poor but she still has her pride. We must think of another way. Something much more devious… A legacy, do you think?'

Angel clapped her hands in delight. 'Yes, of course. It shall be a very distant third cousin, or something of the sort, who has made a modest fortune in the service of his country in…India, do you think?'

'Splendid. And his lawyers have been desperately trying to find an heir for some years. They have only just discovered Louisa's existence since she has been…living rather retired. Will that content you, my lady?'

'Yes. Except that it makes it impossible for me to give her my thanks.'

Max stood up and began to pace, as always when he was disturbed. 'You, madam, are a most unusual female. It is my mistress we are discussing.'

'Ex-mistress.'

'Very well, ex-mistress. You are supposed to be a respectable lady of rank. You should not even acknowledge the existence of such persons.'

'You know very well that I am not in the least respectable. I have been seduced and abducted, I have had my gown ripped from me, I—'

'You have the order wrong, my sweet. Abduction first. Then seduction. And I did apologise for ripping your gown.'

Angel did not answer.

'Now, Lady Rosevale…'

'Yes, Lord Penrose?' she said, looking demurely up at him through her lashes.

'Dammit, woman, don't look at me like that! How am I supposed to think straight?'

Angel tried hard not to smile. Max was doing the same, she noticed. His mouth was clamped into a tight line, but the tiny creases in the corners of his eyes gave him away.

She bowed her head, fixed her gaze on her clasped hands and allowed her hidden smile to broaden.

'A wife is supposed to be a support and a helpmate, not a fiery termagant, Lady Rosevale. How will we ever live together with tempers like ours? No doubt our friends will open a book on how soon one of us will murder the other.'

Max paused and ran a hand through his thick hair. It was one of the gestures Angel loved, for it betrayed the fact that he was so much less in control than he liked to pretend...where she was concerned, at least.

'I might rip up at you—in fact, I am sure I would—but I am not much given to violence,' she said. She looked up at him once more, with her head impudently cocked on one side. 'On the other hand, you might do well to keep your guns under lock and key. You never know what a woman might do...'

Max's eyes widened. Then recognition dawned and he burst out laughing. 'You, madam,' he said, pulling her to her feet and into his arms, 'are enough to drive a man wild. I can see that I shall have to beat you.'

At his words, a shiver ran through Angel's body.

The laughter disappeared from his eyes on the instant. He drew her close, into a comforting embrace. 'Forgive me, my love. That was a wicked thing to say, even in jest. You did not think I meant it?' He put her away from him just enough to look into her eyes.

'No, I— It was just that there are moments that I cannot forget, no matter how hard I try, and when you said—'

He did not attempt to reason with her. He simply kissed her, gently, tenderly, trying to prove with his lips and the closeness of his body just how much he loved and cherished her. She did not resist at all, but pressed herself against him, welcoming the touch of his lips and softening in surrender. It was a long, long kiss. When at last they broke apart, they were both breathless and wide-eyed. It had not been a kiss of passion but a melding of souls. It had shaken them both.

Max pulled Angel into the crook of his arm so that her head rested against his shoulder. With trembling fingers, he began to stroke her silver hair. 'Your hair is like silk, did you know that? And I would do nothing—nothing—

to harm one single strand of it. I swear it. You do believe me, Angel?'

'I never doubted it,' she said in a low, rather unsteady voice. She could not begin to try to understand the meaning of that soul-searing kiss, but the memory of it would go with her to her grave.

Max gave a growl of satisfaction, deep in his throat. Then, in a single swift movement, he sat down on the sofa and pulled her on to his lap. 'That's better,' he said.

'Better than what, sir?' she said saucily.

He groaned. 'I have promised never to raise a hand to you. Heaven help me! How on earth am I to control such a wayward woman?'

She lifted his hand and placed a gentle kiss on his calloused palm. 'I am sure you will find a way, sir.'

'Indeed.' His voice was suddenly a little hoarse. He tried to clear his throat.

Angel was wriggling about to find a more comfortable position on his lap.

Max groaned again. 'Angel, if you continue to do that, I will not be responsible for my actions. You do understand what you are doing to me? Do you really wish to be ravished on the drawing-room floor?'

Another tremor ran through Angel's body at the image conjured up by his words. And she was in no doubt that he was fully aroused. It felt as if the heat of him was burning through her fine lawn petticoats.

'Angel...? Forgive me, I—'

She laid a gentle hand on his cheek. Then in a low voice, she said, 'I am not sure that I wish to be ravished, even by you, Max. But if you want to make love to me, I...I... Wouldn't it be wise to lock the door?'

'I do. And it would.'

'Well, then—' Angel made to rise.

'But we have matters to discuss first,' Max said, closing his arms around her so that she was held fast once more.

'Have we?'

'Yes, you maddening minx, we have. Seriously, Angel, I am still afraid that I might hurt you. Not physically, I promise. In spite of what you once said of me, I am gentleman enough not to strike a lady…even when provoked.' He smiled down at her, waiting for her response. He needed to know that she accepted his word. Her answering smile, when it came, was radiant.

'But I do not always have control over my tongue. I have tried, believe me, but even now there are things that enrage me—'

'Like me?'

He took a deep breath. 'I will not lie to you, Angel. Yes. Sometimes you do infuriate me. As I do you. And I fear that, in a fit of temper, I might say things that were unforgivable, that would drive you away. If I lost you now, my darling…'

'You will not.'

'You do not know what a bear I can be.'

'Do I not? You forget that I am a Rosevale, too, and I have lived with Rosevales all my life. My father had the family temper and his rages were terrible.' She shuddered at the memory. 'Terrifying. And he would never apologise, never admit he had been wrong. If I was the object of Papa's anger, I had to take the blame, and apologise to him, even if Papa was clearly at fault. It was either that, or banishment to the tower, on bread and water.'

'Oh, my love. How could you endure it?'

She shrugged. 'Because I loved him. And he loved me, too, in spite of his forbidding ways.' She pressed a tiny kiss to the corner of Max's jaw. 'And I learned to read the storm warnings at a very early age. When Papa was like to lose his temper, I used to hide until he had taken it out on someone else. Cowardly, I suppose…but I was only a child. And he never did find my hiding places,' she added, with obvious satisfaction in her voice.

Max laughed and dropped a kiss on her hair. 'I promise you that, if I am in the wrong, I *will* apologise.'

'If?'

He grinned. 'Surely you know that husbands are never wrong?'

'Max…'

'Well…hardly ever,' he conceded, still grinning.

'And wives?'

'Now, there you have me at a disadvantage. I have never had a wife, you see, and it would not do to pronounce upon the subject with so little experience. Would it?'

'Indeed not,' she replied, mimicking his mocking tone. 'However, acquiring the experience is not a matter to be taken lightly. It does tend to require a somewhat… permanent arrangement. And a man is permitted the study of only one wife at a time. The law, I believe, is quite precise on that point. I imagine it must restrict the study somewhat. Would you not agree?'

'That depends, my love, on whether you believe all women are alike. If I learn to understand you, will I thereby understand all womankind? I am happy to make it my life's work, you know.'

'I am delighted to hear it. I will settle for nothing less, I promise you. Tell me, sir, just how do you propose to go about this *study* of yours?'

'Ah. Now, I am not sure that I can share those details with you until we are married. You might betray my methods to others, and then what should I do?'

Angel was captivated by the thread of laughter in his resonant voice. She had never imagined that lovers could

be like this, teasing, laughing, trusting… Max was pre
pared to let her see that he was vulnerable, just as she was.
It was not a matter of physical strength. Yes, he could
overpower her in an instant—he was a strong man—but
he would not do so, not unless she wanted him to. And
sometimes—

She gasped. He had begun to nibble at her earlobe. It
was exquisite torture, making her belly turn to water. She
closed her eyes. The sensation became even more intense.
'Is that one of your methods, Max?' she said, her voice
cracking slightly on the words.

Max continued to nibble. 'Mmm.'

One of his hands began to stroke the sensitive skin just
under her breasts with light, flickering caresses. So near,
but… Her breasts felt as if they were swelling, reaching
out towards his fingers so that they, too, could experience
the tiny touches that could ignite fire. She leaned into him
and her breasts brushed his hand. Even through the layers
of clothing, she felt the joining of their flesh.

He lifted his fingers to cup her breast. 'And that, my
love, is doubtless one of yours,' he said softly, moving his
lips to the corner of her jaw and beginning to feather kisses
along it. After a second, he moved his thumb across her
nipple. It was erect, and beginning to ache.

'Max…' She raised a slightly shaking hand to his hair
and drove her fingers into it. 'Max, I need you…'

His lips had almost reached her mouth when he stopped
kissing her. Her eyes flew open. He was gazing at her, his
expression filled with love and—she would almost have
said—wonder. She could not speak.

He took his hand from her breast and laid it on her
cheek. 'We need each other, my love,' he said hoarsely.
'Without you, I am not…complete.' He rested his head on

her hair and began to stroke her face. 'If I lost you, I would lose part of myself.'

Angel put her hand gently over his. 'You will not. "Till death do us part", remember?'

'You would be married to a bear?'

'Even bears can be tamed, my love. I believe they can become…quite acceptable companions.'

Max did not raise his head from hers, but he allowed his fingers to trail tantalisingly slowly down her cheek, her neck, and her shoulder, coming to rest on the naked swell of her breast above her gown. His little finger tucked itself under the neckline and began to circle the puckered skin of her nipple.

Angel groaned aloud.

Max lifted his head at last. 'Is this…acceptable? Or must I be tamed yet more?'

'This is sheer torture…and you know it. Please, Max. Let us lock the door. I cannot—'

With a grunt of satisfaction, he slid an arm under her knees and stood up, cradling her against him. 'Bear-taming, my Lady Angel, should take place in comfort. In your bedchamber, I think.' He started towards the door.

'Max! We are not yet wed! You cannot carry me to my room! Max! The servants—!'

He paid no heed, simply settling her more comfortably in his arms. He even managed to open the door with his elbow.

'Max!'

He grinned down at her. 'Look around you, my love. The whole house seems to be deserted. I'd wager we shall not see a single servant between here and the bedroom door. Do you care to hazard a guinea or two on that?'

Silently, Angel shook her head. The servants did indeed seem to have melted away. As if they knew…

Embarrassed, she hid her face against his coat. But that closeness served only to make her even more conscious of his warmth, and of the strong beat of his heart as he carried her, apparently effortlessly, up the staircase.

She sighed deeply.

He stopped in mid-stride. 'Have you changed your mind, Angel? You have only to say the word. I want you…desperately…but if you would rather wait until after we are married—'

Angel raised her free hand and placed a finger on his lips. 'I have only one word for you, my darling Max,' she said, gazing up at him with all her love shining in her eyes. 'Now!'

* * * * *

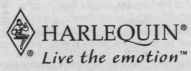

If you enjoyed what you just read,
then we've got an offer you can't resist!

Take 2 bestselling love stories FREE!

Plus get a FREE surprise gift!

Clip this page and mail it to Harlequin Reader Service®

IN U.S.A.
3010 Walden Ave.
P.O. Box 1867
Buffalo, N.Y. 14240-1867

IN CANADA
P.O. Box 609
Fort Erie, Ontario
L2A 5X3

YES! Please send me 2 free Harlequin Historicals® novels and my free surprise gift. After receiving them, if I don't wish to receive anymore, I can return the shipping statement marked cancel. If I don't cancel, I will receive 6 brand-new novels every month, before they're available in stores! In the U.S.A., bill me at the bargain price of $4.69 plus 25¢ shipping and handling per book and applicable sales tax, if any*. In Canada, bill me at the bargain price of $5.24 plus 25¢ shipping and handling per book and applicable taxes**. That's the complete price and a savings of over 10% off the cover prices—what a great deal! I understand that accepting the 2 free books and gift places me under no obligation ever to buy any books. I can always return a shipment and cancel at any time. Even if I never buy another book from Harlequin, the 2 free books and gift are mine to keep forever.

246 HDN DZ7Q
349 HDN DZ7R

Name	(PLEASE PRINT)	
Address	Apt.#	
City	State/Prov.	Zip/Postal Code

Not valid to current Harlequin Historicals® subscribers.

Want to try two free books from another series?
Call 1-800-873-8635 or visit www.morefreebooks.com.

* Terms and prices subject to change without notice. Sales tax applicable in N.Y.
** Canadian residents will be charged applicable provincial taxes and GST.
   All orders subject to approval. Offer limited to one per household.
 ® are registered trademarks owned and used by the trademark owner and or its licensee.

HIST04R   ©2004 Harlequin Enterprises Limited

Harlequin Historicals®
Historical Romantic Adventure!

TRAVEL BACK TO THE FUTURE
FOR ROMANCE—WESTERN-STYLE!
ONLY WITH HARLEQUIN HISTORICALS.

ON SALE JANUARY 2005

TEXAS LAWMAN by Carolyn Davidson

Sarah Murphy will do whatever it takes to save her nephew
from dangerous fortune seekers—including marrying lawman
Blake Caulfield. Can the Lone Star lawman keep them
safe—without losing his heart to the feisty lady?

WHIRLWIND GROOM by Debra Cowan

Desperate to avenge the murder of her parents, all trails lead
Josie Webster to Whirlwind, Texas, much to the chagrin of
charming sheriff Davis Lee Holt. Let the games begin as
Davis Lee tries to ignore the beautiful seamstress who stirs
both his suspicions and his desires....

ON SALE FEBRUARY 2005

PRAIRIE WIFE by Cheryl St.John

Jesse and Amy Shelby find themselves drifting apart after
the devastating death of their young son. Can they put
their grief behind them and renew their deep and abiding
love—before it's too late?

THE UNLIKELY GROOM by Wendy Douglas

Stranded by her brother in a rough-and-rugged Alaskan
gold town, Ashlynne Mackenzie is forced to rely on the
kindness of saloon owner Lucas Templeton. But kindness
has nothing to do with Lucas's urges to both protect the
innocent woman and to claim her for his own.